Holy Moly!

G. W. Reynolds III

This is a work of fiction. While, as in all fiction, the literary perceptions and insights are based on experience, all names, characters, places, and incidents are either products of the author's imagination or are used fictitiously. No reference to any real person is intended or inferred.

Published and distributed by:
High-Pitched Hum Publishing
321 15th Street North
Jacksonville Beach, FL 32250

Contact G.W. Reynolds III at www.jettyman.com

ALSO BY G. W. REYNOLDS III

From the Jetty Man Series: Jetty Man
                            Mullet Run
                            Oak Baby
                            Horny Toads
                            Joe Jumpers
                            Gopher Stew

Other Books: Roads End
              Sin City

Holy Moly!

G. W. Reynolds III

PRELUDE

Jason stood on Mr. Leek's dock looking down at the shrimp boat *Mary C.* He had no idea his mother was holding a set of keys to a new fire engine red Chevrolet Corvette in her hand. Jason wanted to see if the shrimping had been good during his time away at the Giant's Motel. He was glad the sex filled adventure was over and Sofia was back home with her mother and sisters. Jason was ready to start making a living for his son and his mother. His mind was clear as he looked down from the dock at the boat.

Mary C. sat on her bed next to her grandson Billy. The oak baby was awake and making his baby noises. Mary C. was still wrapped in the silky robe she had borrowed from Mr. King. She looked at Billy and smiled. Then she looked at the two envelopes the young and handsome Mr. Malin had given her. Mary C. still held the keys to the car in her hand. She thought about the Crane and smiled in honor of his wonderful surprise and generosity.

Mary C. thought of Hawk and wondered if he was watching her at that very moment. She smiled again when she thought of the carousel not being there to bring Hawk to her. Mary C. was actually hoping Hawk had gone and crossed over to the other side. She knew in her heart if Hawk were still walking Mr. King's halls her dead lover would find a way to get to her. Mary C. was definitely insane.

Mr. Leek and his dockworker, Mathias, stepped up behind Jason on the dock. "Mathias tells me he ain't seen Chichemo in two days. Him and Beanie got the boat fueled, iced up and ready to go, but didn't come back. That ain't a real good sign when Chichemo and Beanie's together. When they do work, they work hard together, but they ain't never been a good influence on each other." Jason didn't really understand, but he was still glad to be home. He stepped off the dock and down to the deck of the boat.

Miss Margaret turned to the door of her store when the bell rang and three of her four daughters walked in. She smiled with pride, knowing they had come to help her get the store ready for the customers who had missed three days of the convenience to shop there. She did not want to question the fact her oldest daughter, Margie, was not with them. She knew how rebellious Margie had been lately, but she was still concerned. She addressed the three of them.

"Is your sister, Margie, all right?"

Peggy answered for them all. "Yes ma'am. She'll be here in a few minutes. She had some bad stomach cramps."

The dusting, cleaning, and stocking the shelves would last until Miss Margaret felt all was in order. She was glad they were all home safe and sound. She had no idea what the four of them had done during their trip away from home. Miss Margaret knew nothing of Sofia's life and death encounter with Carlton Steen and the awful fact that her youngest had actually killed a man.

She knew nothing about the sexual activities of all four girls during their stay at the Giant's Motel. She would never know or believe what Margie had done in the carousel room with Jason, Helga and the pervert Little Tom. Miss Margaret loved her four daughters, but she knew very little about them as adults.

The three working sisters had separate thoughts about their adventure away from Mayport. Susan thought of her wild night away from the others with her new friend, Seth. Peggy had flashes of her sexual demonstrations in the backseat of a car in the Giant's Motel parking lot. Sofia thought of pulling the trigger of a gun and killing a man. She did not think of Jason. Sofia was different. They were all different.

Margie was also thinking about the trip to the Giant's Motel and her vile sexual acts with Jason, the midget and the black Amazon Woman. She wanted to go to the tree, but she knew she should go to the store like her sisters. Margie opened her small duffle bag and took out a few items of her clothing. She smiled as she pulled out the carousel music box and held the beautiful antique in her hands. She placed it on the nightstand next to her bed and pushed up the "on" switch. Margie was insane, too.

Mr. King was headed to his haunted house. He had taken his 1957 Chevrolet to the Big Chief Tire Company out on Mayport Road. He just had to show his new car to his friend Chip Parman. Mr. King smiled as the Chevy leaned into the curve at the Little Jetties. He wanted to get back home and see if his friend Norman Bates, the Skeleton Man, had settled in with the other ghosts. He took his foot off the gas pedal and slowed the Chevy down as he passed Johnny Vona's dock. Mr. King stopped his new car in the middle of the road. His mouth dropped open as he looked out the front windshield. He had to refocus his eyes, because he did not believe what he saw.

Another hard look told Mr. King it was true. He could only shake his head at the pitiful sight of Chichemo, Beanie, Bosco, the spider monkey, and a donkey. Beanie was walking in front of the donkey holding the reins and leading the animal down the road. Beanie wore a child's black cowboy hat with the string tied under his chin to keep the small hat from falling off his big head. It looked more like a pillbox hat sitting in the middle of his head. Chichemo was riding the donkey with Bosco sitting on Chichemo's shoulder. Bosco wore a tiny cowboy hat, too. It was a funny sight. It was also a sad sight, because Mr. King knew both men were too drunk to realize how ridiculous they looked. He waited for the strange foursome to walk by the passenger's side window of the car. Neither of the men looked at Mr. King, nor acknowledged him in any way. Bosco stuck his little tongue out at Mr. King, as they moved past the car. Mr. King watched the Mayport cowboys in his rear view mirror as he drove away.

CHAPTER ONE

The carousel was spinning at full tilt. The music was playing and the lights were bouncing off the walls and ceiling of Margie's bedroom. Margie watched the flashing lights, as they seemed to enter her eyes. Like Helga told Jason, it was hypnotism at its simplest form. The combination of Margie's thoughts and her hypnotic state of mind took her deep into a colorful world of the magic carousel dreams.

Margie stood naked with her hands on the oak tree. She was bending over at the waist and realized instantly there was someone behind her. She felt the person arms and hands grip her waist. Margie lost her breath and moaned out loud with the deep penetration on the first push. Margie liked what she was feeling, but she was curious to see who had made her moan with pleasure. She turned her head as far back as she could to greet her sexual pleaser.

Margie's eyes widened and her throat went dry with fear when she saw the midget, Tom Thumb's smiling face with his chin resting on her left butt cheek. His little hands were digging into her sides as he held on. He was sexually attached to her with his feet dangling off the ground.

Margie screamed and tried to move her hands off the tree. Her fear mounted when she realized the ropes of the tree held her again. She could not pull away from her attacker. Margie tried to move her legs, but the white, soft sand held her ankles tightly. Her only option was to move her buttocks from side-to-side, hoping to dislodge the connection of the perverted little man.

As Margie shifted her hips, the midget tightened his grip. She knew he was still deep inside her, and the harder she thrashed, the harder he fought to stay connected. His little feet rubbed the backs of her legs as they swung back and forth each time she shifted her hips. Margie could not throw her rider off his mount. The nasty little man stayed on way past eight seconds.

Margie stopped moving when she realized there was nothing she could do. She pushed against the tree with her hands and took all the little pervert could give her. Margie knew the attack had ended. She knew his oversized organ had left her. She felt him slide down her left leg like a monkey sliding down a palm tree. Margie watched the little man walk away. He moved to the other side of the tree where she could not see him at first. Then she saw his little head peek around the trunk of the tree. She knew he was going to watch her.

Margie tried to pull her hands free again, but the ropes continued to hold her. She heard another noise behind her and she tried once again to turn her head back far enough to see who was there with her. Margie's stomach burned and went sour when she saw a line of men standing behind her. It was not a line of five or ten men. It was a line of fifty men. It filled the top of the sand hill and snaked its way down the hill and onto the road below. Margie screamed when the next man stepped up behind her, grabbed her hips and pulled her back toward him. It was his turn.

Mr. King stood in his small kitchen. He was sure Mary C. had heard him come in, but she had not joined him downstairs. He thought perhaps she and the child were resting after the long ride home. He poured a cup of coffee and looked around the kitchen.

"Norman, if you're here, let me know somehow when ya can." He held up the cup as if to toast his new ghostly arrival. Mr. King walked out of the kitchen, through the living room and out onto the downstairs front porch. He sat down in his wicker chair and took his usual Mayport watching position with coffee in hand. Mr. King was sorry he had seen Chichemo in his drunken condition. He knew he would have to tell Mary C., but he wished she would find out from someone else.

The carousel stopped spinning. Margie sat straight up in her bed as if two strong hands had pulled her up. She had felt that once before when she had used the carousel for her sexual dreams. She was naked and the bed sheets were wet from her sweating body. Margie sat on the edge of the bed as her legs trembled from fatigue and the rest of her body trembled with fear. There was a small moment of relief when Margie realized she was back in the reality of her bedroom and she knew it was just a dream. She also knew the life-like dream would haunt her for a long time, if not forever. Margie took the music box and put it in the corner of her closet under a blanket. She hurried to the store to join her mother and sisters.

Jason walked out of Mr. Leek's fish house and got into his Uncle Bobby's truck. He started the engine and began to drive out onto the main road. Jason looked to his left to be sure the ferry traffic was not coming his way so he could turn toward Mr. King's house. He looked to his right to be sure the coast was clear in that direction as well. The same incredible sight that Mr. King had seen earlier came into Jason's view.

It was the Mayport cowboys with their donkey. Chichemo was still riding with Beanie walking and holding the reins in front of the donkey. Bosco was still sitting on the donkey behind Chichemo. The foursome stopped on the side of the road. Beanie turned up a pint bottle of clear liquor to his lips. Chichemo did the same with a bottle of Jack Daniels. Jason recognized the square bottle with the black label. Jason could not believe what he saw next. He actually laughed out loud as he sat mesmerized in the truck. The spider monkey, Bosco, turned up a miniature bottle of liquor to his hairy little lips and took a drink along with the other two drunks. Jason watched the comical group as they walked past the front of his truck. He did not know what to do so he just sat there until they went by. Jason had to smile again when he thought that the donkey was the only sober one of the four.

Mr. King watched Margie from his porch as she walked into the front door of the store. Miss Margaret turned when the bell on the door rang again. She was pleased to see that her eldest had joined the cleaning crew. "Thank you for coming Margie, are you feeling better?"

Margie knew the six eyes of her three sisters were staring at her. She smiled at her mother. "Yes mother, I'm fine. My stomach was a little queasy when I first got home. I was probably a little car sick, but I'm fine now. What do you need me to do?"

Margie did not look at her sisters. She knew they were most likely rolling their beautiful eyes at the fact she was late again and they had already done most of the work. They did not know their older sister had just had sexual relations with fifty men. Perhaps if they knew they would not have been so hard on her. Miss Margaret handed Margie a dry rag and a bottle of furniture polish. "How about you making the wood counters shine, dear?"

Mr. King turned when he heard the front screen door open. Mary C. walked out onto the front porch. She was dressed in one of her better outfits. Mr. King knew his houseguest was getting ready to go somewhere.

"Well, well, don't you look nice? I thought you and the child might rest all day. Looks like you caught your second wind."

Mary C. smiled and sat down in the other wicker chair. "I got somethin' to tell ya, John. You ain't gonna believe what happened when ya left. I don't quite believe it all myself, but it seems real enough." Mr. King knew the serious look on Mary C.'s beautiful face. He would tell her about Chichemo another time. Mr. King waited for her to continue and tell him what had happened. Mary C. changed the subject. "John, what's that smell? Somethin's dead somewhere close by."

Mr. King nodded. "It hit me when I walked out here. At first I thought it was the smell of low tide, but it's more than that. You're right, somethin's dead. That dog probably got hungry while we was gone and took somethin' under the house."

Mr. King had not thought of the hound from hell. "I'll bet that's it. That dog's left somethin' dead under the house. I got enough dead in the house. I don't need no dead under the house." Mary C. smiled and shook her head at Mr. King's haunted house humor. She let him continue. "I'll have to give one of those young boys around here a few bucks to climb under there and find out what that crazy dog's left under my house. I'm too old and fat to be climbin' around in that crawl space."

Officers David Boos and Paul Short were standing next to their police car in the parking lot of the Giant's Motel in Gibsonton, Florida talking to the Florida State trooper, Bobby Woolard. The two Mayport policemen were ready to end their search for the fugitive Tom Green and return home. Trooper Woolard was making an observation.

"You two sure brought us some excitement. We had a double murder suspect on the run. A legendary bounty hunter was killed in the line of duty. We got two boys from your hometown just passin' through and now they're missin'. And how the hell does some poor fool get stuck with a name like Moochee?" He smiled and shook his head. "The skinny man died while you boys were here. And, y'all brought the prettiest bunch of women here I ever seen in my life. Yes sir, you Mayport boys know how to make things interestin'. Promise me you won't come back too soon. Our little town couldn't take y'all but once every twenty years or so."

David Boos smiled after Trooper Woolard's humorous, but true commentary. "I'd like to take credit for being that exciting, but it ain't us. It's the woman, her son and the baby. It follows them where ever they go."

Paul Short had to add his thoughts. "The women follow Jason and death follows his mother, Mary C. It's crazy, but we've seen it time and time again. It was driving our boss, Mr. Butler, out of his mind. And, now he's dead, too. He was keeping count of all the deaths that took place with Mary C. involved in some way. Now, his name's got to be added to that list. No telling how many he'd recorded all ready. I'm sure gonna look for that list when I get back home." He opened the door to the car and raised his hand to Trooper Woolard. "Thanks Bobby for your help. Sorry it got so crazy. Time for us to roll."

Mr. King held the keys to a fire engine red Corvette in his hand. Mary C. had told him about her money-carrying visitor and Steve Robertson's gift to her and Jason.

"Mary C., this is a true blessin' for the three of you. Praise God, somethin' good has come your way. This can be a new beginning for you and yours. You can rebuild your house. You can sell the

land and build somewhere new. You can keep the land and still
build a new house on another piece of land. You can do anything
you want. He's given y'all a fresh start. Praise the Lord. If Al Leek
was here he'd be down on his knees givin' thanks right now. I can't
wait to tell him. Have ya told Jason yet?"

Mr. King finally gave Mary C. a chance to talk. "No, he didn't
come back from the dock yet. I was gonna go find him and take him
with me to get the car. I'm gonna get one of Miss Margaret's girls
to watch Billy while I'm gone. That's why I got so dressed up. A
woman can't go pick up her new Corvette without lookin' like a
Corvette woman, now can she?"

Mr. King smiled a huge full teeth grin. "No ma'am, she sure
can't. And may I take the liberty of sayin', you do look like a
Corvette woman."

Mary C. had to smile at Mr. King's attempt to compliment her.
She could not resist. "I think spendin' a little time with the belly
dancer has done you a world of good. You've become a sweet
talker."

Mr. King was embarrassed by Mary C.'s observation. "I think all
the girls are over at the store. I can keep my eye on the little one 'til
one of 'em gets here. But, you know I ain't too good with babies.
Go on now. It's gettin' late. You know it took the whole day for us
to get home. It'll be nightfall before ya know it. Now, go and find
Jason. Get that new car. He's probably on the boat."

Mary C. smiled again and stepped off the front porch. She
looked to her left to see the devil dog, Abaddon, turn the corner of
the porch. The huge dog had chicken feathers sticking out of his
mouth.

"Well, well, there's my bad boy. I knew you'd be fine here
alone. Looks like you've already had your dinner." The Rottweiler
walked closer to his new mistress as Mr. King walked to the edge of
the porch.

"That's one ugly dog, Mary C. He's gonna be trouble if he keeps
killin' them chickens. Somebody's gonna be lookin' for the reason
their chickens are missin'.

Mary C. smiled and reached for the car door. "He ain't gonna
kill no more chickens. I'm back now and I'll be sure he ain't
hungry."

"You know once they get a taste for killin' it don't just go away."

Mary looked up at Mr. King. "It ain't nothin' new for him. He's always had a taste for killin'. I want to be sure he keeps it."

Mr. King did not respond. Mary C.'s comments never surprised him any more. She opened the driver's side door of her Ford Falcon, but before she could slide into the front seat and under the steering wheel, Jason pulled up in Uncle Bobby's truck. She was glad to see her son. Jason could see the excitement in her eyes. He was not accustomed to such a happy expression on his mother's face. He stopped the truck and stepped out into Mr. King's small front yard. Mary C. closed the door to her Falcon and stepped to her son.

"Jason, where ya been? I was on my way to find ya. I've got some crazy news."

Jason put his head down as his mother walked closer to him. "I know, Mama. I saw Chichemo, too." Mr. King's eyes widened when Jason mentioned one of the drunken Mayport cowboys. Mary C.'s expression changed.

"What are you talkin' 'bout? I ain't seen Chichemo. I ain't even thought about him. I got some big news and you're talkin' 'bout Chichemo."

Mr. King stepped to the edge of his front porch so he could hear a little better. He liked the fact Jason would give Mary C. the news about her boat captain falling off the wagon. Mary C. looked back at Mr. King.

"John, don't say nothin' to Jason while I'm gone. I'm gonna go over to the store and get one of the girls to come get Billy." She turned back to Jason. "You go in the house and clean up. Put on a clean shirt. You're drivin' me to Jacksonville Beach."

Mary C. turned and walked away from Jason in the direction of Miss Margaret's store. Jason looked at Mr. King standing above him on the porch. Mr. King shrugged his shoulders. "I think ya need to hurry, son." Jason sidestepped Abaddon as he followed Mr. King's suggestion.

Mary C. knew Abaddon was created to kill. She saw it in the dog's eyes that night in the woods after she killed the Ax, Johnny D. Bryant. Abaddon was a true devil dog and was, along with five other Rottweilers, trained to kill for and protect the man who

considered himself the son of Satan. The other five dogs were all
killed the night Macadoo sent her religious, misguided henchmen to
kill Mary C. and take the oak baby.

When the Ax named his six killer canines he made sure to pay
tribute to the Devil. Each dog was given a different diabolical name
representing the servants of Beelzebub. Abaddon was the leader and
the strongest. He was the Alpha male. He was named for the
devil's destroyer. Johnny D. Bryant called Abaddon his brother
because they had the same evil nature. They both killed with no
feeling.

Habbalah was the creature that invoked the lust for blood.
Calabim was the destroyer that controlled his animal instincts as a
member of society until he was needed for evil. Shadim possessed
wild animals and used them for evil bidding. Djinn was the true
servant to Beelzebub that took the form of an animal to hunt and
track down the devil's victims. Lilin was the servant who brought
the animal instincts out of the other servants.

Abaddon had not been alone, even after the other five dogs were
killed, because he had taken up the duty of protecting Mary C.
When Mary C. left him, the dog was alone for the first time. His
killing nature was ignited once again.

The bell on the door rang as Mary C. walked into the store. Miss
Margaret turned to greet the new customer. She was surprised to see
Mary C.

"Mary C., have you recovered from that long ride?" Mary C.
knew Miss Margaret was still not herself after the run away ordeal
with Sofia and Margie. There was a little coldness in her tone, but
Mary C. understood it completely.

"I'm fine. I hate to bother y'all, but somethin' wonderful has
happened and I was hopin' one of the girls could watch Billy for an
hour or so for me. I've got to go to Jacksonville Beach on business.
I need Jason to drive and well, we all know John's not the
babysittin' kind. Besides, I'd be too worried if the master of the
haunted house was responsible for the safety of my only grandchild.
I might find the child hovering above the bed when I got back." The
girls all smiled. They knew Mary C. was just joking. "You could
go get him if you didn't want to stay at John's. I know you're busy
and tired, but I wouldn't ask if it wasn't important."

Miss Margaret was her gracious self. "Of course we can, dear." She looked at her four daughters. "Sofia, you and Peggy go get Billy and bring him over here. We'll all baby sit until Mary C. returns." She turned to Mary C. "Now you go take care of your business and don't worry about Billy."

Mary C. knew Miss Margaret would not question her about the important business. Miss Margaret was shocked and surprised when Mary C. stepped to her and hugged her neck.

"You're a wonderful friend. I'll never forget what a true angel you are. I love you."

Mary C. released her hold on Miss Margaret's neck. Sofia and Peggy followed her out the door. Margie turned to her mother.

"Miss Mary C. was sure excited about something. I wonder what's going on?"

Miss Margaret shook her head. "If she wanted us to know she would have told us. Perhaps she will tell us another time."

Mr. King was still standing on the porch and Jason was standing next to Uncle Bobby's truck. He was wearing a clean shirt as his mother had instructed. He saw Peggy and Sofia. Jason was always nervous and uncomfortable when more than one of the sisters came calling. Sofia's eyes met his, but she did not smile. She looked away from Jason. She had never done that before. He did not like it. He felt empty and his stomach burned. Mary C.'s voice interrupted Jason's uncomfortable moment.

"John, the girls are takin' Billy to the store. Don't scare 'em when they go upstairs to get him. No noises, no stories and don't call for Norman."

Mr. King smiled. "You're afraid he might just show up, huh?"

Sofia and Peggy looked at each other and then at Mr. King. Mary C. could not resist the opportunity to join Mr. King's philosophy.

"I'm sure he's already here, John. Nobody, dead or alive, would have let you take that car without comin' with it." Peggy and Sofia looked at each other again and then at Mary C. Mr. King had to continue.

"Don't worry girls. It's too early in the day for the big boys to come out."

Mary C. looked at Mr. King. "John, don't you dare." She turned to Jason. "Let's go, son. I'll explain it all to you while we ride." Mary C. and Jason got into the truck and drove off, leaving Sofia and Peggy to the mercy of Mr. John King and his haunted house.

Sofia stepped up onto the porch first. Peggy was a few feet behind her. Peggy had acted brave about the haunted house before, but she did not like the feeling she had at the moment. She had an idea. "Mr. King, would it be too much trouble if you went in and brought Billy out here to us?"

Sofia was appalled at her sister's question. "Peggy, I can't believe you said that." She turned to Mr. King. "I'm sorry. I didn't know my sister was afraid of your house. Please forgive her."

Mr. King looked at Peggy. He could not miss the opportunity to exploit the fears of others. She felt he was looking deep into her soul. "There's many who will not enter my house. It's fine that you are counted amongst them. I understand. Very few are comfortable with the creatures from the other side. And if Norman has settled in, he could very well appear. They like to let me know when they've arrived. It's just common ghost courtesy." Mr. King got a whiff of the carrion rotting under his house. He could tell that Peggy and Sofia smelled it, too. "I'm sorry about the odor ladies. We think that crazy dog left a dead animal under the house while we were all gone."

Peggy nodded. "Yes sir, I smell it, now. She looked at Sofia. "Let's just sit out here and wait for Mary C. to come back. We can hear Billy if he cries."

Sofia was scared and furious at the same time. "That's ridiculous! You know as well as I do, he never cries. We told mother we would come here and get him. She's expecting us to be back at the store with him." Sofia got a big whiff of the odor. She turned to Mr. King. "Oh my, that does stink. Mr. King, if you will show me what room he's in, I'll take Billy to my mother."

Mr. King smiled. "Right this way, Sofia." He turned to the front door and entered the house. Sofia looked back at Peggy as she slowly followed Mr. King into the house. Sofia's heart jumped in her beautiful chest when she saw Mr. King walking up the stairs. She did not think about the possibility that Billy was in one of the upstairs bedrooms. Sofia heard the ghost stories and knew a great deal of the ghostly activity was in the upper level of the house, especially in the bedrooms.

Jason was at the wheel of his Uncle Bobby's truck. He was waiting for his mother to tell him where they were going and why. He knew she was playing with him when she remained silent as they passed Johnny Vona's dock. He was glad when she broke the silence.

"Son, you ain't gonna believe where we're goin' and what's happened to us." Jason could hear the unusual excitement in his mother's voice. He was more than ready to hear what she had to say. Jason saw her facial expression change when she looked out of the front windshield of the moving truck. Jason looked, too. He had already seen the sight his mother was now seeing. Mary C. could not contain herself.

"What the hell is that?"

Jason looked out the window and knew she was referring to the Mayport cowboys and their donkey. Mary C. was speechless as she watched the strange quartet walking on the side of the road. Jason had to speak up.

"I was gonna tell ya about this when we was at Mr. King's, but I didn't have a chance. You was so excited. I didn't want to spoil it for ya."

Jason stopped the truck as the foursome came near. Beanie passed the passenger's side window first. He was still holding onto the reins leading the donkey. Mary C. could only see the ears of the short donkey as its head passed the window. The next thing she saw was Chichemo's red face. He smiled and saluted Mary C. as if they were in the military. Mary C. moved her head back when the spider monkey jumped from the back of the donkey and landed on Chichemo's shoulder. Mary C. turned slowly to look at Jason.

"Is the boat okay?"

"It seems fine. Mathias said Chichemo got the boat ready to go out, but didn't come back. The boat's been at the dock for two days."

Mary C. surprised Jason when she smiled. "About every year or so Chichemo does this. Sometimes he lasts a little longer, but it's usually once a year. Beanie adds to the problem, but Chichemo gets weak when it comes to that booze. He's still a good man, but like us all, he does have his weaknesses. He looks and acts a fool when he gets like this. Your Uncle Bobby used to be the one who would get Chichemo away from here and dry him out when he got on a drinkin' binge. Now, that Bobby's gone I wonder who'll save Chichemo from the bottle? Let's go. They'll be fine. Nothin' ever happens to drunks. Don't you worry, nothin' can spoil my surprise." Mary C. had something else to tell Jason as they drove away. "If there's still light when we get back, John needs you to climb up under the house and find out what stinks. If it's too dark you can do it in the mornin', if we can stand the smell all night."

Mr. King stood at the door of the bedroom. Sofia was still walking slowly up the stairs. The hallway to the bedroom looked to be a mile long to the scared young woman. Mr. King opened the door to the room. "He's in here. This is one of my most haunted rooms, but Mary C. didn't care. I'm not sure why, but she actually wanted to stay in here."

Sofia finally made her way to the door of the room. She did not like the comment about the room being the most haunted. She looked into the room and saw Billy on the bed. He was wide-awake lying there wedged between two pillows. Mr. King stood back from the door so Sofia could go in. He knew she was still afraid even though he was standing with her. The beautiful young woman took a deep breath and stepped into the room. Mr. King smiled and had to relieve her apprehension.

"Nothin's gonna scare ya, Sofia. Just get the child. I promise you'll be fine." Sofia smiled a weak smile and walked to the bed.

Miss Margaret stepped out of the store and looked toward Mr. King's house. She saw Peggy standing at the foot of the front steps. Peggy was holding her nose with one hand and waved to her mother with her other hand. Miss Margaret was worried about why it was taking so long for the girls to come back with Billy. She yelled to Peggy.

"What's going on over there? Where's your sister?"

Peggy looked toward her mother. "She's getting Billy."

Miss Margaret had to smile at Peggy's fear of Mr. King's ghosts. "Peggy, don't tell me you're scared to go in there? Why are you holding your nose?"

Peggy did not hesitate to yell back to her mother. "It stinks over here. I won't tell you I'm afraid if you don't want me to, but that doesn't mean it's true. I don't even like standing here."

Sofia picked Billy up off the bed. She turned to Mr. King, who was still standing at the door. "Are there really ghosts here, Mr. King?" She moved into the hallway.

"You better believe it. It's the perfect setting for the souls who have not passed over to the other side. It's a waiting room for the spirits trying not to leave this Earth. Some say it's because the house was built over a Timacuan Indian burial mound. Some say it's sitting on a Spanish graveyard. Maybe it's both. No matter the reason, the atmosphere here is perfect for attracting the dead. You felt it when you came in. Everyone does. When you walk through that front door you know something's different. You feel it deep inside. You felt it when you came in. I've learned to live with it. I've actually learned to like it. You might say I've become the caretaker for the lost souls in search of a place to be until they find their way. You'd be shocked at the things that happen here on a daily basis."

Sofia understood what he was saying about the way the old house felt. It was different than other houses she had been in before. It smelled old and wet. The antiques and old pictures added to the strange atmosphere. Sofia held Billy close to her body.

"You're really not afraid here are you, Mr. King? Have you ever been scared?"

"Oh, I've been scared lots of times. Especially, when it first started for me. I had heard about the ghosts before, but that was in the original boarding house that burned down. When the house was rebuilt the haunting ended and the ghosts were gone for many years. When the ghosts reappeared, they were not the same one's from the first haunting. It was as if the new house attracted new ghosts. I became the new host for the new ghosts." Sofia smiled at Mr. King's little ghostly humor. She turned with the child and walked toward the top of the stairs.

Peggy looked up at the front door when Sofia walked out onto the porch holding Billy in her arms. A feeling of relief ran over her body. "You all right?"

Sofia moved down the steps. "I'm fine." She turned back to Mr. King at the door. "Thank you Mr. King. We'll see you later."

Mr. King couldn't resist. "Bye Peggy, nice to see you again. Come back sometime when you can come in and stay longer. Bye Sofia. Sorry about the smell, ladies."

Margie was polishing the wooden items in the store. Her thoughts were of the carousel and the oak tree. She knew as soon as she got the opportunity she would visit the tree. Margie turned to the front door when the bell rang. Miss Margaret, Peggy and Sofia walked into the store. Sofia was carrying Billy, the oak baby. Miss Margaret was talking.

"Peggy, I can't believe you stayed outside while Sofia went into the house. I didn't know you were that scared of Mr. King's house." Miss Margaret turned to Sofia. "Did you see any ghosts?"

"No ma'am, but that doesn't mean they weren't there. I believe in the ghosts, too. I was nervous, but I trusted Mr. King to protect me. Besides, I had to get Billy, ghosts or not. I used to be scared, but I'm not any more." She looked at Margie as if to say, *I killed a man. I created a ghost. Why should I be scared?"* Margie knew Sofia's thought and tried to change the subject for her little sister.

"Now Mother, you know it's hard not to be afraid of that house. Mr. King makes sure the thought of ghosts stays in your head. He's pretty good at scaring us all."

Miss Margaret nodded her head. "He is the master at ghost stories and scaring folks. He's been doing it for years, now."

Mary C. directed Jason to drive into the parking area of the Thor Chevrolet dealership. It was the only new car dealership at Jacksonville Beach. Jason stopped the truck and turned off the engine. He looked at his mother and waited for her to give him more instructions.

Mary C. knew she had to tell him the good news. "I know I've been silly about my good news, but it was fun for me to play with you a little bit. You're so damn serious all the time, son."

Jason had to respond. "Well, when ya think about it, we ain't had much to laugh about lately."

Mary C. nodded. "That's true, but all that ends today. We need to start smilin' again. Let's start right now."

She handed Jason his envelope with his $25,000 check. He took the envelope, opened it and took out the check. Jason had seen a check before when Steve Robertson gave him money for saving the crane operators life at the jetties. He looked at the check and then at his mother.

"It's for you, Jason; $25,000. The Crane left it to you in his will. He left me one, too, $25,000 for each of us. This'll change our lives." Mary C. shook her head. "Is there any emotion inside you at all, son? We've got $50,000. Do you understand what that means? We can do what ever we want." She did not wait for Jason to respond. She did not care. "Oh, and we came here to get my new car."

Mr. Leek was standing with Mathias when they heard a loud voice. They both turned to the large front double doors of his fish house as the Mayport cowboys made their grand entrance. Chichemo was still riding the donkey and Beanie was still leading the way. The donkey's hooves made a clacking noise of the floor of the fish house. Beanie stopped their forward motion when he saw Mr. Leek. Beanie was still wearing the child's black cowboy hat. It had the white lacing embroidered on the brim of the hat. When the donkey stopped, Chichemo, Beanie and Bosco all saluted Mr. Leek at the same time.

It took all Mr. Leek's intestinal fortitude not to burst into laughter. It was a funny sight. He was able to maintain his stern facial expression. He did not want to condone the drunken state the two men were in. It was all Mr. Leek could handle when Chichemo remained on the donkey as Beanie guided the animal closer to Mr. Leek. Chichemo grinned an idiot's smile and ended Mr. Leek's attempt to hold his laughter when Chichemo saluted again and made his declaration.

"Captain Chichemo Singleton reportin' for duty sir. My mama calls me Earl Todd."

Chichemo sat on the donkey with his saluting hand to his forehead, waiting for Mr. Leek to acknowledge him. Mr. Leek started laughing, but he did return the salute. Chichemo motioned for Beanie to continue leading the donkey toward the main dock area where the boats were tied to the pylons. Mr. Leek signaled to

Mathias to stop Beanie from taking the donkey out onto the dock. Mathias stepped in front of Beanie. Mr. Leek did the talking.

"Fellas, y'all can't take that animal out there on the dock. It's too dangerous. I don't think y'all are in any condition to be out there near those boats. I'd hate to see one of ya fall in the river."

Beanie looked at Mathias with a mean glare in his bloodshot eyes. Mathias did not care. He was going to do whatever Mr. Leek told him. He would have done anything to keep Beanie from going out onto the dock. Beanie turned to face Mr. Leek.

"We need to lie down and sleep this off. I'm clearin' a little, but I need to lie down."

Mr. Leek stepped to Beanie. "Why don't y'all come to the office? I'm afraid for y'all tryin' to get on the boat. One of y'all can sleep it off on the couch and I've got that little cot in the back. It would be better for everyone if y'all go in there."

Mr. Leek motioned to Mathias and he walked over to help Chichemo get down off the donkey. Chichemo mumbled as Mathias walked him into the office and took him to the cot in the back. Beanie smiled at Mr. Leek.

"You always rescue somebody, don't ya Al? You want me to take Blossom outside?"

Mr. Leek had to smile again. "No, I'll take care of Blossom. You go lay down on the couch. Get some sleep."

Beanie nodded his head and dropped the reins from his hand. Mathias walked back into the fish house. Mr. Leek motioned for him to take the donkey outside. Beanie went into the office and fell face first, down on the couch. Mathias walked past Mr. Leek leading the donkey.

"Mathias where's that damn monkey?"

"He's in the back room layin' next to Mr. Chichemo. He passed out, too."

Jason stood next to a new fire engine red Chevrolet Corvette. His mother was sitting in the bucket seat under the steering wheel. The salesman who helped her was walking back into the main building.

"Thank ya, Frank." Mary C. looked at Jason. "I'm takin' the money to the bank. Follow me so you can put yours in, too. We'll keep some cash and put the rest in that account the Crane started for you when he gave you that other money. Jason followed her out onto Beach Boulevard. They were headed to the Ocean State Bank in Neptune Beach.

The store had been cleaned and prepared to Miss Margaret's satisfaction. She surprised her four daughters with her announcement.

"The store looks wonderful, ladies. Now, I'm going to stay and work the rest of the evening. It's something I need to do for myself, so don't make a big deal out of it, please. I don't want any arguments about it and that's final." The four girls looked at each other. "Now, you four go on home, relax, go to bed, eat, take showers, what ever you want. I'll close the store at ten o'clock and I expect one of you to be here to pick me up. Margie, drive your sisters on home and let me be here alone now, without any of you around. You four decide who opens in the morning and work out a new schedule for everyone. I'll work three afternoon shifts and two nights. Add me to the schedule. Peggy, you do it. You write down the times each of you wants. You're the best at making everybody happy. Margie and Sofia, the next time you are going to run away, please just tell me so I won't worry so much. Sofia, take Billy to the house so he'll be more comfortable. I'll send Mary C. to get him when she gets back."

Each daughter wanted to say something to their mother, but they knew that was a bad idea. Sofia took Billy. They did not understand the unusual request, but Margie led the way to the door and the family station wagon. They got into the car. Margie turned the key and started the engine. As the family station wagon began to move away from the store, Susan could not contain her thoughts.

"Well now, that was interesting, wasn't it?"

Peggy responded first. "I don't think interesting is the word. Strange sounds better."

Sofia blew air from her mouth. "Margie, we really hurt mother's feeling when we left. I'm so sorry and sad about that stupid mistake. Just think of all the things that happened because of me. None of this would have happened if I hadn't left."

Margie had to add her thoughts. "You can let mother make you feel guilty if you want. And yes, you're right. Some awful things happened because we left, but things are going to happen. Do we stay here and never try to do anything else? Do we stay scared our entire lives?" Margie pulled the car up next to their house and turned off the engine. She turned to her sisters. "We've got to talk. You might not like what I'm going to say, but I'm depending on the fact that we're sisters and we can talk to each other openly."

All three sisters nodded their heads at Margie. "Good. Now, we've had a lot of wild things happen to us because of Jason and Miss Mary C. I think we're stronger and better off because of it. I know you three think I've gone crazy with the tree and trying to think like Miss Mary C., but you have to admit our lives are much more exciting with those two in it. And as for the tree, I like believing in something. Something I can see and feel."

Sofia's eyes lit up. "What about God? Don't you believe in God?"

Margie took a deep breath. "Yes, Sofia I still believe in God. I don't see Him very often though, do you?"

Sofia did not like Margie's tone. "Margie, you're scaring me."

"Sofia, you killed a man so you could continue living. Nothing should ever scare you again. We've got to learn from these things that are happening to us and get stronger."

Peggy joined in. "That's all good talk, but people are dying around Miss Mary C. all the time. I would hate it if one of us got killed because we were with them. It almost happened to Sofia. It was because she was with Jason." Peggy looked at Sofia and then at Margie. "And you Margie, you had to run and hide because Miss Mary C. shot another man. I'm just afraid one of us, especially you two, is going to get hurt. You spend more time with them than we do." Peggy looked at Susan. Susan nodded her head and joined the conversation.

"Peggy's right. Even though we all like being with Miss Mary C., with all the excitement that follows her, we should realize for some reason they are both very dangerous. Someone is always after them about something."

Margie lit up. "That's right! Someone is always after them and the baby. We're part of something special, here. It's our opportunity to do something besides work in that store. We can do our family duties for mother and the store, but can't we help keep that baby safe just in case he is a true oak baby?" She looked at Sofia. Sofia joined in.

"The priest said the baby was special and I believed him. But, I do agree with Peggy about being scared one of us will get hurt or even killed. I know being with Jason has changed my life in more than one way, but I have to admit, I'm not sure it was in a good way. When I think about it, more bad things have happened than good things."

Susan had to add her thought at the moment. Even though Susan had been with Jason sexually she was the one sister who had spent the least amount of time with him.

"And let's talk about Jason for a minute. I can't believe we have all had sex with him." Margie, Peggy and Sofia were shocked at Susan's comment. Susan knew they were speechless at the moment so she continued. "How could that have happened? We all know he loves Sofia. If they get married, how will she be able to look at us? How does she look at us now?" Sofia put her head down. Margie had to speak up.

"I blame Jason for all that. He knew he had been with all of us, but we really didn't know at first. We were just reacting to his charm and I think each one of us thought he was reacting to our charming personalities, too."

Peggy smiled. "I wonder if four sisters have ever been with the same man before? I hope no one finds out about it. How embarrassing would that be? We don't need to talk about it any more. If Sofia wants to be with Jason and she can put our past mistakes out of her mind, then that's fine." She looked at Sofia. Sofia gave a half smile. Margie had a different suggestion.

"Peggy, you have to be honest. You know good and well if you were alone with Jason at this very moment you would be naked in a heartbeat. We all would." Sofia's eyes lit up as Margie continued. "I know I would. I don't think he gives a rat's ass about any of us, including you." She looked at Sofia. "Now, I do think he likes Sofia the best, because she is the prettiest and she was innocent when he finally got to her. But, let's face it. When we first met him, he was devoted to two people, his Uncle Bobby and his mother. Now, he's devoted to his mother and his son. A son, I might add, from another woman he was with, not one of us."

They were all silent as they absorbed what their older sister was presenting to them. Margie knew she had them as a captive audience. She would not let go.

"Now, it's true we all love the baby. There is something special about him. I believe he is the greatest oak baby of them all. You three can say I'm crazy, but I would have Jason's next oak baby tomorrow if he took me and layed with me under the oak tree." She looked at Sofia again. "You know in your heart, Jason will not stay with you. I know it hurts, but you really do know it's true. Jason has been enjoying us all for two years now. I say if any of us gets the chance to enjoy him, do it. Why do the men of the world get to enjoy the women? What ever is inside all of us comes from our blood. We all seem to have a man's appetite for sins of the flesh."

Peggy could not maintain her silence. "You sound like a preacher going in the opposite direction. The sad part is, you're right. We talked one time about this, but we were all too drunk to complete the subject." She looked at Sofia. "We all know you and Jason have been together. We know how hard it is to stay away from him. What are you thinking? How do you feel about what we're saying?" They were all surprised when Sofia did not hesitate with her answer.

"The first thing on my mind is how scared I am that I will soon be arrested for killing that awful man. I've tried to put it out of my mind, but that will never happen. Every time I see a police car, I think they're coming to get me. I feel it will haunt me the rest of my life. I also know I have waited too long to turn myself in. I am locked into the fact I ran away. As for Jason, it does hurt that he will never be completely mine. He has never been and he never will be. I'm happy and sad I ever met him. I will always have feelings for him, as we all do, but all of the sadness in my life has come from knowing Jason." She put her head down and then lifted it to look at Margie. "If I'm ever alone with Jason, I will most likely take my clothes off again. If any of you are alone with him I'm sure you will do the same." The other three sisters were silent after Sofia's declaration and permission for her sisters to enjoy Jason sexually. She had one more thought for Margie. "I do not want to be the mother of an oak baby. That's really looking for trouble, don't you think? It was funny when you said, 'rat's ass'. Where did you get that from?"

Mary C. and Jason had finished their business at the Ocean State Bank. Mary C. was sitting behind the wheel of her new Corvette and Jason stood next to the car. Mary C. was still smiling.

"You go on back to Mayport and check on Billy. I don't want Miss Margaret to have to keep him too long. She ain't gonna be herself for a while. Not 'til a little time passes, anyway. And remember, she ain't gonna be real friendly to you. You ran away with her baby girl. Somethin' like that just don't bounce off a mother like her. Just be polite and don't hang around. Time'll heal it all." She turned the key and the Corvette engine roared like a lion and then calmed down and purred like a kitten. "Now, that sounds like a car should sound, don't it?" Jason smiled and nodded his head as his excited mother continued to talk. "I'm too dressed up and excited to go home. I'm gonna take this baby down Seminole Road and see if I can hear those crickets when I fly by. Then, I'm gonna park her next to the steps at Bill's Hideaway. Then, I'm gonna go over to the Fish Bowl. I'll be home when I get there." Mary C. pushed the gas pedal down with her foot and the red Corvette blasted out of the small parking lot.

CHAPTER TWO

The Florida sun was on its way down on the west side of the St. Johns River. Jason was driving back to Mayport and had reached the dangerous curve at the Little Jetties. He knew it was where the Crane had flipped his Corvette and was killed. Jason thought he would give up the money if it would bring Steve Robertson back, but he did not think his mother would give up the car. Jason smiled at his funny but true thought. He knew how sharp the curve was ahead of him so he slowed down Uncle Bobby's truck and took the turn at a safe speed.

Mr. John King sat on his front porch. It was one of his favorite things to do. The sound of the ferry horn blasted, shaking the evening air. He was alone, but talked out loud. "I hope some of y'all let me know who's still here. I hope everyone stayed in place, especially you Norman. If you've settled in, give me some sign so I'll know."

Mr. John King did love his resident spirits. He waved to Jason as he drove past the house and stopped Uncle Bobby's truck in front of Miss Margaret's store.

Jason was hoping he would not have to face more than one of the sisters. His wish came true when the bell on the door rang as he walked in and found what appeared to be Miss Margaret minding the store alone. He looked for the sisters as Miss Margaret gave him the perfect greeting.

"Good evening, may I help you with something." Miss Margaret shook her head. "Oh Jason, I'm sorry. That's just a habit with me. I even knew it was you and still said it. I already know you're here for Billy." Jason wanted to say he thought the greeting was great, but he did not want to say too much. Miss Margaret carried the one sided conversation. "The girls took Billy to the house so he would be more comfortable. Those girls do love that baby. They've only been gone an hour or so."

Jason nodded his head. "Thank you for taking care of Billy. I'm sure Mama will tell you all about why we had to go."

Miss Margaret smiled. "If she wants."

Jason smiled, too. "Oh, she wants to. She'll probably come see you in the mornin'." Jason reached for the handle of the screen door. Miss Margaret was a great woman. "Jason." He turned back to face her. "It's hard for a mother to let her children go. You have won Sofia's heart and I think Margie's, too. How you will deal with that dilemma is far beyond me. I'm trying not to blame you for running away with Sofia. I know such thoughtless acts are in the nature of men, especially men around here. I actually blame myself for not teaching my girls about life. I'm mad at myself because I know about these things and still did not teach the lessons properly. It's difficult for a mother to admit she has failed with her children. This too will pass and we'll all move to another lifetime crisis. They seem to come around faster and faster. With four beautiful daughters, what in God's name should I expect? I was just asking for trouble. You go on now, get Billy."

Jason was more than happy to leave Miss Margaret with her philosophical moment. Even though he heard her say it was not all his fault, he knew she thought it was. Jason would try and stay clear of Miss Margaret like his mother had suggested. He avoided the four daughters as a group and now he would avoid their mother.

Mr. King waved at Jason again as he turned the truck around in front of the store and passed the haunted house. Jason blew the horn to acknowledge Mr. King's kind gesture.

Mary C. sat on a stool at the bar in Bill's Hideaway. She did not recognize the young bartender behind the bar. He was a handsome, square-jawed young man. He did not look old enough to be tending bar. He stepped up to Mary C. "Good evening ma'am. What's your pleasure?"

Mary C. smiled. She was in her element, she had money and she had her new car waiting outside. "That's a loaded question young man. I have many pleasures; too many to pick just one. But, for now, let's make it Jack Black and coke. Are you sure you're old enough to pour it for me?"

"You got it." He did not respond to her questioning his age.

Mary C. turned on the stool to look around the room as the bartender mixed her drink. She had a mental flash that surprised her. She saw the Crane sitting on one of the bar stools at the end of the bar. He raised his glass to her and then he was gone. She turned away from the strange vision to see Mr. Butler sitting at one of the tables. He raised his glass. Mary C. remembered she had seen them both at the same time the last time she was in Bill's Hideaway. She did not want to turn and adjust her eyes again for fear Hawk would be the next ghost she saw. Mary C. commented out loud. "Where the hell is John King when ya need him?"

"Excuse me, ma'am."

Mary C. looked up to see the young bartender standing in front of her. Her Jack Black was on the bar. Mary C. recovered from her visions. "Oh, don't mind me. I always talk to myself when the ghosts are following me around."

"A woman like you should never have to talk to her self, unless she just wants to."

"I'm old enough to be your mother, but it was nice of you to say that."

"No problem." The young man moved away from Mary C. and began cleaning his bar glasses. Mary C. felt different. She had never told a man she was old enough to be his mother. Being a grandmother had its downside. She smiled and sipped her Jack Black.

Mr. Leek stood near the double door entrance to his fish house with the head dockworker, Mathias. Mr. Leek was a good man and treated everyone with respect.

"You did a great job for me while I was gone, Mathias. The boat captains all say we never missed a beat. Thank you for takin' such good care of things for me."

"Yes, suh. But, you was only gone two days, Mr. Leek."

"Well, at least I know I can trust things to be done right around here, if I decide to go away for a longer time." He handed Mathias a white envelope containing two twenty-dollar bills as a bonus for his good work. Mathias took the envelope and opened it. His eyes lit up like flares.

"Oh sweet Jesus, Mr. Leek. That's too much, suh. Let me give one back, suh. You can give it to the church."

Mr. Leek had "glory chills" run through his body when Mathias offered to give half his bonus to the church. "Praise the Lord Mathias, that's the kindest, most unselfish offer I've ever heard a man make to the Lord. I feel Jesus standing with us right now."

Mathias looked around the big fish house with his eyes wide open. "I feels Him, too, suh. I always liked that feelin', even when I was a little boy. You know how it feels when the hair stands up on the back of your neck? That's usually the Lord standin' near by." Mathias thought for a second. "Now, I did have them chills and the hair raised on my neck over at Mr. King's one night. But, I don't think the Lord had much to do with that one."

Mr. Leek could not resist. "What happened at the King house that night?"

Mathias took a deep breath. "I ain't sure, suh, why I even mentioned that. I ain't never told nobody 'bout that night over there."

"You don't have to tell me, Mathias, if it bothers you."

"It ain't just what happened at the house. It's a lot of different things, lately. I never had no dreams. I always sleeps like a rock. For some reason, that's all changed now. It all started the day you left. The day Junior Pane and Moochee come here to find that boy, Jason. I knowed somethin' was bad wrong." Mathias' eyes revealed his fear to Mr. Leek.

"Just take your time and tell me what's happened."

Mathias took another deep breath. "I was sure Junior and Moochee was up to no good the way they come over here lookin' for that boy. I seen Clayton Demps with Moochee that mornin' and now he's gone. He just disappeared. His family can't find him."

"You think Moochee did somethin' to Clayton?"

"I know he did. It was in my dream. Moochee was part of it, but Junior did the killin'."

"They killed him? What on earth for?"

"Don't know that, Mr. Leek. I just know they done it. I knows I can't prove it with a dream, but I knows it's true."

"People have dreams all the time, Mathias."

"I don't."

"You had just seen Junior and Moochee. You heard Clayton was missing. You hate Junior. It all fits together. It was all sitting right there in your mind. You had the responsibility of taking care of the dock and it all came together in one of your rare dreams."

"That ain't all, Mr. Leek." Mathias licked his dry lips. I'm gonna get me a cold RC out the box. I'm getting' the cotton mouth with all this talkin'. I don't usually talk this much. My glands ain't used to it. Can I get you a cold drink, suh?"

"I believe I will take a cold one."

The young bartender was standing in front of Mary C. again. "You ready for another, ma'am?" Mary C. put her hand over the top of the glass.

"I'm ridin' light tonight. This was fine. Is Hank still workin' here?"

"No ma'am. I took Hank's place. You a friend of his?"

"I've known him since I was a child. It was good seein' him in here the last time. I knew he wouldn't stay around too long. He's always on the move. He was a good friend of my daddy's."

"I guess you ain't heard what happened then."

Mary C.'s stomach went sour. She had an awful feeling. "No, I ain't. What happened?"

"Hank got beat up real bad two nights ago. He's in the hospital. They ain't sure he's gonna make it."

Mary C. was trying to register what the young man had said. "What do ya mean, he got beat up?"

"I heard he left here about two in the mornin'. Somebody either followed him home or was waiting for him at his cottage. He was staying in one of those old cottages on the beach. The police said it might have been a robbery and he walked in and caught 'em. They say he put up one hell-of-a fight, but they think there was more than one man beatin' him. Who ever did it, hurt him pretty bad."

Mary C. was sick to her stomach. Her wonderful new attitude was blasted from her mind. "What would they want to steal from Hank? He ain't never had much. He lives a simple life that's for sure. Hell, he's always helping folks."

"I never met the man. I've heard people sayin' the same thing you are. 'He's a good man'. My daddy knows him, too."

Before the young man could continue a new voice joined them. "Evenin' Mary C." She turned to see her good friend Bill the owner Bill's Hideaway.

"Hey Bill. I can't believe what happened to Hank. I just talked to him a week ago. He was funny about bein' back behind the bar. He laughed when I called him the Wizard."

Bill nodded. "He told me he saw you. He was excited about you comin' in. I had to sit here and listen to him talk about the old times with your daddy. He's got some great stories about those days."

"What do you think happened?"

"I don't know, but I think it's more than somebody robbing him and then beatin' him. I just got a feelin' that's all." He looked at the young bartender. "Have ya met my nephew, Joe? He's fillin' in 'til we get somebody full-time. He's my sister's oldest boy. He was helpin' in the kitchen. He just turned nineteen, but he looks older. He's like his mama. He matured early."

Joe stuck his hand out to Mary C. "I'm sorry I didn't introduce myself. I'm Joe Croom. Nice to meet ya. I hope your drink's okay. I'm kinda new at this."

"The drink's fine, Joe. I can't believe you're Stella's oldest son. I would have never recognized you. You have really turned into a man. I know ya mama good. Our birthday's in the same month. We spent a lot of time together as children. She tried to keep us all out of trouble. She acted like a mama even before she was a mama."

Bill smiled and nodded his head again. "That's a damn truth. I hadn't thought of that in years. She took care of everybody and everybody's business. Now, all she does is try to keep her younger boys in line. That's become a full-time job. Joe here, is the only one can make 'em act right."

Mary C. nodded. "You're talkin' 'bout them twins, ain't ya? I heard them little fellas is hell'yuns."

Bill shook his head. "Hell'yuns might just be the proper word for those two. Stella's thinkin' 'bout sendin' them off to a private Catholic school. One of them schools where the boys live there and don't come home, 'cept Christmas."

Joe Croom smiled. "Now, Uncle Bill, you know Mama ain't gonna send Chuck and Buck nowhere. She just gets frustrated and says all kinds of silly things."

Bill wanted to continue his thoughts. "Now, she ain't never had no trouble from Joe, here, or Pee Wee. Pee Wee's 'bout the best little fella around. But, that Chuck and Buck's got mean streaks a mile long; pure meanness." It was strange to Joe and Mary C. when Bill completely changed the subject. "What brings you out this evenin', Mary C.?"

She took a deep breath. Joe watched her chest rise and then go down. She was good to look at. Joe had done his share of looking at pretty women lately. He still had not recovered from his wild, foggy night on the sand hill with Margie under the oak tree.

"I had some good things happen today 'til I heard about Hank. It kinda takes away from the good stuff. Why ya feel like somethin's strange about this thing with Hank? Who would want to hurt him?"

Bill lowered his voice as Joe moved away to help a new customer who sat down at the far end of the bar. "I'd rather talk to you about it privately. You're one of the few people I'd trust with my thoughts 'bout this. You're one of the few who would understand. I need to talk to John, too."

Mary C. nodded. "I'm stayin' at John's for a while. Why don't you come over there and talk to us both?"

Bill nodded his head. "I think I need to do that. When ya think would be a good time?"

"None better than right now. I'll take you for a ride in my new car. We'll go talk to John and I'll bring ya back later. You're gonna like my new car."

Mr. Leek and Mathias sat on the side railing of the shrimp boat *Mary C.* They both held their cold drink bottles to their lips. Mr.

Leek pulled his away from his mouth first to watch Mathias drink his down with one long swallow.

"Holy Moly, Mathias, you were thirsty."

"I always drinks 'em like that. Cools me down and fills me up fast. I like that feelin'. It's a habit I got when I was a boy. I used to guzzle gin and cold beer like that, too, 'til the Lord sent you to find my drunken body face down in that ditch off Mayport Road."

Mr. Leek's eyes filled with tears. He had no idea Mathias thought about the time he found him lying in the ditch near the Oak Harbor Baptist Church. Mr. Leek was cutting the grass of the churchyard and as he pushed the lawnmower to the edge of the ditch he found Mathias. He took him into the back of the church, cleaned and sobered him up. He gave Mathias a job on the dock. Mr. Leek could see the gratefulness in Mathias' eyes.

"That was a great day for us both. We both found a friend that day. Now, stop all this sentimental foolishness and tell me about your dreams and what happened at Mr. King's house."

Mathias smiled and nodded his head. "That was funny, Mr. Leek when ya said, "Holy Moly. I ain't sure what a Holy Moly is, but it sounds funny when a growed man says it."

"Well Mathias, I'm glad you like it. I call it a religious expression of excitement."

Mathias grinned a big white teeth smile. "Now, you just funnin' with me, ain't ya, Mr. Leek?"

"I never make fun of the expressions from the bible. I believe I read "Holy Moly" in the book of Genesis. It was when God first saw Eve standing naked with Adam. He said "Holy Moly, what a difference!" They both exploded with laughter at Mr. Leek's out of character, humorous explanation for the first "Holy Moly".

Jason pulled Uncle Bobby's truck up to the front porch at Miss Margaret's house. He experienced a mild body shiver at the prospect of seeing all four sisters at one time. He knew he had to get Billy, but he was afraid of what he might have to face in the house. Sofia and Margie together would be hard for him to handle.

He ran away with Sofia. They slept together a number of times. Sofia killed a man who would have kidnapped her. Jason made love with Sofia in the carousel room. He had sex with Margie in her room and then spent one night in the carousel room with Margie,

Little Tom and Helga. His sexual cup did runneth over when it came to Sofia and Margie. His heart began to pound in his chest when he saw Sofia walk out of the front door of the house. She was holding Billy and stopped at the edge of the porch. Jason got out of the truck. Sofia was talking to the child.

"There's your daddy, now. He is a handsome man, don't you think?"

Jason gave a half smile. "Hey Sofia. How's he doin'?"

"He's always fine when he's with me."

"That sounds like somethin' mama would say."

"I'm getting more and more like your mother everyday. You think that's good or bad?"

Jason thought it was a strange question. He had just left strange talk behind him with Miss Margaret at the store. He did not need any more. He knew he had to respond.

"Mama's got some good ways, but she's got other ways, too. You know that. Just keep your own good ways Sofia. You're one of a kind, please stay that way."

"We all change as time goes on. In fact, in the blink of an eye we can change. Or better yet, in the squeeze of a trigger. You talk about growing up in a hurry. First, I made that ridiculous decision to leave with you. I shared your shower and your bed. Then, I killed a man. Then, I shared your bed again; tried to treat it like it was all a dream and didn't happen. Then, my mother and sisters found it necessary to rescue me. Your mother and my sister Margie had to defend themselves on their way to find me. I love you so much and Margie does, too."

Sofia began to cry. She stepped on the top step and held Billy out to Jason. Jason took the child. As soon as Sofia released Billy into the safety of his father's arms, she turned and ran crying into the house. Jason was lost as usual for the proper reaction. He lay Billy in the front seat next to him and drove away.

Margie walked around the corner of the room to see Sofia run up the stairs. She looked out the front window and saw the truck moving away from the house. She looked up the stairs as she heard Sofia's bedroom door close. Margie turned and followed Sofia up to the room.

Mr. Leek and Mathias were back to the serious subject of Mathias' dreams and his encounter at the haunted house. Mr. Leek would not interrupt Mathias as he talked.

"I saw Clayton Demps in my dream the night of the same day I saw him with Moochee. I knowed then, he was dead when Junior and Moochee was over here. They had already done the killin'. Clayton could only tell me with his eyes. I don't think he could talk. I don't think he had no arms either. I didn't want to be in that dream. I was fightin' to get out of it. I knowed Clayton was tryin' to tell me about Junior and Moochee."

Mathias stopped for a second. He was breathing deeply. Mr. Leek could see it was a struggle for Mathias to relive his nightmare. Mathias began again.

"When I heared Clayton was missin', I knowed what he was tryin' to tell me. That's why I went to Mr. King's house. I 'member hearin' Mr. King talkin' 'bout the way some folks fight to stay alive if they's bein' killed. They tries to stay with the livin' and refuse to cross over to the other side. When they do finally give in and cross over they leave somethin' behind. What ever they leave behind becomes their ghost and will appear now and then to the livin', just to tell someone what really happened to 'em. Clayton was fightin' to stay, but he was too weak. He had to tell me in my dream. I was kinda hopin' if Mr. King could tell me if Clayton had made it over there. I was gonna tell Mr. King 'bout my dream and if we could do somethin' to Moochee and Junior." Mathias stopped again and licked his full lips. "I might have to swill down another cold one. Let me get some water."

Mathias stood up and walked over to a facet that was attached to a thick, two inch wide, rubber hose. The end of the hose was lying close to the water over the edge of the dock. When Mathias turned the round knob they could hear the icy cold water splashing into the river water, under the dock. Mathias stepped to the edge of the wooden dock planks and bent over to pull the hose up so he could cool and fill his mouth.

Mathias stood straight up with the hose in his hand when a huge female Manatee came up out of the river water and grabbed the end of the water hose with her mouth. The creature did not release the hose as she fell back under the water. Mr. Leek was startled when he heard the loud splash and saw Mathias fall back onto the dock. Mathias got to his feet and looked over the edge of the dock and down into the water.

"Hurry, Mr. Leek. You ain't gonna believe what I's seein'."

Mr. Leek rushed to Mathias' side and looked down into the water. It was truly a wonderful sight of nature. The huge Manatee cow had pulled the hose down into the water so her single calf could drink the clean, cold water from the hose. The mother manatee pushed the end of the hose in the baby's mouth. It sucked on the hose and then released it. The mother took a drink and then gave it back to the baby. Neither man had ever seen such a sight. It was one of those times you wished everyone you knew could be there with you, mainly, because no one would believe it. The huge sea cow dropped the hose from her mouth and pushed the calf away from the dock. They both sank into the deep river water and were gone. Mathias looked at Mr. Leek and smiled. "Holy Moly!"

The new fire-engine red Chevrolet Corvette took the curve at the Little Jetties like it was floating on air. Mary C. smiled at Bill in the passenger's bucket seat. He smiled back. "Don't worry 'bout me. You can't go too fast for me. I been crazy 'bout speed my whole life. If I had my wish I would have been one of them race car drivers at Daytona. I raced a little on the street and on the beach. I like fast cars, always have."

"Well Bill, ain't you just full of surprises here tonight. I never heard 'bout you doin' no racin'."

"You know how it is when ya get married and have to grow up. Responsibility ain't worth a shit, is it?" They both laughed as the car flew past Johnny Vona's dock.

Jason drove Uncle Bobby's truck up to the front of John King's haunted house. Mr. King was still sitting on the porch. As Jason stepped out of the truck, holding the oak baby, the bright lights of Mary C.'s new car lead the way for the rest of the red Corvette.

Mr. King stood up when he realized Mary C. was the driver of the beautiful new sports car. He walked to the front porch railing and stood with Jason. Bill got out of the car and walked to the porch. He looked up at Mr. King. "Damn John, it stinks out here."

Mathias had started to tell the rest of his story. "I know I ain't 'spose to be believein' in no ghosts. But, it's hard to change the way you was raised. Everybody in my family believed in the other side. We talked about ghosts all the time. The dead had as much to do with our lives as the livin'. My gramma talked to 'em all the time. She loved Mr. King's house. If ghosts is real, she's probably over there right now, with the rest of 'em." Mr. Leek tried not to smile at Mathias's serious, but humorous thoughts. Mathias continued. "When I got there and saw that Mr. King was gone, I shoulda just left right then. I don't know what made me stay. I even thought about my gramma bein' there. Maybe she could tell me 'bout my dream. I had a bad feelin' while I was standin' on the porch. I wanted to pray, but I didn't think it would be proper to pray when I was on a ghost hunt. I looked into the window of the front door. Ain't that crazy? I knowed Mr. King was not there and I still looked through that window. That's when I saw 'em. At least I think I saw 'em." Mathias stopped again. Mr. Leek remained silent. He knew Mathias was collecting his thoughts and the story would continue when he was ready. "You gonna think I'm crazy, Mr. Leek."

"I don't judge folks. We're all a little crazy. Some more than others. I just spent two days at the craziest motel on the face of the Earth. I was with a perverted midget. I watched a fat woman play the piano like an angel. I watched a belly dancer dance almost naked. I slept in a room near a dead man because his friend didn't want to tell the others about the death. It would ruin their show at the lounge. No sir, I would never judge anyone's sanity. No matter what you say, I'll believe that you believe it."

Mathias took one more deep breath. He would complete his story. "What I saw through that window really scared me, but I couldn't look away. I seen Moochee first. He was sittin' on the stairs about half way up. He was holdin' his head down in his hands. I couldn't see his face, but I knew it was Moochee. That's another thing I can't explain. He lifted his head and I could see half his face was gone. It was a nasty thing to look at. I wanted to run, but I seen a huge shadow at the top of the stairs right above Moochee. My feets was stuck to the porch floor. I couldn't run if I tried. I guess I was frozen with pure evil and fear. It was of the devil. The shadow I seen was Junior Pane. He walked down the stairs and stepped over Moochee, like he wasn't there. The front of

Junior's shirt was soaked in blood. He walked all the way to the window of the door and looked out at me, kinda like he was surprised to see me lookin' in at him. He looked scared as I was. I think that was the moment he realized he was dead and was a ghost at Mr. King's. Junior screamed a horrible, painful sound. That's when that big, ugly dog ran up on the porch and bit my leg. He tore the crap out of my pants. I knew if I fell down that demon dog would'a got his big teeth on my neck. One time while I was tryin' to kick myself free of the dog, Junior was screamin' for the hound to eat me. Even as a ghost he's pure evil."

Mr. Leek was speechless at first. Mathias's story had been incredible. Mathias seemed to be resting after his Mayport ghostly tale. Mr. Leek had to know one more thing.

"Mathias, how'd ya get away from the dog?"

"It was the craziest thing of all. I don't know where he come from, but the skinniest man I ever seen in my life come walkin' 'round the corner of the porch. He looked like a skeleton covered in skin. The dog let my leg go and ran growlin' and barkin' toward the skinny man. The dog jumped up off the porch and the animal went right through the man and slammed into the railin' of the porch. I jumped off the porch and started runnin'. I figured that skinny ghost could take care of his own self. I heard that damn dog barkin' durin' the night. I think he was huntin' for me. You know Mr. Leek, I don't think my gramma's over there."

Mr. Leek wanted to laugh out loud, but he knew Mathias was serious and afraid. "I think you need to tell John what happened. He may know somethin' about it."

"I don't think I'm goin' over there ever again. For some reason I ain't that scared of the ghosts, they're dead. It's that dog. He's alive." Mathias pulled up the leg of his pants to expose the bite marks. It was scary, sad and funny all at the same time. Mathias had lived one of the better unbelievable Mayport stories.

Mr. King examined the new Corvette. He did love a beautiful car. Mary C. told her story about the money and the car. Bill told of Hank's critical condition after he was attacked. The group moved into the house and was sitting in Mr. King's living room. Billy was lying at the end of the couch. Mr. King looked at Bill.

"I'm sorry about Hank. He's one of the better men I've known. You got some personal thoughts about what happened to him?"

Bill wasted no time getting straight to his thoughts. "They beat Hank for Elizabeth Stark's necklace."

Mr. John King's mouth fell open and the color left his face. Mary C.'s eyes lit up. Jason had no idea what Bill was talking about. Bill had more.

"I know that sounds crazy, but he told me he thought he found it. He had it hidden at the cottage. He only had it a few days. Hank wanted me to see it. I was gonna go by the cottage that mornin'. They got to him the night before."

Mr. King finally found some words. "Do you know what that necklace would be worth today? The historical value alone would be worth a million dollars. The size of the twelve diamonds and twelve rubies and the gold chain would add millions to it's worth. This is crazy. Do you think he really had it in that cottage?"

"He seemed pretty sure it was the necklace. His excitement was real enough." Bill nodded. "Yeah, he had it. That's why he's in the hospital right now. The police are hoping he'll come around and tell them the names of his attackers. Now, someone else has the necklace."

Mary C. was more than interested. "Did he tell ya how he got it?"

"Yeah, he did. And that part of his story was believable, too. He said he was headed to work. He was a little early so he turned on Wonderwood Road leading to Miss Starke's old house. Hank used to go out there when his son was little and let the boy run around and chase her goats. Miss Stark would bring them cookies or candy, what ever she had made. She was always givin' goodies to the young people. Hank told me he got out of his car and walked around the yard thinkin' of the good old days. He stopped next to the big empty wadin' pool and sat down on one of the plaster benches. That's when he heard the plaster crackin', but he didn't get off the bench quick enough. He crashed to the ground with chunks of the plaster underneath him. He got up and was brushing the white dust off his pants. He looked down and saw a small black leather bag. He said he thought it was an old time water pouch. When he picked it up he knew there was somethin' in it. He opened the bag and there it was. The damn fool said he went to work and even left it in his car. When he got back to the cottage he hid it somewhere."

Mr. King took a deep breath. "Ya do know it's probably gone forever? Who ever did this, knew the value of the necklace and took it to sell it, or sell it in pieces. I'd like to know if Hank told anyone else about it. You can bet your bottom dollar he told somebody and they took it. A thief didn't just go to his cottage and was lucky enough to find that treasure. They knew what they were after. Hank probably came in on 'em while they were in the cottage."

Jason ended his interested silence. "Where did it come from in the first place? Why did Miss Stark have it? How rich was she?" Jason had always been a three-question man. Mr. King had the three answers and he was more than willing to tell what he knew of the antique necklace.

"I've always felt honored that I was one of the few people who got to see the necklace. I don't know to this day why Miss Stark trusted me enough to show me that amazing piece of history. The stories about the necklace ranged from it being stolen from the Queen of England by someone who worked for Miss Stark. That was the reason she left England and moved to a far away place like Mayport. It was rumored that every time she needed money she would sell one of the gems from the necklace and live off the money for years. Others said the Czar of Russia owned the necklace and pirates took it off a Russian ship. The stories never said how Miss Stark was able to get the necklace from the pirates. The pirate story's probably not true. It was even said the necklace dated back to Cleopatra. I doubt that was true either, but those stories sure added to the mystery surrounding such a mixture of gold and precious stones. I saw it about three years before Miss Stark died. I realized then, she had not been selling it piece by piece. She told me the real story about it. Or at least what she knew to be true. There was one part of the story she speculated about. It was of a delicate nature. It was interesting how she spoke freely with me about a woman's anatomy."

Mary C. had to speak up. "When she died why didn't they look for it?"

Bill knew the answer. "Oh, they looked for it all right. It was like a treasure hunt out there. The children of Mayport hunted

Easter eggs at Miss Stark's for years when she was alive and the adult citizens hunted for treasure when she died. I always wondered why she didn't leave it to a relative or someone she grew fond of as her years here went by."

Mr. King smiled. "I don't think she thought about dyin'. Miss Stark thought she had all the time in the world. It's the way the affluent and spoiled think. It was as if nothin' could touch her. I don't think she meant to leave it hidden. Time just ran out on her. At the end she probably didn't even remember where it was or if it existed at all. I want to find it. I want to find out who took it away from Hank." Mr. King thought for a second. "I guess it would sound better if I changed the order of what I want to do."

Mary C. smiled. "I'm sure Hank understands and forgives you. John, tell us what Miss Stark said about where the necklace came from. And what was the delicate nature you mentioned?"

Mr. King nodded. "Miss Stark found the necklace in the shallow water on the bank of Ribault Bay when she was living at Miramar. It was about three years before the Government took her land and home to build the Mayport Navy Base. She said she was just wading in the water on a hot day and saw the necklace shining in a few inches of water. She knew it was of great value when she held it in her hand."

The group was silent wanting to hear more about the necklace. Mr. King had the floor and he loved telling the great Mayport story.

"Miss Stark found out the necklace was treasure from a shipwreck that took place over a hundred years before. There were remains of ships still stuck in the sand near the lighthouse and along the sandy shores of Ribault Bay. I remember some old wooden ribs of huge ships stickin' up out of the sand when I was a boy. The shoreline of the Atlantic and the mouth of the St. Johns River were not kind to the old ships. Miss Stark told me the day came when fate took a strange turn. A woman named Mattie Bridge arrived in Mayport. She was a writer and historian. She was also a true treasure hunter. That was pretty odd for a woman in those days. Miss Stark said Mattie told everyone she had come to write a book about the beautiful beaches along the Atlantic shores for the tourist in the North. When Miss Stark met Mattie she realized the woman was actually looking for treasures from some of the ships that had fallen near Ribault Bay. Mattie knew all about the ships, the cargo they carried and the necklace. Miss Stark never revealed the fact she already had the necklace. She was a smart woman."

Mr. King stopped talking to allow the others to respond to his story. No one wanted him to stop. He went on. "It seemed that Mattie was trying to recruit Miss Stark and her money to search for the treasure from the shipwrecks. Mattie had an interesting story to tell. It was about a group of so-called fallen women from England. They were prostitutes and criminals who had to leave their homeland, so many chose to come to America. The women were used for the pleasure of the officers and crew during the voyage. When the ship hit a sand bar near Ribault Bay and began to break up, the crew and officers lowered the small boats, filling them first with the men. They rowed all the men to safety, but never returned for the women. When one of the women realized the men were not going to return to the sinking ship to save them, she jumped into the water and floated to the other shore holding on to a small empty rum keg. She was the only woman to survive the ordeal. The woman actually made it to the shore on the Fort George side of the river. She considered going back to face the cowards who left the women to die, but she was afraid they would kill her because of what she knew. Strangely enough, the lone woman survivor made it to Fort Clinch in Fernandina. She walked north along the Atlantic Ocean shoreline, hiding in the thick wooded areas during the nights. It rained one evening and she was able to quench her thirst. She swam across small bodies of water to make it to the island. Three days of walking and swimming brought her to a small village of fishermen and their families. A group of women and children fed her and gave her shelter. The men of the village were out hunting and fishing. When the men returned the woman knew she had found a new home.

Mattie Bridge was visiting Fernandina to write about the many shipwrecks and the pirates of the area. She met the survivor's great granddaughter and the woman told her the story of the necklace."

Mr. King was telling a classic. No one in the room had thoughts of interrupting him in any way. He knew they wanted to hear it all.

"The survivor's last name was Weatherby. I can't remember her first name. The great granddaughter's name was Ethel Drew. The story had been passed down throughout the years and Ethel told it to the historian, Mattie Bridge. This is where the delicate subject matter comes into the story. Miss Stark never hesitated to tell me the details. She was an interesting woman. I think she got a kick out of her graphic presentation."

Mr. King continued to hold the full attention of his listeners. All eyes were on him. "It seemed that the resourceful Miss Weatherby was one of the better whores of the time. She was even used by the aristocrats living in the actual palace in England. Somehow she was able to steal the great necklace from the queen, or the king, or somebody. She knew they would find her so she joined the group of fallen women as they boarded the ship for America. They knew her as a local prostitute and took her with the others. She had the necklace with her during the entire journey. The part of the story Miss Stark liked telling me was that Miss Weatherby's reputation for bizarre sexual activity won her a place in the captain's bed and his bed only. She was a woman who survived at all cost. You would think that keepin' the necklace a secret would have been a great problem for her, but she was a survivor. She knew she would live a life of riches if she could just make it to America."

Mr. King hesitated and allowed the suspense to build. He was a master storyteller and he knew he had his audience in the palm of his hand. "It seems that Miss Weatherby would hide the necklace somewhere in the captain's cabin while she satisfied him and she would push it up inside her when she was left alone."

Mr. King nodded when all eyes in the room were wide open. "That's right, evidently she had enough room to hide all twelve stones up inside her body. Miss Stark said, when she heard that part of the story from Mattie Bridge, she took the necklace later that evening and boiled it."

Mr. Leek stood next to Mary C.'s new car. The devil dog Abaddon was lying next to the front steps. He sidestepped the dog and walked up onto the front porch of the haunted house. Mr. Leek had to tell Mr. King about Mathias' ghost story. Mathias did not come with him.

Margie sat on the edge of Sofia's bed. Her little sister had her beautiful face buried in a big white pillow. Margie touched Sofia's shoulder. "You all right, Sofia?" Sofia turned her head out of the pillow and faced the wall next to her bed. "Sofia, please talk to me."

"I don't know what to say. I'm so sad and confused over all these awful things that have happened to me. I'm afraid again. This time I'm afraid I'm different and I know I will never be the same."

"You can't stay the same. You're not supposed to stay the same. We're all supposed to change and be different. Some, more than others, but we have to change. I'll admit you're dealing with drastic changes because drastic measures had to be taken. Sofia, we are not little girls anymore, but we are better and stronger women. I want to accept and grow with these changes. Let's grow together."

Sofia turned to her sister. "I've never heard you talk like this. I like what you're saying, but what about Jason? I've never been in love before. I know I love him and at times, I really think he loves me. Then, I don't know if he does or not. Most of the changes in me good or bad, are because I've been with him. That scares me, too."

"There's one thing you have to accept about Jason. He's not capable of a relationship. We all forget about his troubled past and his dark mental state. I've realized he will never come completely out of the darkness. If you want to be the one who tries to save him and have your heart broken in the end, go right ahead. That's what love does to you. I like Miss Mary C., but she will always control Jason. He will never belong totally to anyone, but her. You need to look at it through your new eyes as a woman and not that little lovesick girl you've been. I'm growing up, why don't you join me?"

Mr. Leek was sitting with the group in Mr. King's living room. Mr. King was telling Mr. Leek about Hank's misfortune and Bill's necklace theory as the others recovered from the story of Miss Weatherby, her survival skills and hidden necklace. Mr. Leek knew about the necklace, but had never seen it. After Mr. King finished talking, Mr. Leek had to tell Mathias's ghost story. The group would listen to another unbelievable Mayport story.

Mary C.'s eyes lit up when Mr. Leek said that Mathias saw Junior Pane at the house and Moochee was there too, with half his face gone. Mary C. looked up at James Thorn's skull over the fireplace mantle. She was worried about two more evil ghosts being in the house. Mary C. knew she was the reason Moochee was there and the thought of another hostile spirit did not set very well with her at all. She wondered if she was also responsible for Junior being there. Perhaps the pellets from her shotgun found their way to Junior and he died later. No matter what happened, Mary C. knew Mathias was not dreaming or imagining what he saw. They all knew the skinny man was Norman Bates. Only Bill had no idea what was going on. He just listened.

Miss Margaret was at the store and her four daughters had left her as she requested. Margie and Sofia had their talk about Jason, being brave and growing up. They did not really settle any of those points, but the sisterly dialog would continue at another time.

After Susan and Peggy took baths, they dressed up and drove the family station wagon to Seminole Beach for a shrimp dinner at Bill's Hideaway. They would pick up their mother at the proper time. The two sisters asked Sofia and Margie to join them. Sofia was going to rest in her room for the remainder of the evening. Margie declined the offer, but gave them no reason. She just said, "No thanks".

Mr. King and Mr. Leek continued a private conversation, while Jason was being a good father taking care of Billy. Mary C. and Bill were headed back to Bill's Hideaway. Bill was at the wheel of the Corvette. He was grinning from ear-to-ear.

"I can't believe you let me drive your new car. This is the nicest thing anyone has done for me in a long time." The red rocket ship flew past the curve at the Little Jetties. They both loved speed.

Margie stood at the bottom of the sand hill looking up at the great oak tree. She had been wanting to get there ever since she returned from the wild trip that afternoon. She had to walk, so she was on the grape arbor side of the sand hill. Margie knew the climb to the top was difficult, but it would be worth the effort. She took her first step in the soft sand.

Bill drove the Corvette up under the stilt pylons of his restaurant. The tide was low and the beach sand under the building was hard. Mary C. recognized Miss Margaret's family station wagon parked near the steps of Bill's Hideaway. She was interested to see who was away from home. Bill hugged Mary C. with genuine respect when she stepped out of the car.

"Thank you, Mary C. I had an interesting evening. I want to go with y'all to see Hank. I want to help y'all get the necklace back. I need a little excitement. It keeps us young. That's why you never change. You're always surrounded by excitement. You don't run from a fight. You don't sit on the fence watchin'. You jump into the fire. Let me know what I can do to help."

Mary C. smiled and they walked up the steps. Her heart jumped when she heard one of her brother Bobby's dancing songs coming from the jukebox. It was the song *Teddy Bear* by Elvis. Mary C. had to smile when she thought of the dancing fool.

Bill's voice ended her thoughts of Bobby as they walked through the two swinging doors at the top of the steps. "Dinner and drinks on the house for you, Mary C. Your money ain't no good here tonight. Please stay, relax and have something to eat. I need to check on things in the kitchen. When the cat's away the mice will play. I got a bunch of new young cooks back there and they can get silly if I ain't around to keep 'em workin'. If we don't get a chance to talk again tonight, thanks a lot."

Mary C. smiled. "I think I will relax a little and have somethin' to eat. I don't mind payin'. You're in business to make money ain't ya?"

"Not off you on this night." Bill left Mary C. and went to the kitchen. Mary C. turned to walk into the restaurant. She was interested in who was driving Miss Margaret's green family station wagon.

The restaurant area was filled with customers enjoying the seafood dinners with all the trimmings. The aroma of frying hush puppies filled the air. Most of the customers, mainly the men, watched Mary C. walk across the floor of the dining area. She liked the eyes being on her. She was used to it. There were a few empty tables in the bar area. Mary C. decided to eat her meal at one of those tables. It was strange that she did not see anyone from Miss Margaret's family at the tables in the dining room. She entered the bar area and saw what she was looking for. Peggy and Susan were sitting at the bar, talking to the new young and handsome bartender, Joe Croom. The girls did not see Mary C. as she walked up behind them. Joe saw Mary C. first. He smiled when Mary C. reached the bar. Mary C. smiled back at him.

"Well, well, I didn't think I'd see you two here tonight. I saw the car outside, but didn't think it was you two."

Peggy was the more outspoken. "Mother gave us a little freedom and it has gone completely to our heads. I'm not sure what we're doing here either, but here we are."

Mary C. knew sarcasm when she heard it. She also knew that Peggy had been drinking. "Peggy, you've grabbed freedom by the horns. Good for you." Mary C. looked back at Joe. "Hey, Joe. Ain't these some pretty girls?" The two girls looked at Joe.

"Yes ma'am, they sure are."

Mary C. nodded. "What y'all drinkin', girls?"

Peggy was still the talker. She had a loose tongue. "We wanted to try something different. Joe suggested a rum and coke with a lime. It's called a *Cubie Lubie* or something like that."

Joe and Mary C. smiled at the same time. Susan smiled, too. "Peggy, that's not it. It's a *Cuba Libra*. Are you getting drunk?"

Peggy had a silly look on her face. "I'm just feeling good, that's all. Excuse me for not pronouncing the drink correctly."

Mary C. thought the girls were funny and entertaining. She looked at Joe. "Another round for these two beauties and I'll take a *Cubie Lubie* myself."

Mr. King and Mr. Leek sat on the front porch at the haunted house. They were still discussing the necklace. Mr. King was talking. "Al, I want to find that necklace. I think somebody local took it, because Hank probably wouldn't have told a stranger about it. We need to talk to Hank. Let's go to the hospital in the mornin'."

Susan did not take Mary C. up on the second round drink. She knew they had to pick up their mother in a few hours. Susan did not intend to be drunk at the time. Peggy, however, had finished the second rum and coke and was sipping on her third. She was drunk and her tongue had found a new freedom. She leaned over the bar, exposing the cleavage of her breasts to Joe Croom.

"You are the best looking bartender I've ever seen. Who are you, anyway?"

Mary C. smiled and answered for the young man. "Peggy, you don't recognize Joe Croom. His brothers are the bad little Mayport twins."

Peggy and Susan looked at Mary C. and then back at Joe. Susan just listened. Peggy was still the talker. She moved even closer to Joe. "Boy, you've really changed." She looked back at Mary C. "Are you sure that's him?"

Mary C. smiled again. "Yes Peggy, that's Joe Croom, our new bartender."

Peggy stuck out her hand to Joe. "Pleased to meet you again."

He smiled and shook her hand. "Nice to meet you again, too, Peggy." Peggy sat back on the barstool. Joe looked at Susan. "And you're Susan, right?"

Susan nodded. "How'd you know that?"

"I don't think there's a man within fifty miles of here that don't know y'all's names. Susan, Peggy, Sofia and Margie, the four sisters."

Mary C. was still smiling. "Damn, girls, I think Joe here's tryin' to tell y'all somethin'. It's a good thing when people talk about you. You girls didn't know you had a reputation did ya?" Both girls smiled at the thought of having a reputation. Mary C. was hungry.

"Come sit with me and have dinner. I'm in the mood for some fried shrimp and hush puppies." She put her arm on Peggy's shoulder. "I think a little food will absorb that alcohol and you'll sober up faster."

Peggy grinned another silly grin. "I'm just very happy. I'm not drunk."

"Of course you're not. Happy's good. Now, come eat with me."

Margie sat on the lower limb of the oak tree once again. She actually thought about Joe Croom watching her from the tunnel of palmetto fans. Margie had no idea her two sisters had just met the new, matured and adult version of Joe Croom. Margie began her hip and pelvic movements to create the erotic feelings with the tree limb she needed for her orgasmic release. Margie would have no audience on that particular night. She did not use the carousel. The ropes would not hold her. The sand would not cover her feet. She was alone with the tree. Margie knew the great oak tree recognized her. She was becoming one of the insane.

Mr. Leek walked to his truck. "Good night, John. I'll call the hospital in the morning and find out if we can see Hank or not. It would be somethin' else if we was able to recover Miss Stark's necklace. See if one of your ghosts know anything about it."

Mr. King smiled. "You're talkin' about my ghosts a lot lately, Al. I didn't know you ever thought about my dead houseguests."

Mr. Leek smiled and nodded his head "If they can help us find the necklace, I believe in 'em. Damn John, it really stinks out here." It was going to be another interesting night in Mayport, Florida, U.S.A.

CHAPTER THREE

A blanket of clouds covered the moonlight that was usually visible over Mayport. The true veteran shrimpers could feel the elements of an approaching late November Northeaster. The change in the weather would last for three days. The Mayport shrimpers would not take their boats out into the ocean until the storm lifted. Margie felt the first breeze from the storm as she sat on the lower limb of the oak tree. Her limb rubbing ritual was over and she was climbing down to stand on the soft white sand. Once again, her legs trembled as they tried to support her on the ground. She looked around, but could not see any spectators. Margie was disappointed Joe Croom was not hunting for his bad little brothers.

Mary C., Peggy and Susan sat at one of the tables in the bar area of Bill's Hideaway. The food had not completely absorbed the amount of alcohol Peggy had consumed. She was still under the influence of the rum ingredient in the *Cuba Libra*. Her tongue was still very loose. Peggy was talking to Mary C.

"Can you believe Mother took us to find Sofia and Margie? We'll never get away from her. She'll hunt us down like a hound dog if we try to run."

Susan shook her head. "Miss Mary C., I don't think the food sobered Peggy up at all. She's still drunk."

"I am not drunk! I told you I'm not drunk, I'm just happy."

"Please stop telling us how happy you are. You sound like an idiot."

Peggy smiled at Mary C. "Can't I be happy?" Mary C. had to smile at Peggy's silly face and silly question.

"Yes, Peggy, you can be happy."

Peggy turned to look at Joe Croom working behind the bar. Her loose tongue shocked Mary C. and Susan. "I'd really like to get my lips on his *thing*."

Susan looked at Peggy. "Oh my God, I can't believe you said that! You stop talking like that. I don't care how drunk or happy you are. Stop saying those things." Susan looked at Mary C. "She's really drunk. I'm so sorry about this."

Peggy ignored Susan's reprimand. "Hey, Joe!" She waved at the handsome young man. Joe smiled and waved back as he washed the bar glasses. Susan was still upset.

"Stop it, Peggy. You're making a fool of yourself. Let's get you home. I've got to pick up Mother in a little while. I think I should take you home and put you to bed before I go to the store. If she sees you like this, she'll have a fit."

Peggy turned to Joe. "How about him taking me to bed?"

Susan looked at Mary C. "It's time for Peggy to go home, don't you think? She's going to embarrass us all if she continues with this foolishness."

Mary C. smiled again. She thought how funny it was that Susan had gone from being Peggy's sister out at the bar, to a protective mother figure. Mary C. had to support Susan. She looked at Peggy.

"I think maybe it would be a good idea for y'all to call it a night. You don't want to be late pickin' up your mama." Mary C. turned to Susan. "You drive don't ya, Susan?"

"Yes ma'am."

Peggy stood up. "Well then, let's go. I don't think I'm that happy any more."

Mary C. almost laughed out loud at Peggy's statement and the silly expression she had on her face. Susan stood up, too.

"I hope I can get her to the car. I'd hate for her to fall down those steps."

Mary C. had the solution. She motioned to Joe Croom. "Joe, we need a strong man. Help us get Peggy down the stairs and into the car."   Susan looked at Mary C., but did not say anything.   Joe walked from behind the bar and moved next to Peggy.   She looked into Joe's eyes.

"Hey, Joe."

Joe put his arm around Peggy's waist.   "Hey, Peggy."

Peggy touched Joe's face and looked at Mary C.   "Look at this face, Miss Mary C."

Joe's face turned red, as his blood seemed to run in different directions.   Peggy put her arm around Joe's shoulder and whispered to Susan.

"I can really walk on my own, but why would I want to if he's going to walk me down the stairs."   Peggy looked at Mary C.   "Smart, huh?"

Mary C. nodded.   "Real smart, Peggy."   Mary C. motioned for Joe to start moving Peggy toward the door.

Margie walked into the store, sounding the bell on the door. Miss Margaret turned to see who her next customer would be. "Margie, what are you doing here?   You don't need to be out in this weather.   You'll have a relapse and be sick again."

"I'm fine, Mother.   I thought you could use the company.   I took a little nap and I'm wide awake."

Miss Margaret looked out the front window of the store. "Where's the car?"

"I walked over.   Peggy and Susan took the car.   They went to get something to eat."

"Why didn't you go with your sisters?"

"I was tired.   Sofia and I stayed home.   I'm sure they'll be here to get us in a little while."   Miss Margaret had no idea her oldest daughter had just had a sexual encounter with the oak tree.

Joe Croom supported Peggy until they got to the passenger's side door of the green family station wagon.   Mary C. stepped up and took Peggy's arm, guiding her into the back seat.   Peggy grabbed Joe's arm and tried to pull him into the back seat with her.

"I really want my lips on it."

Peggy reached down and grabbed Joe between his legs. He stepped back from the car before she could get a good hold on him. If it had been up to him, Joe would have joined Peggy in the back seat of the family station wagon.   He knew Mary C. was watching so he knew it was best for him to be a gentleman at that particular moment. Peggy fell back and lay on the seat.

"Oh my, I'm a little dizzy."

Susan got into the front driver's seat. "You're more than a little dizzy."

Peggy still had her sarcastic wits about her. "Yes, Mother." Peggy held her open arms out to Joe. "Come here, Joe. Kiss me good night." She puckered up her full lips and kissed the air.

Joe smiled. "Maybe next time, Peggy. When I kiss you I want you to remember it in the morning."

Mary C. had to smile, too. She liked the young Joe Croom. He had a certain way about him. There was something unique in the way he carried himself. Mary C. closed the backside door on the station wagon and stepped to the passenger's side window to talk to Susan.

"Be careful drivin' back. Take her home first and then you go get your mama. I'll follow y'all."

Susan nodded her head. "Yes, ma'am." She understood and liked the fact Mary C. would be following them back to Mayport. Susan started the car and drove down the beach. Mary C. turned to Joe.

"You need a ride home, Joe?"

Joe looked at Mary C.'s new red Corvette. He would have loved to ride home in that car with a woman like Mary C. next to him. "I'd like that, but I'm workin' 'til midnight. Thanks anyway. Besides, I've got my mo-ped." Joe turned and pointed to, what looked like, a wide tire bicycle with a gas tank and motor attached.

Mary C. looked at the contraption and then back at Joe. "You ride that thing all the way from Mayport to here and back again?"

"Yes ma'am. You gotta use what ya got. That's all I got. I'm savin' up for a car, but seems like every time I get a little saved up I have to spend it. And sometimes I give up and just spend it on stupid stuff. Savin' money ain't one of my good points."

Joe looked down the beach and saw the tail lights on the back of the family wagon flash red when Susan stopped before she turned up onto the wooden beach ramp that led to Seminole Road.

"I need to get back to the bar and I guess you need to catch up with the ladies."

Mary C. looked down the beach as the family station wagon drove onto the ramp and the red taillights disappeared. "Oh, I'll catch 'em."

Mr. John King sat on his front porch with a Mayport Northeaster swirling around him. The cool air tossed his thinning hair. It was another dreary night made for the spirit world. He left Mayport to go visit Ana Kara during a heavy fog and now he was home, surrounded by bad weather again. It was another perfect night for the eccentric ghost watcher and caretaker. He saw the family station wagon and the red Corvette roll past. Both cars turned in the direction of Miss Margaret's house. Mr. King thought of all the beautiful women he saw on a daily basis. Ghosts and beautiful women, he did feel blessed.

The family station wagon pulled up to Miss Margaret's front porch and the red Corvette pulled up behind the wagon. Susan and Mary C. helped Peggy get into the house, up to her bedroom and into her bed. Sofia got up and helped them with her drunken sister, and then she went back to bed. Susan left to pick up Miss Margaret and Mary C. drove off in her new car.

Jason sat on the hold cover at the stern of the shrimp boat. Billy was sleeping in the warm bunk on the *Mary C.* Jason looked up when he heard a noise on the dock above him. A man was standing in the dark. Jason did not recognize the man's voice.

"I'll bet you're Jason, ain't ya?"

Jason looked into the darkness as the man walked under the dim light on a metal pole. Jason stood up when he saw that he did not recognize the intruder. "Can I help you with something?"

The man jumped down to the boat. "I'm Beanie. Folks in Mayport call me Beanie."

Jason responded in an out of character and strangely cleaver way. "I didn't recognize you without your cowboy hat and your donkey."

Beanie smiled a "no front tooth" grin. "I'm sobered up now. That was pretty funny, what ya just said. I heard a lot about you, but you being funny wasn't one of the things I heard. Nobody ever said you was funny. But, I've been known to bring out the humor in some real hard cases." Jason did not respond. He had already said more than he intended.

"You mad at us, ain't ya?"

Jason had to answer the strange man. "I ain't mad, mister. I don't even know you. Why would I be mad at you?"

"Don't you and ya mama think I'm the reason we didn't take the boat out? Don't ya mama say I got Chichemo drinkin' again?"

"I don't know what my mama thinks. You'll have to ask her." Jason had another out of character moment that surprised Beanie. "Listen mister, you need to get off my boat. I don't want you on my boat."

Beanie changed the expression on his face. "I thought you ain't mad at me."

"I ain't mad at ya. I just don't like you bein' on my boat."

Beanie's face turned red. "I'll wait for Captain Chichemo to tell me that."

A voice cut through the tension filled air. "Come on, Beanie, get off the boat." Beanie and Jason looked up and saw Chichemo standing on the dock above them. Beanie stared at Jason. Chichemo barked again. "Beanie get off the man's boat. He has the say-so here."

Beanie kept his mean expression, but he did climb off the boat to stand on the dock with Chichemo. Jason looked up at them both. He had no more words, but Chichemo did.

"Tell ya mama I'm sorry. I didn't mean to cause her no trouble. She let me keep workin' the boat after I messed up last time. I can't do her like that again. I'm gonna go down to Fort Meyers and see if I can get on a boat to Texas. Tell ya mama thanks for everything and I'll see her when I see her."

It was after midnight when Joe Croom walked down the steps at Bill's Hideaway. He had finished his night shift behind the bar. His mo-ped awaited him in the sand under the building. Mary C. was standing at the bottom step. Joe did not see her at first. He was looking down at the steps as he descended toward the sand. Mary C.'s voice got his attention and he looked up.

"I was thinkin' 'bout you ridin' that motor thing all the way home, tonight. After the way you handled our sweet Peggy, you deserved a ride home." Joe could not believe Mary C. was standing there. She continued. "You can put that mo-bike, or what ever you call it, in the trunk."

Joe scanned the white beach sand for Mary C.'s red Corvette, but he did not see the new shiny machine. Mary C. stepped to her blue Ford Falcon as Joe reached the bottom step. She unlocked the trunk and held open the cover.

"Put that thing in here."

Joe's mo-ped was leaning against one of the pylons under the building. He pulled it away from the huge post and rolled it to the back of the Falcon. Mary C. held the trunk open so Joe could lift up the bike and put it in the back. Mary C. pulled the trunk cover down until it hit the bike. She handed Joe a piece of rope.

"It ain't gonna close over those handlebars. Just tie it off. Keep the trunk from floppin' up and down."

Joe followed her instructions. Mary C. stepped to the passenger's side of the Falcon. Joe finished tying the rope and looked up. Mary C. threw the car keys to him. "You can drive a car, can't ya?"

"Yes ma'am."

Jason decided he and Billy would sleep on the boat that night. He did not trust the man called Beanie, but he did not think Chichemo would allow Beanie to do any thing to the boat. Jason wasn't sure what they were going to do about the boat and a new place to live, now that they had money. He would tell his mother about Chichemo's message in the morning.

Mary C. had the radio in the Falcon at full blast as they rolled down Seminole Road. Joe had not made any conversation at all. He was nervous and not quite sure of himself, or what to make of Mary C. He was attracted to her, but he knew to be smart about his thoughts. Mary C. liked teasing men, young or old. She reached over and turned down the radio.

"Peggy's pretty ain't she? She sure seems to like you."

"Yes ma'am she's real pretty. All those girls are pretty. I don't know if she liked me or not. That rum had a lot to do with her talkin' crazy, I guess."

"I think Peggy knew good and well what she was doin' the whole time. She can use being drunk as an excuse if she needs one later. And yes, you're right, they're all pretty." Mary C. could not let up on the nervous young man. She was having too much fun. "You really wanted to climb into that back seat with Peggy didn't ya?"

Joe did not hesitate with his answer. "Yes ma'am I sure did." Mary C. smiled and turned the radio back up. She liked Joe Croom's honesty.

Susan was sitting in the family station wagon in front of the store. Miss Margaret was locking the front door and Margie was getting into the back seat of the car. Susan was surprised to see Margie.

"You helping Mother again? You sure have become helpful lately."

Margie smiled. "I just had some new energy after my nap. I wished I had gone with y'all."

"Well, you would have seen Peggy make a complete fool of herself over that Joe Croom." Margie's eyes lit up when Susan mentioned the handsome young man. Margie had a memory flash about her sexual encounter with Joe. Miss Margaret was approaching the car. Susan started the car. "Here comes Mother. I'll tell you all about it when we get home."

The four sisters had their arguments and differences, but they usually did not tell on each other. They were becoming experts at keeping each other's secrets. Miss Margaret did not know her four daughters at all.

The Falcon approached John King's haunted house. Mary C. knew Joe Croom lived about a mile farther down the road. "Joe, stop here at Mr. King's house."

Joe took his foot off the gas pedal. The Falcon began to slow down. He saw the red Corvette parked in front of the porch.

"We're stayin' here at John's for now. We'll be movin' out soon."

Joe stopped the Falcon next to the Corvette. He got out of the car and walked to the trunk. He was going to take his mo-ped out and ride it the rest of the way home. Mary C. got out of the car. She knew what Joe was doing.

"You don't have to take that thing out of there. The Falcon's yours."

Joe stopped in his tracks and looked at Mary C. She smiled. "I don't need two cars and you need one. Be nice to her and she'll always start for ya."

Susan was in Margie's bedroom telling her about Peggy's antics at Bill's Hideaway. Margie really just wanted to know about Joe Croom. Peggy was in a deep *Cuba Libra* induced sleep. Sofia was tossing about in her own restless sleep. She would have many uncomfortable nights in her future. Jason would have a good night's sleep. Beanie would not bother the boat and none of the four sisters would show up to sexually please Jason.

Mary C. was settled in her haunted house bed. She would have no dreams, but she would think of her future before she fell asleep. The ghosts of the house would move about, but the carousel was not there to open the door to the other side and release them. The devil dog, Abaddon, was at his guard post on the porch of the haunted house. Mary C. thought Jason and Billy were sleeping in the other bedroom. Jason and Billy were asleep on the boat.

CHAPTER FOUR

Mary C. was on her way to the kitchen for a cup of morning coffee. She looked out the front window to see her blue Falcon roll up to the front porch. She opened the door of John King's haunted house to greet Joe Croom and his father, Joe Croom Senior. Most people called him Big Joe.

"Hey, Joe. Hey, Big Joe." She knew Big Joe Croom from their younger days growing up in East Mayport.

Mr. Croom spoke up quickly. "Hey, Mary C. Sorry to bother you so early, but Joe's been tellin' me a strange story. He's a good boy, but this don't add up."

Mary C. looked at Joe. "The car got you in some trouble, huh?"

Mr. Croom chimed in again. "I'm sure you didn't give him the car. You let him use it, but I think he misunderstood the whole thing. He just gets excited sometimes."

Mary C. stepped out onto the front porch. She wore the silk rope Mr. King had given her. It was very short and revealing. It clung to her body. Her legs were beautiful. Joe looked directly at her round breasts as her nipples pushed against the silk material. He was nineteen years old. He could not help it. Big Joe could not help it either.

Joe Junior continued his stare with the double-breasted whammy. Mary C.'s voice got Big Joe's attention away from two of her female attributes.

"They're ain't no misunderstandin' at all. I got a new car. I gave Joe my old car. He helped me out and he needs a car. It's his. It ain't no big deal. I hope you let him keep it."

Mr. Croom looked at his son. Joe finally broke his lustful stare. "I didn't ask for the car, daddy. It was a surprise for me, too."

Big Joe looked back at Mary C. "Let's just see how he does with it. If you decide you want it back, let us know."

Mary C. shook her head. "You've always been such a rock head, ain't ya? The car belongs to Joe. I ain't gonna change my mind and take it back. A workin' man needs a car. He oughta drive that death trap motor bike of his off one of the docks."

Big Joe nodded and smiled. "You know Mary C., the last time somebody called me a rock head was about twenty years ago. I'm pretty sure it was you."

"I believe you're right, Big Joe. I do believe you're right."

Mary C. and the two Crooms turned to see Mr. Leek drive up to the house. He stuck his head out the window. "Mornin' Mary C, Big Joe, Little Joe. Sorry to interrupt y'all. Got some boats comin' in." He looked at Mary C. "Can't see Hank today. I'll call again tomorrow mornin'. He's still in critical condition. They say he's got head injuries. His brain's swellin'. Don't sound too good. Good to see ya, Big Joe." Mr. Leek began to drive away. He looked back out of the truck window. "Tell John, it really stinks out here."

Jason woke up when he heard a boat coming into the dock. He had almost gotten a full night's sleep. He did have to attend to Billy one time during the night. Jason needed to tell his mother about Chichemo leaving.

Mary C. walked out of John King's house. She was glad Big Joe Croom decided to allow his son keep the car. Mary C. was dressed to kill and craving the feel of speed her new car could give her. Mr. King was driving up to his house in his new Chevy as Mary C. opened the door of the Corvette. Mary C. smiled at her friend.

"You doin' some early mornin' ridin'? Hell John, you're ridin' around as much as I am. A new car sure feels good, don't it?"

Mr. King walked up the steps. "Your new car sure agrees with you, Mary C. I'm really happy for you and Jason. Ya ain't seen Norman Bates yet, have ya?"

Mary C. shook her head. "No, and I don't want to see him either. I didn't like the way he looked when he was alive. I sure as hell don't want to see that bag of bones now that he's dead. Besides John, we ain't got the carousel no more. It's gonna be hard for your ghosts to show up. Speakin' of sightings, have ya seen Jason and Billy?"

"I'm sure they stayed on the boat last night. Jason likes to have Billy close by."

Mary C. climbed in behind the wheel of the Corvette, showing her firm thighs, muscular calves and the edge of her white panties as she sat down in the bucket seat. Mr. King felt his manliness push against the zipper of his pants. He enjoyed seeing the physical attributes of his houseguest. At his age, he was extremely proud of his quick reaction to the sexy vision. Mary C. looked back at Mr. King.

"Al was here earlier. We can't see Hank today. He's hurt real bad. Al's gonna try and find out more tomorrow. Damn John, it really stinks out here." The Corvette disappeared within seconds. Mary C. had no particular destination. She just wanted to ride.

Mr. King looked toward Miss Margaret's store and saw the Croom twins going in. He stepped to the side of his porch that faced the store and waited for the boys to come back out. The ferry horn blasted. Mr. King was just like Jason. He liked hearing the sound of that big car carrier.

Jason walked through the busy fish house with Billy in his arms. Al Leek's wife, Eloise, came out of the office and walked to Jason. "Oh, this must be Billy! I haven't held a little baby in the longest time." She took Billy out of Jason's hands. "Let him stay with me a little while. This is a real treat." Jason would help in the fish house while Miss Eloise enjoyed Billy.

Margie opened the door of her bedroom closet. She bent down and picked up the carousel she had left there wrapped in a blanket. Her last encounter with the magic music box scared her, but she had recovered because she knew it was a dream. She knew she would use it again. Margie wanted to tell Mary C. about keeping the beautiful antique, but she wasn't sure if that was a good idea. She also wanted to open the door to the other side at Mr. King's haunted house. Margie had an hour before she would relieve Sofia at the store. She took the blanket off the carousel and placed the box on the floor. She turned it on. The music played, the lights began to flash and the carousel began to spin. Margie was addicted to the sexual dreams.

The twins walked out of Miss Margaret's store. One of the boys was carrying a bag. Mr. King yelled to get their attention.

"Hey, you boys. I need to talk to y'all. Come on over here." Both boys looked toward Mr. King when they heard his voice. "Over here, boys. I need your help. I'll pay y'all two dollars each for a few minutes of your time." Chuck looked at Buck. They hurried to see what Mr. King was yelling about.

Mary C. was already out on Mayport Road. She slowed her red rocket down and looked to her right. She wanted to see Miss Carolyn's Jim Walter Home. She drove off the main road and up into Miss Carolyn's pine needle covered front driveway. She had to stop and wait for a truck that was pulling a car out onto the main road.

Earnest Coolie was driving the truck and his son Bucket was behind the wheel of the car being pulled. Mary C. was excited when she saw Miss Carolyn sitting on her front porch. There was a wooden shrimp boat hanging on the front of the house above Miss Carolyn's head. Mary C. got out of the car and walked up to the porch. Miss Carolyn smiled.

"Well hello, darlin'. What a wonderful surprise. What brings you out my way on this beautiful mornin'?" Mary C. smiled at Miss Carolyn saying it was a beautiful morning. Miss Carolyn smiled, too. "I love the cool wind of a Northeaster. I wish I was on the beach watchin' the salty foam tumble on the wet sand. God's big finger's stirrin' up those rough waves right now." Mary C. had forgotten how Miss Carolyn saw the good in everything and everybody. It was her trademark, that and calling everybody, *darlin'*.

"I hope I didn't come at a bad time. I been wantin' to come out and see your house. I'm thinkin' 'bout movin' out this way. If you wouldn't mind some new neighbors?"

"That would be a blessin' darlin'. I can't think of a better person to call my neighbor. There ain't never a bad time for you to come see me. You're welcome here anytime."

Mary C. looked out toward the road. "That your car?"

"Yeah, old Betsy ain't been runnin' so good lately. Mr. Coolie keeps it runnin' for me. He don't charge me a arm and a leg. He let's me pay when I can. I know he's a rough character, but he's always been respectful to me." Miss Carolyn looked at the red Corvette. "That your car?"

"Yes ma'am." Mary C. had an idea. "I want to see your house, but let's take a ride to the beach first and see that foam tumble."

Mr. King stood on his porch above the bad Croom twins. They looked up with no fear in their eyes. Mr. King explained his predicament. "Y'all smell that. boys?" Both boys lifted their identical heads and took a big sniff of the foul air that surrounded Mr. King's haunted house. They both made unpleasant faces and nodded their heads at the same time. Mr. King had to smile. They were strange little boys.

"A big dog's been killin' chickens and maybe other animals around here. I think he's been eatin' what he wanted and leavin' the rest under my house. That's what stinks so bad. I'll give both of y'all two dollars if you'll take a croaker sack under the house and fill it up with whatever's stinkin' the place up. I got some gloves y'all can use so ya don't get nothin' nasty on your hands. I'm sure it's some chickens, but I'm also sure there's something else. Maybe a cat or another dog. The smell's gettin' so bad we can't sleep at night. After you fill the sack up just throw it in the river. Once the carcasses are gone the odor will be gone, too. What'a say fellas? Can ya do it?"

Chuck and Buck did not say one word while Mr. King was telling them what he needed. They looked at each other. Chuck did the talking. "We gotta take this stuff to Mama. She told us to hurry. We'll come right back."

Mr. King smiled down at the two little boys. "That's great. I'll be here."

The twins turned at the same time and began to walk away. Buck looked back at Mr. King. He was the talker now. "It'll cost ya three

dollars each. You ain't gonna get nobody to climb under a haunted
house for two dollars. It's worth three."

The boys walked away. Mr. King had to smile at the rationale
and bargaining ability of the bad little boys. He had to admit they
were right. He would have the six dollars ready on their return.

Mr. King looked to the front of his porch when he heard a truck
engine. He turned to see his good friend, Mr. Leek, driving his truck
up to the front porch. Mr. Leek stepped out of his truck, walked up
the steps and joined Mr. King.

"Damn John, it really stinks bad out here."

"I know. I wish I had a dollar every time somebody said that to
me lately. I just hired them Croom twins to go under the house and
find what's causin' it. We think Mary C.'s ugly dog went on a
hunger killin' spree and left the remains of his daily meals under the
house. I wish Mary C. would'a put that dog down."

Mr. Leek nodded. "Well, somebody's gonna do it. Folks talkin'
'bout some missin' chickens, a fightin' rooster, even a couple of
cats. If he keeps killin', he'll be dead, too." Mr. Leek always knew
what was going on in the town of Mayport. "You heard 'bout this
mornin's kidnappin'?"

Mr. King's eyes widened. He had no idea what Mr. Leek was
talking about. "There's been a kidnappin'?"

"Early this mornin'. Theda Moore's new baby. He's a week
old."

Mr. King knew whom Mr. Leek was referring to. "Theda's just a
baby herself. I didn't know she was even with child. How old is
she, anyway?"

Mr. Leek had the correct information. "She just turned fifteen.
They say Earnest Coolie's boy, Duck, is the baby's daddy."

Mr. King knew the Coolie's. "That Duck's twenty years old if
he's a day. What's he doin' with Theda?"

"I can tell ya ain't seen Theda lately. She ended up being one of
those girls that turn into a woman way ahead of their time. She
looks like she's well into her twenties. Duck probably knew how
old she was, but I can understand it not mattering to him at the time.
I ain't sayin' its right, I'm just sayin' I understand how it could have
happened.

The police arrested Duck about an hour after he took the child. He's in jail, but ain't sayin' where the baby is. Everybody thinks he's hidden the boy somewhere across the river with friends or family members. The Coolies all come from Black Hammock Island. Ain't nobody wanna go up in there. Folks out there don't take to strangers. I don't know of any lawman who'd go out there without an army. It might just take an army to get this baby back to Mayport. He just might be gone for good."

Mr. King needed more answers. "Why ya think Duck had to kidnap his own son?"

Mr. Leek was a well full of information. "Theda's mama and daddy sent her away to have the baby. They didn't want anything to do with Duck and his crazy family. For some reason the girl came back ready to drop that baby at any minute. Duck hadn't seen her during the entire nine months. When Duck heard Theda was back he tried to see her, but ol' Stoddard Moore refused to let Duck get anywhere near Theda. Stoddard and Duck had words in the front yard with Theda yellin' out the window that she loved Duck. When Theda's brother joined the ruckus Duck decided to leave before he got hurt. He did swear he'd have Theda and the baby. Stoddard sent the police after Duck as soon as the baby was gone."

Mr. King had another question. "How'd they let Duck take a one-week-old baby?"

Mr. Leek was ready for any question. "Theda was hangin' a load of clothes out on the backyard line real early this mornin'. She took the baby out with her. He was settin' in one of those wicker clothes baskets all wrapped up in a baby blanket. Theda remembered she had left some blue crabs boilin' on the stove. She said it took her less than a minute to run into the house and get back out side. The basket was empty and the baby was gone. They say you could hear Theda screamin' all the way to the ferry slip." Mr. Leek changed the subject. "Holy Moly, John, it really stinks bad out here. You better get them boys under that house and see what's dead. I'm goin' back to the dock where it smells better."

John smiled. "It's low tide ain't it?"

"It might be low tide, but it smells better than this."

They both turned to see Jason drive up in Uncle Bobby's truck. He got out of the truck with Billy in his arms. Mr. Leek shook his head. "Y'all should'a stayed on the boat. It smells much better over there. I'll see y'all later."

Officers David Boos and Paul Short sat in the office at the police station across from, Officer Larry Dean, the temporary police chief. Debbie Butler was sitting to the left of the desk that used to belong to her father. Miss Butler was angry as she addressed the new chief.

"How can one old man find a way to elude the authorities and kill a professional bounty hunter with the experience and caliber of Mr. Shackleford? Somebody explain this to me. My father's killer still walks free. A man who's killed four times that we know of. No telling how many we don't know about."

Officer Dean took a deep breath. "I can't answer those questions. Desperate men on the run can do more than you expect when losin' their freedom's at stake. This is a cunning man. He ain't your run of the mill criminal."

Officers Boos and Short looked at each other, but did not speak. Miss Butler had more. "Perhaps I should have given you two more time, but I was just hurt and frustrated. Sending Mr. Shackleford was my mistake. I'm sorry he lost his life. I just wanted one person dead. I'm sick about the whole thing. I'm not sure what to do next."

Officer Dean had some information. "The authorities down in the Ruskin area will keep a look out for Tom Green. He's known around there. If he stayed around or comes back may be somebody'll turn him in."

Miss Butler's eyes lit up. "That's it? I'm supposed to wait on some local to turn him in? I'll go down there and post a reward for who ever turns him in. Can I write "wanted dead or alive" on it?"

The three lawmen looked at one another and then back at Miss Butler. She was serious with her thoughts of giving a reward for Tom Green's capture or death. She was a hard woman and she was not going to give up her quest to see Tom Green dead.

The red Corvette rolled off the wooden ramp and turned onto the hard sand at Seminole Beach. There was only about twenty yards of sand left with the tide so high from the storm. The seagulls stood on the ground at the foot of the sand dunes facing the wind. They knew better than to try and fly with the northeast wind swirling above them. The beach was loaded with the tumbling sea foam Miss Carolyn had mentioned. Mary C. had another idea.

"How 'bout an early lunch at Bill's, Miss Carolyn?"

"My goodness, darlin', you are full of surprises, today. I ain't ate at Bill's in two years. I'm ridin' with you, darlin'.."

Margie was in a deep carousel dream. It was colorful and peaceful. She was standing naked next to a huge bed. Margie saw herself lying naked in the middle of the bed. She liked to watch, but had never watched herself. Jason crawled into the bed and turned her over so he could enter her from behind. It was Margie's favorite sexual position. The Margie standing next to the bed moaned and groaned with every hard stroke from Jason. He moved off the bed and knelt down in front of her as Joe Croom took his turn with the other Margie in the bed. Again, the Margie in the bed took her lover from behind. The spectator Margie grabbed the top of Jason's head as he shoved his tongue inside her. She wanted to join the other two in the bed. When Margie climbed into the bed she got up on her hands and knees facing the other Margie. They smiled at each other as the two men entered them from behind. Each time the men would push forward the two Margies would bump foreheads.

Debbie Butler stood next to her car in the Atlantic Beach police station waiting for Officers Boos and Short. They both saw her when they walked out to the parking lot. She motioned to them to come to her. The two officers joined her at her car. She had a question for them.

"What do I do, now? I just can't let it go. I'll hire you two to go back down there. Name your price."

Officer Boos shook his head. "We've got jobs here. We can't just leave and go on a revenge hunt for you."

"You must have vacation time. You could make a lot of money during your vacation. You're the only ones I know who might be able to find him. You found him once, you can do it again." She opened her car door. "Just think about it. You know how to get in touch with me."

Mary C. and Miss Carolyn were back at Miss Carolyn's Jim Walter Home. She was giving her guest the complete tour. They were walking down the hall to the bedrooms. Miss Carolyn was explaining about the bedroom doors.

"Now, as you can see we ain't been able to finish the inside trim. You can buy these houses at different stages. I couldn't afford the deluxe model, but I'll get it finished when I save the money. I did get a door on my bedroom and the bathroom. I made some curtains out of old sheets for the other bedrooms. It oughta be private enough for the children." Mary C. could see Miss Carolyn did not have much, but she was proud of her new Jim Walter Home. Miss Carolyn smiled.

"It don't look too bad with out the baseboard trim down, does it darlin'?"

"It's a beautiful house, Miss Carolyn. I'm gonna build me one, too."

"Try to save up for the deluxe model if ya can, darlin'."

The carousel stopped spinning and Margie woke up from her strange, but not so scary dream. She got off her bed, wrapped the blanket around the music box and put it back in her closet. She looked at the clock on her dresser and she still had a half hour before she had to go to the store. Margie knew she needed a shower. She looked into the long body length mirror on her closet door. There was a red mark in the middle of her forehead.

CHAPTER FIVE

Mr. King looked out his front window and saw the Croom twins, Chuck and Buck. They were standing in the road directly in front of the house. Mr. King noticed that the two boys were looking up at his upper level porch. He opened the door and stepped out onto his front porch. The boys continued to stare at the upper level.

"Thanks for comin' over boys. Come on and I'll show y'all the best place to get under the house." The boys did not respond to Mr. King's invitation. One of the boys pointed up at the top porch. Mr. King knew something beside him had their utmost attention. He stepped off the porch and walked to where the boys were standing. He turned to see what had taken their interest.

Mr. King's heart jumped in his usually calm body. He could not believe what they were looking at. At least fifty big, black turkey buzzards had landed on the top porch of his house and were perched on the railing and chairs. Mary C. drove up in her red Corvette. She stepped out of the car and joined Mr. King and the twins. She stepped up next to Mr. King.

"What the hell is this?"

John talked to Mary C., but he did not look away from the spectacle. "I ain't never seen nothin' like this in my life. I got to get a picture of this. Don't scare 'em off."

Mary C. looked at Mr. King. "Don't scare 'em? How 'bout them not scarin' us." She looked at the Croom twins. "You boys all right?" Both boys nodded their heads but did not say anything. Mr. King walked slowly up the front porch steps and into the house. Mary C. looked back up at the nasty birds. She talked out loud. "I ain't believin' he's gone to get a damn camera."

Mr. King came out of the house with his box camera and Jason. "I always keep this ready just in case one of the ghosts materialize and I can get a picture. This is just as good. This should prove once again that the dead reside here."

Mary C. smiled. "It might prove that dog pulled a cow under your house. You do realize the smell attracted these things." Jason joined his mother. Mr. King did not care why they were there. He knew it was going to be a great picture for future Mayport haunted house stories.

A number of the Mayport citizens stopped their cars in front of Mr. King's haunted house. People stopped to see the strange sight as they were on their way to take the ferry across the river. Seeing such a sight was a once in a lifetime event. A crowd began to gather. It wasn't long before the spectators outnumbered the buzzards. The stench was so strong and enticing to the carrion eaters that the birds did not panic and fly away as the people talked and pointed. It was just another bizarre, but classic moment with nature for Mr. King's haunted house and the residents of Mayport,

Florida. Mr. King was in "haunted house heaven" as he snapped pictures and watched the crowd react to the situation.

Mr. King stood next to Chuck and Buck. As usual they were not talking. "Well boys, y'all got a hell-of-a audience to see what y'all pull out from under that house."

Chuck broke their silence. "Them birds ain't under the house, are they?"

Mr. King smiled. "They're here 'cause of the smell. They know when somethin's dead. They must be real hungry. I ain't never seen so many at one time. I thought they would have been scared off by now. The possibility of a meal seems to be keepin' 'em here."

The ratio of man to bird had changed again as more buzzards flew in and landed on the house. The foul fowls numbered at least a hundred, perhaps even more. No one would ever know they were looking at the same flock of buzzards that had eaten Mr. Butler for breakfast. No one would ever know one of the larger males was the same buzzard that plucked out one of James Thorn's eyes, while James was tied to a tree in the woods. No one would ever know that those particular birds had a gruesome history, both past and future, with the citizens of Mayport.

Sofia was standing in front of the store. She could see the crowd and the large black birds. She walked to the edge of the building to get a better look. Joe Croom walked up to the front of Miss Margaret's store. He left his car at home and followed his younger brothers to the store. Sofia turned to him and smiled as he walked closer. The handsome and manly Joe Croom returned a smiled and walked to where Sofia was standing. He looked at Sofia and then at the crowd in front of Mr. King's house. Joe was captivated by Sofia's natural beauty. He had seen her many times before, but this time was different. He was calm, cool and confident.

"What's goin' on over there?"

"They're looking at all those big black birds. I wonder why they landed there, like that?"

Joe took a better look. "Those are turkey buzzards. I never seen 'em do that before. That don't make no sense."

Sofia had an observation. "Isn't it odd that they landed on Mr. King's haunted house?" Joe Croom was like Jason. He loved the way Sofia talked. It took him only a few seconds to see and feel Sofia's unique nature.

Joe found it hard to believe he was standing with the fourth and most beautiful of Miss Margaret's daughters. He had wild sex with Margie at the oak tree, he assisted Peggy and Susan at Bill's Hideaway and now he was with Sofia. Sofia saw the twins standing with Mr. King.

"Look, your little brothers are over there."

Joe focused in on the two boys. "They were supposed to be coming here, but they always seem to get sidetracked. If somethin's goin' on you can bet you'll find those two little toe-heads right in the middle."

He had no idea the twins were preparing to enter the animal graveyard filled with victims of the killer Rottweiler, Abaddon. Sofia smiled when Joe called his brothers, toe-heads. She remembered the attack of the Joe Jumpers.

"My sister, Margie, told me about the Joe Jumpers. That was awful."

Margie's naked body flashed in Joe's head. He would always enjoy that particular memory. Sofia's voice caused the vision to fade away. "I guess the boys recovered."

"Like I told Margie, they're pretty tough little fellas. Even though they are 'bout as bad as they come, I felt bad for 'em that day. They were really hurtin'."

Sofia had another observation. "I've watched you with your brothers. They're very lucky to have a big brother like you."

While John King was in haunted house heaven, Joe Croom was in Sofia heaven. Sofia saw a customer walk into the store.

"I've got to get back to work." She left Joe standing there. He wanted to go join the excitement at the haunted house, but his desire to see more of Sofia eclipsed his thoughts of buzzard watching. Joe followed Sofia into the store.

Mr. King walked up to Chuck and Buck and handed them each a pair of cotton yard gloves. "Here ya go boys. There's probably gonna be some nasty stuff under there." Both boys took the gloves. "The best place to go under's on the side over here." Mr. King walked to the side of the house as the boys followed him. Mary C. and Jason walked behind them.

The crowd realized what was happening and a few of the people moved to the side of the house to see what was to come. Mr. King bent down and moved a square piece of plywood that was covering an opening in the latticework that surrounded the outside of the house. He turned to the boys.

"The dogs been goin' under out back through a broken piece of wood. This is a bigger openin' and it'll be easy for you boys to move in and out." Mr. King handed them both a brown croaker sack. "Just put what ever you find in these sacks and we'll throw it in the river. We can feed the fish with it."

The odor was heavier when Mr. King removed the board. One of the spectators stepped up to Mr. King. "Excuse me sir, I just got this out of my car. It'll help the young men clean up under there." The man held out a small jar. Mr. King looked at it. "It's Vick's Salve sir. If the boys put it under their noses, they won't have to smell that stench. It really will help."

Mr. King took the jar. "Thank you, mister. I hadn't thought about that." He turned to the boys. "Put this under your noses, boys. It'll make things easier on ya."

Mary C. took the small jar from Mr. King and stepped to the boys. "Put your gloves on, boys. I'll put this stuff under your nose."

Chuck and Buck put their gloves on while Mary C. dabbed the salve out of the jar with her finger and placed it under each boy's nose. They both made a face of dissatisfaction as they took a deep breath of the menthol ointment. Mary C. smiled.

"You'll be glad we did this in a few seconds. Trust me. You boys be careful under there."

Mr. King had forgotten something. "Here boys. You need this for the dark corners. He handed Chuck a flashlight. "Just got one boys. Work together with it."

Chuck and Buck did not hesitate. They both got down on all fours. Chuck turned on the light and crawled under the house. Buck was right behind him. They both carried a croaker sack.

The dog's killing spree had only been raging for three days. In that short amount of time, the evil canine had taken his toll on the weaker creatures on the streets and in the yards of Mayport. His first kills were due to hunger, but his more recent kills were due to the dog's instinct and killing nature. The animal population of Mayport had diminished and the remaining animals were in grave danger.

As soon as the boys crawled a few feet under the house a swarm of green butt blowflies flew up toward them, hitting them on their faces. The light from the flashlight reflected off the back shells of three dead armadillos. The odor from the three rotting armadillos penetrated the Vick Salve shield Mary C. had created. Chuck gagged, but did not throw up. Buck grabbed the three shells and put them in his sack. When Buck moved the shells, Chuck saw armadillo legs and claws covered with maggots. He picked up the decaying legs and placed them in his sack.

There was a pile of chicken feathers in the middle of the area. It was obvious the dog had eaten the chickens. As the boys gathered the feathers and put them into the sacks, they found the feet of the chickens under the feathers. The chicken remains were placed into the sacks. A dozen fish heads were stinking the most. Mr. King's voice interrupted the twin's concentration.

"You boys all right?"

Chuck answered. "Lot'a stuff here. Lots'a chickens and fish heads."

"Make sure y'all look in those dark corners. Use those bags. Be careful."

Chuck turned the flashlight to one of the dark corners as Mr. King had suggested. The light fell on some type of dead animal. The boys crawled slowly toward the corner. When they stopped they realized it was two cats. The cats had been killed and chewed up, but not eaten. Some of the animals were not eaten at all. The wild dog had just killed his prey and carried it back to his layer. The maggots had taken their toll on the carcasses. Buck gagged again as he put one of the cats into his sack. Buck picked up the other cat and held it up by it's broken tail. "Ain't this the cat Miss Millie was lookin' for yesterday?"

Chuck nodded his head with a smile. "It's a Persian cat. She called it a Persian cat. Wonder if she wants it back." They both smiled at the thought of returning the cat to Miss Millie. They were strange young boys.

The first corner and the middle area were clean of a number of Abaddon's victims. Chuck aimed the light toward the second dark corner. It was clear of any rotting animals. Chuck aimed the flashlight again in the direction of one of the darker corners at the back of the house. His little heart jumped when he saw something moving on the ground. He jumped back, bumping into his brother who was close behind him. Chuck dropped the flashlight into the dirt and yelled, "The dog! It's the dog!" Chuck dropped his croaker sack, but for some reason Buck held his tight as they crawled toward the opening where Mary C. and Mr. King were still standing. Jason had gone into the house to check on Billy. The scared boys emerged from under the house. Chuck was the first.

"The dog's under there! He tried to bite us!" The twins stood up and moved away from the house. Buck dropped his sack on the ground. Mr. King took the square piece of plywood and covered the opening to keep the dog from getting out that way. Mary C. reacted.

"I'll get my gun."

Mr. King nodded. "I'll stay here, but he's got that other opening at the back of the house. If he wants out, he'll go out there." Mr. King turned to the twins. "You boys hold this board so he can't get out. I'll go to the hole out back. Mary C., bring my gun, too. We'll be ready at both places."

The twins reluctantly stepped to the opening and Chuck was first to lean against the board. Buck stuck his foot against the board in a ready to run position. They were both still scared. Mr. King left them and walked to the back of the house.

Mary C. and Jason stepped out onto the front porch carrying shotguns. Mary C. had her favorite pump action and Jason carried Mr. King's double barrel .12 gauge. As they both walked down the steps, a police car rolled up and stopped on the road behind the crowd that had gathered to see the buzzards. Officers Boos and Short looked up at the buzzards at the same time. David Boos reacted first. "Would ya look at this? Only in Mayport. And at the haunted house. What the hell's goin' on?"

Officer Short saw an even more troubling sight. It was Mary C. carrying the shotgun. Jason had already walked to the back of the house with Mr. King's gun. "Looks like our girl's gonna do some shootin' again."

Officer Boos saw what his partner was referring to. "Oh no! I hate to get out of this car, but you know we have to?"

They jumped out of the car and moved through the crowd trying to get to Mary C. They reached her as she walk to the side of the house. Officer Boos was closest to her.

"Hold on there. There's a lot of people out here. Please be careful with that gun."

Mary C. turned to the policeman. "I said if that dog caused any trouble, I'd put him down myself. I guess it's time. I ain't asked all these people to come here."

"Well, they're here no matter what the reason. I can't let ya shoot that gun with all these people out here. Please understand that. What's goin' on here anyway?"

Mary C. did not want to spend any more time with the two policemen, but she stopped and tried to explain the situation.

"My dog's killin' other animals. Eatin' 'em, I guess. He's been leavin' the remains under John's house. I'm sure you can smell 'em. John had two boys go under the house to clean up the mess. They just saw the dog under there. Me and John's gonna shoot it before it can get out from under the house."

Officer Short stepped up to his partner and Mary C. "Is it that big dog you took in?"

Mary C. nodded. "I guess he got hungry while we was gone. He just kept killin'."

Mr. King yelled from the back of the house. "He ain't come out yet, Mary C."

Officer Boos turned to Officer Short. "Go around there and tell him you'll handle it. I'll stay here." Officer Short hurried to the back yard. Officer Boos had a request for the gun totting, Mary C. "Please put the gun down. Give us a chance to handle this."

Mary C. leaned the gun against the railing of the porch. "I don't think y'all can kill him, but go ahead. I won't go against the law."

Officer Boos gave a little smile after Mary C.'s ridiculous statement. He knew she broke the law on a daily basis. He turned to the crowd. "I know y'all want to see what's gonna happen, but if I can just get y'all to move to the other side of the road, it will be safer and better for us all. I'd like to have y'all move along, but I know that ain't gonna happen. If that dog comes from under that house and people are in danger, we won't be able to fire our guns with everyone standing around. We'll have two dangerous situations; the dog and the guns."

Some of the spectators began to move farther away from the house. Some even got into their cars and headed to the ferry. The Mayport citizens were there to stay. Officer Boos had another announcement. He yelled it loud enough so his partner and Mr. King could hear him. "I'm gonna shoot my gun into the air and see if I can scare these buzzards away."

He pulled his gun from his holster and aimed it into the air at an angle toward the river. He pulled the trigger three times. The noise caused the buzzards to explode from their perches. It was a solid wave of flapping black wings in motion. Some of the crowd screamed and ducked their heads thinking the nasty black birds were coming toward them. The entire flock flew high above the house and began to circle as if they were going to wait for another opportunity to land and have dinner. The odor continued to entice them and hold their attention. Mary C. took Officer Boos to the opening where the Croom twins were on guard duty.

"These boys were under the house when they saw the dog." Chuck and Buck stepped away from the plywood that was covering the opening. They were more than happy to see the policeman. Officer Boos stepped to the hole.

"Where's the dog?"

Chuck spoke up. "He's in the corner near the back. Right where the other hole is. Mr. King's back there."

Mary C. had a thought. "You might be able to get a good shot from that opening if he's just layin' there in the dirt."

Officer Boos looked at the boys. "You boys need to move back with the crowd. I'll get somebody to hold this wood up here." The boys moved away quickly. Mary C. had an idea.

"I'll get one of the men to stand here with me. You go find out if y'all can see the dog from where John is." Mary C. saw the man who gave her the Vick's Salve. He was not from Mayport. "Can you help me keep this closed?"

The man walked to Mary C. "Yes ma'am." Officer Boos went to find Mr. King and his partner.

Joe Croom stepped out of Miss Margaret's store drinking an orange Nehi. He enjoyed being with Sofia at the store, but he knew she was working and he did not want to bother her. Joe walked toward the haunted house. Chuck and Buck saw their big brother and ran toward him. They began to tell Joe what was happening and what they found under the house.

Officer Boos joined Mr. King, Jason and Officer Short. "The boys say the dog's layin' in the corner right here by y'all." He pointed to the left corner.

Mr. King tried to look into the hole the dog was using to go under the house. The odor was terrible. Mr. King backed away from the hole. Jason got on his knees and looked under the house.

Mary C. turned to see Joe and the twins standing together. Her heart raced in her chest when she looked past the Croom boys and saw Sofia standing in front of the store. Sofia was petting the devil dog, Abaddon. Mary C. had no gun. She yelled so Mr. King and the others could hear her.

"John, the dog ain't under the house! He's over at the store right now!"

Mr. King, Jason and the two officers heard Mary C. loud and clear. They heard something else, too. All four men had a look of disbelief and shock on their faces. They knew they all heard the same sound. The noise was coming from the nearest corner under the house. It was a baby crying. Jason was still on his hands and knees. He pushed the latticework with his foot until it broke and he could pull away the pieces of wood to form a larger opening. He lay down on his belly and crawled into the opening he created. His hand touched a pile of slimy maggot covered animal remains. Blowflies flew up into his face. He looked to his left when he heard the baby cry again. He saw movement in the dirt. Jason's heart pounded and his blood ran cold when he saw a dirty blue blanket move. He reached out and picked up the blanket. Jason knew he held a baby in his hands. He held the blanket to his chest with one hand and crawled toward the opening on his other hand. When Jason reached the opening he handed the baby to Officer Short.

Mary C. was walking toward the store with her shotgun at her side. Sofia was still petting the dog. She looked up to see Mary C. Sofia smiled.

"Hey, Miss Mary C. Abaddon stopped by to say hello." Sofia saw the serious look on Mary C.'s face and then she saw the gun. "What's wrong? You look mad."

Sofia's heart jumped when Mary C. pulled the pump handle down and loaded a shell in the chamber. "Move away from the dog, Sofia."

Mary C. did not aim the gun, but she was ready to lift it when Sofia was out of the line of fire. Sofia was surprised and scared. She was frozen with fear. The dog stood next to her. Mary C. talked to the dog.

"You know what's comin' don't ya, boy. You seen this gun before, ain't ya? Sofia, get back in the store."

Sofia found the courage to talk. "Are you going to kill him?"

"He needs killin'. Now, go in the store."

"But why? You love this dog."

Abaddon must have sensed Mary C.'s intentions. The devil dog turned and ran around the corner of the store. An explosion of cheers and voices took Mary C. and Sofia's attention. They both looked toward Mr. King's haunted house. They could not see what all the commotion was about. Mary C. left Sofia at the front of the store and walked back to join the crowd. The man who was holding the board for Mary C. was the first one to approach her. He was excited.

"They found a baby under the house! It's a miracle! The baby's fine! They found a baby under there!"

Mary C. saw Mr. King and Jason standing with the two officers. She walked to them quickly. Mr. King turned to her and she saw the dirty blanket in his arms. Her heart jumped. Mr. King was beside himself.

"Look! Look, Mary C.! It's Theda's baby! I know it is! He's been missin' since this mornin'! He ain't hurt; he's just dirty and hungry. Jason crawled under the house and there he was. Officer Boos went to get his mama."

Mary C. looked at her son, Jason, and shook her head. She smiled at him, but had no words as she scanned the shocked and excited crowd. She knew Jason would always be the humble hero. Mr. King got her attention.

"That crazy dog must have carried him here, holdin' that blanket in his mouth. It's a good thing the blanket stayed wrapped around him. I don't know what would have happened if we didn't find him. The dog wasn't eatin' all the things it brought here. He was just killin' some things. Only God knows why he didn't kill the baby."

Mary C. had her thoughts. "He just ain't got around to it yet, but he was gonna kill the baby. We gotta find that dog."

Officer Short joined the conversation. "We'll find the dog."

Mary C. smiled. "Well, while y'all was findin' a baby, I was findin' the dog. He was at the store with Sofia. When I got there with my gun he run off. He knows I'm comin'. He's gonna be hard to kill." Officer Short knew Mary C. was insane.

The police car rolled up in front of John King's house. The now larger than ever crowd stepped to the side, clearing a path for the slow moving patrol car. The car stopped. Theda Moore and her father, Stoddard, jumped out. Mr. King was still holding the baby. He had not even thought of putting the infant into anyone's hands, but Theda's. The teenage mother ran to where Mr. King was standing. Mr. King extended his arms and held the child out to the young girl. She took the baby, held him to her chest, fell to her knees and began to cry.

Stoddard Moore stepped up behind his daughter and knelt down with her. He looked up at John King and nodded. John returned the respectful nod. Stoddard reached around Theda and moved the dirty blanket that covered his grandson's little round head.

Theda looked down at her son. Mr. King wanted her to know he had examined the child. "I didn't see no injury to the baby at all. He's dirty and probably hungry, but I don't think he's hurt. Stoddard, y'all probably need to take him to the hospital so a doctor can take a look at him. Just to be sure."

Stoddard stood up with tears in his eyes. He looked deep into Mr. King heart. Stoddard Moore had no words. Mr. King smiled. "I know Stoddard, I know. Y'all get that baby to the hospital." Theda stood up, hugged Mr. King's neck with her free hand and whispered in his ear.

"God bless you."

Mr. King had to give the credit to the right people. "Jason went under the house and found him. The Croom twins brought all this to our attention. They all had a hand in it."

Officer Boos stepped up to Stoddard Moore. "We can take y'all in the patrol car. We'll get there faster than you can."

Mr. King walked to Officer Boos as the others walked to the police car. "You might want to think about callin' the station and tellin' 'em they need to let poor Duck Coolie out of jail." Officer Boos, Officer Short, Theda Moore, Stoddard Moore and one of Abaddon's more fortunate victims were all on their way to the hospital.

Mr. King motioned to Mary C. as the police car disappeared down the road. She looked up to see some of the buzzards returning. The odor of the decaying dead animals was still enticing the nasty birds. The crowd was moving around, discussing the events of the last hour. Everyone was trying to talk to Mr. King. He was a true hero. He wanted to talk to the well-wishers, but he also wanted the get the dead animals from under his house. His eyes fell upon the Croom twins. They were still standing with their brother, Joe. Chuck saw Mr. King looking at them. He poked Buck so he could see Mr. King, too.

"Boys, look here." Mr. King motioned for the twins to join him. He got Joe's attention, too. "Joe, bring your brothers over here."

Joe walked toward Mr. King with the twins following slowly behind him. Joe reached Mr. King first. "Yes, sir?"

"You think the boys can finish the job now, or has all this been too much for 'em?"

Joe turned to his little brothers. "It's up to them, Mr. King. Ya'll gonna finish the job ya started, or ya gonna quit and go home?"

Buck looked at Joe. "You gonna stay here and watch us?"

"You two helped save that baby. I'm gonna be right here with ya. Let's get Mr. King's house smellin' good again."

Margie pulled up to the store in the family station wagon. Her magic dream was very satisfying to her and she was in a good mood. She liked watching herself and the fact there was more than one man participating. It was her turn to mind the store and Sofia could go home. She had no idea about all the earlier excitement. She got out of the car and looked over toward Mr. King's house. She saw Joe

Croom and Mr. King standing next to the house. They seemed to be just talking. A memory flash took her back to the oak tree with Joe Croom, but Sofia's excited voice ended Margie's trip down memory lane.

"I'm so glad you're here. Have you heard what happened?" Sofia took Margie by the arm and pulled her into the store. She was ready to tell all she knew.

Duck Coolie walked out of the police station. Officer Boos had called the station and explained about finding the baby and that they were in route to the hospital. Duck Coolie was glad to be free, but he was mad. The Coolie's were known for their mean ways and thieving nature. Earnest Coolie and his three children lived out at the end of Mayport Road next to a marsh area near the Intracoastal Waterway. They made a living by collecting junk metal and iron and sometimes repairing cars in their yard. Their home was more of a junkyard, with car parts and old rusty vehicles all over. No one knew anything about Mrs. Coolie. Earnest moved to Mayport about ten years before with the three children. He did not own the property they were living on. He moved into an old shack out there when he first arrived and started his junk business. Earnest Coolie was not the type of man someone questioned. Folks pretty well stayed clear of the Coolies.

The two Coolie sons, Duck and Bucket, were both in their twenties and they were always dirty from the grease they worked with each day. The daughter was eighteen. Her real name was Rebecca. She was as dirty as the two boys. Her life was cooking for her father and brothers and helping in the junkyard during the day. She had a very shapely body under the dirty overalls she usually wore. She also had a beautiful face even when it was covered in grit and grime. They called her Becky during her childhood, but as she matured, the three male members of the family gave her a new name because the maturity process began in her breasts and did not stop until they fit tightly into a 38-D cup bra. Becky hated it, but her chauvinist pig family called her Milkduds.

Chuck and Buck had finished the nasty cleanup job under the haunted house. The spectators were gone and there were no more buzzards sitting anywhere on the house. Only a few of the big black birds continued to circle in the sky above Mayport. The twins dropped their croaker sacks, filled with animal remains, at Mr. King's feet. Joe smiled and nodded to his little brothers. Mr. King reached in his pocket and pulled out a roll of money.

"I tell ya what, boys. If y'all will throw those sacks in the river for me, I'll make it an even five dollars apiece. How's that sound?"

It sounded like a fortune to the two boys. Their eyes lit up. Joe was surprised, too. Chuck and Buck stepped to Mr. King and he gave them their money. Both boys held a five-dollar bill in one hand and a croaker sack in the other. They turned away from Mr. King and walked toward the river. Joe smiled at Mr. King.

"That was nice of you. Thanks. They don't say much to folks. I'm workin' on that, but Mama says it just ain't in their nature to talk much. It's like they don't need nobody but each other. Mama says twins are different. I think they just need their little butts tore up every now and then, but Mama ain't never beat none of us. I need to go down there with 'em and be sure they don't fall in the river. Thanks again, Mr. King. It was a crazy day at the haunted house."

Mr. King grinned a big one. "It damn sure was, Joe. It damn sure was."

Sofia finished telling her story about the buzzards, the baby and the dog. Margie was trying to absorb all the bizarre information. The bell on the door of the store rang and they both turned to see Joe Croom and the twins enter the store. Joe was surprised to see Margie and Sofia standing there together. He went there to see Sofia again. Joe did not expect a double sister treat, but he liked it. Margie and Sofia smiled at the handsome, Joe Croom.

Chuck and Buck hurried to the cold drink icebox where the sodas were covered in ice and cold water. It was fun sticking your hand into the freezing, cold, ice water to find a favorite drink. It did not matter if your hand got wet. It still felt great. The twins always played a game with the icy water. They would stick their hands in the water and the first one to pull his hand out of the freezing water was a sissy.

Sofia started the conversation. "I was hoping you'd come back over here so I could congratulate the boys for finding the baby. They're real Mayport heroes." The twins did not respond to Sofia's comment. They had their hands in the cold water waiting for the sissy to pull his hand out first.

Joe smiled at Sofia. "They're heroes all right. I'm treatin' 'em to a drink. They're pretty rich at the moment, but I'm still treatin'." Joe looked at the boys. He saw the painful expressions on their faces and he knew what they were doing.

"Y'all get ya hands out of that water. You're gonna get frost bite and ya fingers are gonna fall off." The boys pulled their hands out of the water at the same time. They were both holding a bottle of strawberry Nehi. Joe heard Chuck whisper something to Buck. He knew it was a smart remark by the way Buck laughed. Joe got a mean look on his face.

"What did he say, Buck?"

Buck looked at Chuck and smiled. Then he looked back at Joe. Joe knew the twins did not tell on each other very much, but he also knew if Buck thought it was funny enough he would say it to shock the girls.

"Come on, Buck. What did he say?"

Chuck smiled. It was obvious he did not really care if Buck told. Buck could not resist.

"He said why don't ya stick your wacker in there so it'll freeze and fall off."

Before Buck finished his sentence of brotherly betrayal, Chuck was out the door and down the street. Buck tried to stand there, but looking at the girls made it impossible. He shrugged his shoulders and ran out the store, too. Joe turned to the ladies.

"Sorry about that. I should'a known better and just left it alone. How much do I owe ya?"

Sofia's heart was always in the right place. "I'm sure Mother won't mind us rewarding the two Mayport heroes with a cold drink."

Margie changed the subject. "Sofia told me what happened. I wish I'd been here. It sounds so exciting. I'm sorry I missed it."

Sofia did not like Margie joining her conversation with Joe. "Well, it's the first time you've missed anything." She looked at Joe. "Margie's just like the twins. She's always right in the middle of the excitement."

Margie shook her pretty head. "Oh, like you're not." Margie looked at Joe. "My little sister's always got something exciting going on around her."

It was Sofia's turn. "I watched her put that dog's eye back in his head. She helped you when the Joe Jumpers attacked the boys. I think Margie beats us all when it comes to excitement."

Joe looked at Sofia, but Margie knew he was talking to her. "I'm sure you two ladies will always have plenty excitement around you."

Joe Croom was a young Mayport man with a silver tongue. Margie and Sofia both liked him, but for different reasons at the moment. Margie seemed to have a knack for beating Sofia to the men of interest.

The buzzards, the odor and Mary C. were gone. The open road was calling her again. Mr. Leek was standing with Mr. King on the front porch. Mr. King had told him the wild story about the baby. Mr. Leek was shocked.

"We just talked about that baby. John, this is crazy. What are the odds of this happenin'? Amazin', absolutely amazin'."

Mr. King had an interesting thought. "Ol' Stoddard Moore sure owes Duck Coolie a big apology. I'd hate to face that Coolie bunch after Stoddard had that boy arrested."

Mr. Leek wrinkled his brow. "Holy Moly, I hadn't thought of that. We just might have a Mayport family feud brewin'. We've had our share of families fightin' around here. I wonder what'll happen next with Theda and Duck. The whole thing's a real powder keg and that baby's the fire to set it off. I'd hate to know the Coolie's was mad at me. They're a scary bunch. They say that Coolie girl fights just like a man. You seen the titties on that girl?"

Mr. King shook his head. "No, but I'd like to. I heard about 'em."

Mr. Leek nodded in agreement and smiled. "We'll I've seen her and they're definitely worth a 'Holy Moly'!"

CHAPTER SIX

Margie was upset that Sofia had offered Joe Croom a ride home. Sofia said she would pick up the twins if they saw them along the way. Joe and Sofia were getting into the family station wagon. Margie stood at the door of the store. The twins were hiding on the side of the store and ran out when Sofia started the car. They jumped into the back seat laughing and pushing each other. A serious look from Joe made them stop playing.

Margie did not like the fact she had to stay at the store while her baby sister drove away with Margie's new *one time so far,* sex partner. She did not like the shallow wave of jealousy that washed over her thoughts. They were uncomfortable and disturbing, but the feeling was there and she could not stop it.

Sofia was all smiles. "Have a good afternoon, Margie. I'll take these heroes home."

Joe was sitting up front next to the passenger's side window. Margie licked her lips at him when he looked up at her. As the car pulled away, Chuck and Buck pushed their faces against the glass on the backside window. They both licked their lips at Margie, too.

Margie watched the station wagon turn the corner. She turned to face Mr. King's house. Mr. King was going into the house and Mr. Leek was driving away in his truck. The sound of an approaching car took her attention. She turned to see a rusty, gill net skeeter that had a wooden flatbed, drive up to the front of the store. The cut-down vehicle had no doors. There was a black man driving and another man sitting on the flatbed holding a young boy in his arms. Margie could see the boy was hurt. His leg was mangled and bleeding. The driver jumped from the front. Margie had not seen him before.

"Please ma'am, y'all got somethin' to clean my boy's leg? A big dog just bit him and he's hurt bad. I had to stick the dog with a gig pole before he'd turn the boy loose."

Margie ran into the store and grabbed a bottle of rubbing alcohol and a bottle of peroxide. She was calm enough to grab some gauze and bandages off the shelf, too. She ran back to the skeeter to render her nursing expertise to the suffering young black boy. Margie was a true woman of action.

The man took the bottle of alcohol and stepped to the boy. Margie stopped him. "I don't mean to interfere sir, but the peroxide will clean the cuts and won't sting as bad as the alcohol. Please try the peroxide first.

The man stopped. "What ever you think is best ma'am."

Margie moved to the boy. She leaned over the flat bed and poured the peroxide on the open wounds, dabbing the openings with the soft gauze. The boy grimaced in pain as the peroxide foamed up around the dirty gashes. Margie blew cool air from her mouth onto the boy's wounds hoping to take away any of the stinging pain he may have been feeling. She knew it was not as bad as the alcohol would have been. Margie looked up at the man as she dabbed another cut.

The man was scared and nervous and he needed to talk. He repeated himself. "We was fishin' off Mr. Leek's dock when the dog jumped the boy. I had to stick him with my gig pole to make him let the boy go."

Margie had to know more. "Did you kill the dog?"

"No ma'am. It's gonna take more than a gig pole to kill that dog. When I stuck him he chased after me. I jumped on Mr. Pack's boat and that crazy dog jumped on the boat right behind me. I got to the wheelhouse and closed the door. That gave Lew, here, time to get the boy into the fish house. Mathias closed the door to the fish house 'til the dog left. I ain't never seen a dog act like that before."

Margie had to change the strange subject. "These are really deep bites. He needs to see a doctor. I'm sure he needs stitches."

The black man said the strangest thing to Margie. "With Aunt Matilda gone, we ain't got no doctor close by."

Margie used the gauze to stop the bleeding from the dog bites. She wrapped the boy's leg with the gauze after she cleaned his wounds with the peroxide. Something came over Margie as she administered first aid. She looked at the black man. Margie knew what to do. She saw Chichemo do it before.

"I can stitch up his cut, if you'll let me. If we can get some ether and put him to sleep, I can do it." Both men looked at each other with eyes wide open. The driver was still the talker. "You can do that?"

"I really can. I think I can get some ether, too." Margie looked at Lew in the back of the skeeter. "Bring him into the store and put him on the table in the back room. There's some blankets back there you can put under him." She looked at the other man. "Take me over to Mr. Leek's dock. We need to get on the *Mary C.*"

Mr. King stepped out of his haunted house in time to see Margie and the man drive away from the store in the gill net skeeter. He knew Margie was up to something, but nothing would ever surprise him. He sat down in one of his porch chairs and breathed in the cool Northeaster breeze. He knew Margie would not leave the store very long. He would wait for her to return.

Sofia stopped the family station wagon in front of the Croom house. Chuck and Buck jumped out of the back door and ran laughing into the house. Joe looked at Sofia. "I know they're strange little boys, but I'm stuck with 'em."

Sofia smiled with her perfect teeth. "You're wonderful with them. It's easy to see you love them and they love you."

"What makes you think that?"

"I see how you make sure they're safe and how you give them good directions when you have the opportunity. They'll be good men because you are with them."

Joe Croom could not help himself. He leaned over on the front seat and kissed Sofia on her lips. She did not return the kiss, but she did not move, either. The kiss ended and he stayed close to her.

"If I just did the wrong thing for you, I'm sorry. But, it was the right thing for me. I couldn't help it. I won't kiss you again unless you ask me to."

Sofia's sweet voice was music to Joe's ears. "Kiss me again."

Mathias was hosing down the floor when he saw Margie and her companion walking through the fish house. He knew the black man. "What's goin' on, Elmo. That boy of yours all right?"

Elmo stopped, but Margie kept walking. "Little Elmo's hurt bad. This nice lady's gonna doctor him up. She needs somethin' off one of the boats." The two men went to see what Margie was going to do.

Joe Croom and Sofia were sitting in the car and they were kissing up a storm. There was a Northeaster blowing outside the car and a kissing flurry inside the car. It was only the second man Sofia had kissed. At one time she thought Jason would be the only one, but Sofia was different. She was not the same girl who fell so deeply in love with Jason.

Jason was standing on the stern deck of the *Mary C.* when Margie jumped onto the boat. When he first saw her he thought she was being her brazen self and had come there for one of their impromptu physical encounters. It did not take him long to realize he was not the reason Margie was there.

"Jason, is Mr. Chichemo here?"

"No, he's gone. What's wrong?"

"Help me find that little bag that he uses when he's playing doctor."

Jason led her to the wheelhouse. Jason reached under the narrow bunk bed and pulled out Chichemo's generic and illegal medical bag. He handed it to an excited Margie.

"What's goin' on?"

"Everything! I don't have time to explain. This is one of Mayport's crazy days. I'll tell you all about it later." She kissed him. "Maybe we can get together tonight."

Margie came out of the wheelhouse of the *Mary C.*, carrying Chichemo's little bag of medical goodies. Jason walked behind her. She held her hand out so Elmo could help her get back up onto the dock. She hurried to the skeeter with Elmo following her. Mathias shook his head. He knew trouble was brewing. He went back to cleaning the fish house.

Joe Croom was too smart and mature to take liberties with Sofia the first time he was with her. The kisses were very passionate, but he did not try to touch her in any other way. It was Sofia who reached down and touched him first. Joe was surprised, but pleased.

Sofia's soft voice and nature did not fit her forward and aggressive action. Joe took Sofia's move as a green light for him to explore her incredible body. Her lips had been exceptional. Joe knew the rest of her would feel just as wonderful. Sofia responded to his intimate touches. She whispered in Joe's ear. "Let's go somewhere else."

Margie stood next to the table in the back of the store. Little Elmo, Big Elmo and Lew were all there with her. She held Chichemo's bottle of ether in her hand.

"I'm gonna put this cloth over his nose and mouth. You two are going to have to hold him until I finish." She could see the fear on Little Elmo's face.

"This will help you sleep. It won't hurt at all. I promise." She looked at Big Elmo and nodded. He took the boy's arms and held them down on the table. Lew held the boy's legs. Margie turned the bottle over and poured the liquid ether onto the white gauze she was holding in her other hand. It felt cool on her hand as she placed the wet gauze on the child's face, covering his nose and mouth. Little Elmo started to fight to free himself from the feeling of suffocation. It only took ten seconds for him to stop fighting. He was in a deep and painless sleep. Margie removed the gauze as the two men released the hold they had on the boy. Margie opened a round sewing tin and took out the needle and thread she would need to close the deep gashes. Margie was a woman of action, but she was also mentally disturbed.

Joe Croom was surprised again when Sofia drove the station wagon behind the Mayport lighthouse. The car was hidden behind the small building next to the tower, but it was still broad daylight and the possibility of someone seeing them was at a high level. Sofia stopped the car and climbed over the front seat and into the back seat. "There's more room back here." Joe Croom did not hesitate to follow her into the back seat. He did not care if they got caught or not.

Margie had finished sewing up the biggest and deepest gash. She had done a great job and moved to the next cut. The bell on the door rang. She knew they had a customer.

"I can't go out there." She looked at Big Elmo. "Go see who it is. Help them find what they need. Tell them they can pay us later."

Before Big Elmo could leave the table, Mr. King walked into the back room. His eyes widened when he saw Margie with a needle and thread in her hand and blood on her arms. He looked at the boy on the table and he knew right away Margie was practicing medicine illegally. He stepped up to the table. Margie nodded and continued her sewing chores. Mr. King shook his head and moved closer so he could assist Margie if she needed him.

Sofia sat across Joe Croom's lap in the back seat of the green family station wagon. She left her shirt on, but it was unbuttoned, exposing her bare white breasts and pink nipples. Her pants and panties were somewhere on the floorboard. Joe was deep inside the beautiful young woman. It was a dream come true for any man, young or old. She pushed her body down as Joe pushed his up. Her kisses were more than kisses. They took Joe to a different dimension of pleasure. They were intoxicating and made him dizzy. Sofia threw her head back, making her hair slap against her shoulder. Then she dropped her head down causing her long blond hair to fall all over Joe's face and chest. He could not see her through the thick hair, but he could still feel her as she moved her hips from side-to-side for more penetration and pleasure.

Mr. King stood next to Margie while she stitched up the last and smallest gash on Little Elmo's leg. The child had slept through the entire ordeal. She used the alcohol to clean off the dried blood. She wrapped the leg in white gauze, taping it tightly. Margie looked at the child's father.

"He should wake up in a little while. Don't let him get out of the bed for a few days so those stitches don't break." She sounded like a real doctor. Lew picked the boy up off the table and carried him back out to the skeeter. The others followed him. Lew got in the flatbed holding Little Elmo in his arms. Big Elmo stepped to the skeeter.

"Thank ya ma'am for your kindness. I won't never forget what ya done here today, ma'am."

Margie smiled. "You're welcome Mr. Elmo."

He looked back at Lew and his son on the flatbed. "We gotta get Little Elmo home and in the bed. Then, we goin' on a dog hunt. I'll have more than a gig pole with me next time I see that dog." He nodded to Mr. King and then got into the driver's seat of the skeeter and drove away. Mr. King looked at Margie.

"This crazy day just keeps gettin' better and better."

Margie smiled. "You think this can be our little secret, Mr. King?"

"Consider it done."

They both turned when a car horn sounded. It was Sofia in the station wagon passing the store on her way home. She waved out the window and blew the horn again. Margie knew her little sister had taken far too long to take Joe and the bad twins home. The shallow wave of jealousy ran through her veins again. Mr. King waved back at Sofia, but Margie did not.

Mr. King looked over at his haunted house and saw the fire engine red Corvette roll up next to his porch. Mary C. got out and went into the house. He turned to Margie.

"You done good with that little boy as long as he don't get no infection. That's the only thing about them dog bites, the possibility of getting' infected. Don't be doctorin' nobody else now, ya hear?"

"No sir, I won't."

Mr. King could not leave without some ghost talk. "I need to get back home and see if my friend, Norman Bates, might be tryin' to contact me. See ya on the flip side."

Margie smiled at Mr. King's attempt to talk cool. "Say hey to Norman for me."

"I'll do that, Miss Margie."

Margie went back into the store and Mr. King walked back home. As he approached his front porch, Mary C. walked out of the house with her pump action shotgun at her side. They met at the bottom of the steps.

"I'll bet you're goin' dog huntin'."

"You'd win."

"You think that's a good idea with the law tellin' you to let them handle it?"

"I don't think it's a good idea, but I'm the reason he's here. I need to kill him. I don't feel to good about this whole thing, but I'd feel a little better if I was the one that put him down. You know, John, he would have killed that baby sooner or later. It was just a matter of time. I should have listened to Jason in the first place."

"I just saw his latest victim. He chewed up Little Elmo's leg pretty bad. When the police hear about him attackin' people on the docks, they'll come in force and kill him. If Elmo don't get him first."

Mary C. walked past Mr. King and stood at her new car. "I'm gonna ride around and see if I can spot him. I think I just might know where he'd go since he can't come here. If I get close enough I'm gonna kill him. No tellin' who he'll hurt next while we're waitin' for the law." She opened the door of her new car. Mr. King had a suggestion.

"I'll drive you. We'll take my car and you can see better if you ain't driven. I'll get my gun."

Duck Coolie was sitting on a bar stool in Silver's bar and package store drinking with his brother, Bucket. Duck was closer to being drunk than Bucket. Duck was talking through numb lips and he had a thick tongue. He leaned toward Bucket. Duck's words were slurred, but slow and deliberate. "They done let a dog take my baby. They put me in jail, Bucket. I wouldn't hurt my baby."

Bucket was always the more reasonable of the two. "I know Duck. We need to get you on home before they arrest you again."

Duck was not listening. "Pa's gonna be mad, ain't he?"

"We're all mad, Duck, but we can't let bein' mad mean we do stupid stuff. You do stupid stuff when you're drunk."

Duck stood up and puffed up his chest. "You're stupid!"

Bucket took his brother by the arm and escorted him away from the bar and out into the parking lot. Duck had an idea as Bucket got him into the car. "Let's go get my son and my woman. We can kill the ol' man and that muscle bound son of his while we're there."

Bucket started the car. "We'll talk about what to do after you sober up."

Duck closed his eyes and took a deep breath. "Pa's gonna be mad, ain't he?"

Officers David Boos and Paul Short delivered the baby to the hospital. Stoddard Moore followed them in his car so they knew Theda and the baby would have a ride back to Mayport when the doctors finished examining the infant. One of the doctors had already told the two policemen that he was pretty sure the baby was not injured in any way. The child was dirty and exposed to the elements for a few hours, but there was nothing seriously wrong. The two officers left the Moore family to their business.

Miss Margaret and her daughter Peggy sat on their front porch as the family station wagon rolled up to the house. Sofia got out of the car and walked up the steps. She was excited. "Mother, Peggy did you here what happened?"

Miss Margaret was concerned. "Sofia, are you all right? Your clothes are so wrinkled. What's happened?"

Miss Margaret's observation caused Sofia to have a brief moment of indecision on what to say next. Her hesitation got a smile and sarcastic comment from her sister, Peggy. "Sofia you look like you've been rolling in the hay. But, there isn't any hay around here, is there?"

Miss Margaret did not like Peggy's remark. "That's enough, Peggy." She turned back to Sofia, who had collected her thoughts. Sofia lied.

"This shirt wrinkles real easy. I've been working. Sorry I can't look perfect all the time."

Miss Margaret did not care about the wrinkled shirt. "What are you so excited about? What has happened, now?"

Mary C. looked out the front windshield of Mr. King's 1957 Chevy as he drove past Miss Margaret's store. "We need to ride out to my house. Like I said, he might be out there."

Mr. King agreed. "Yeah, that's a good idea. He just might go somewhere familiar."

Jason was back at Mr. King's house. He was hoping to talk to his mother about Chichemo leaving. He saw the red Corvette and thought she was inside the house. He took Billy off the front seat once again and went into the house.

The Coolie family sat at a wooden picnic table in the junkyard outside the shanty house. Earnest Coolie stared at his drunken son, Duck. Bucket and Milkduds knew to remain quiet. Duck was right about his father. Earnest Coolie was mad.

"Are you always gonna be so damn dumb? The first thing you do when ya get out of jail is go get drunk. You can't think clear when ya drunk." He looked at Bucket. "And you took him."

Bucket spoke up. "He needed somethin' to calm him down. He was talkin' crazy 'bout goin' and getting' his baby. I knew that would be even more trouble. I didn't think he'd get drunk."

Earnest looked at his daughter. "Make Duck some coffee. I want him able to remember what I'm sayin'."

Rebecca never smiled. She had no reason. She was miserable living with her two nasty brothers and her abusive father. Rebecca suffered mental and physical abuse as a child after her mother left. It was as if Earnest Coolie was punishing her for his wife running away. She understood her mother leaving, but she would never understand why she left her own daughter behind. That was another reason she never smiled. She had an empty and far away look in her eyes. It was the look of a mentally and sexually abused young woman.

Her father and her two brothers were nasty enough when they were sober, but all three were demons from hell when they filled their guts with hard liquor. The sexual abuse had escalated since she began to physically develop and become a rare and exceptional figure of a woman. None of them had actually performed any complete sex acts with her, but she knew it was becoming more difficult for them to keep away from her. She knew the night would come when one of the men got drunk enough and she would not be able to fight them off. She was afraid of all three of them.

On a number of occasions she had caught her brothers, together and separately, peeking through a crack in the boards of the bathroom wall when she was taking a shower. It was easy to see through the old wood and she had seen her brothers, too. They watched her quite often and they did not care if she knew it. They had also started walking in on her when she was changing her clothes, or drying off with a towel. It had gotten to the point where Rebecca only changed or showered when she was left alone at the yard. Sometimes she went for days before she found a private moment. It was driving her crazy.

One time she woke up and her father was sleeping next to her in her bed. He was drunk and he passed out. She did not think he had done anything to her, but she was afraid of what might happen when he woke up. Rebecca got out of bed and left him there. He got up later and never mentioned the incident to her.

There was another time when she woke up and realized her brother, Duck, was standing in the corner of the room. He was sweaty and naked. Duck did not see if she was awake or not. Rebecca did not move. She knew he was masturbating. She was petrified, but when he was finished he left the room.

Bucket always slapped her on her behind and pretended to be playing, by wrestling around with her. She knew he was just finding a way to touch her breasts. He even tried to kiss her on her lips one time when he was holding her down on the floor. She was able to get away before he lost total control. Both brothers would walk through the house naked from time-to-time.

Rebecca Coolie had no idea what a good night's sleep felt like. She was afraid she would spend the rest of her life trapped as an incestuous sex slave to the three men in her life. When a person's life seems hopeless, killing yourself seems to be the only option. Rebecca "Milkduds" Coolie was thinking about suicide on a daily basis.

The bell rang on the door as Jason entered the store. He held Billy in his arms. Margie was excited to see them. "Jason, I didn't expect to see you so soon. Didn't mean to run off from you a while ago, but it was an emergency. Thank's for your help. Let me hold him."

"You're welcome." Jason handed Billy to her. "You seen my mama? Her car's over there, but she's gone."

"No, I haven't."

"Why'd ya need Chichemo's bag?" Margie was ready to tell her story.

The Coolies were still sitting at the outside table. Duck took the coffee cup from his lips and placed it on the top of the table. "We gonna go get my woman and my baby, Pa?"

Earnest Coolie was still mad. "I don't give a rat's ass about your child whore or your bastard son. What eats at me is the way Stoddard Moore has the power to have 'em throw your ass in jail on just his say-so. You was marked as a kidnapper, a baby thief. What gives him the high and mighty right to slanderin' the Coolie name? He needs to pay restitution for his lies. When this is all over, if you want to lay with that girl and take care of that baby, that's up to you. Just don't bring 'em 'round here." He looked at Bucket. "Is that oldest boy of Stoddard's still here?"

"I think so, Pa. Duck said he was at the house when he tried to see the baby. Fabian made Duck leave. I think he's here to stay. That Fabian's a mean one. He was in the Army or somethin' for four years. He was one of them soldiers that did some kinda trainin' so they could wear them green hats. You get one of them green hats, you're supposed to be a bad ass."

Duck jumped into the conversation. "I ain't scared of no hat. I'm a bad ass, too. Hell, I got a hat." He looked at his sister. "Milkduds, find my hat."

Earnest Coolie interrupted Duck's alcohol induced ranting. "Get him some more coffee, girl. He ain't right yet." He looked at Duck. "Shut the hell up 'til you know what you're sayin'. You're talkin' like a damn fool again."

Mary C. stood next to a pile of black burned wood that used to be her home. The cold-hearted woman had a rare sentimental moment. "I wish this was just a bad dream, John. But, you know I ain't never had many dreams, good or bad."

John King had his own observation. "I don't know if that's a good thing or not. I think maybe we're 'spose to dream from time-to-time. I dream every night. Don't know if that's good either." He changed the subject. "You know you can rebuild if ya want to. Y'all got the money."

Mary C. did not look away from the charred wood, but she did talk to Mr. King. "I'm gonna sell this place and build me a Jim Walter Home out on Mayport Road near Miss Carolyn. I'm buildin' the deluxe model. And while they're buildin' my house I'm gonna have 'em give the deluxe treatment to Miss Carolyn's house. We're both gonna have the deluxe model." She turned to Mr. King with an out of character smile. "And then I'm buyin' Miss Carolyn a new car. Don't you tell her nothin'. It's gonna be a surprise."

Sofia was finishing her story of the wild events she had witnessed during her time at the store. She left out the part about her sexual encounter with Joe Croom. Miss Margaret and Peggy were speechless after Sofia had given them her dramatic interpretation of the bizarre morning events. Susan had been standing at the screen door and heard the majority of the story. Susan's voice made the others turn toward the screen door.

"Oh my God!" The three on the porch saw the fearful look on Susan's face. "Look!"

Susan pointed toward the road in front of the house. Miss Margaret, Peggy and Sofia turned together to see the *wanted dead or alive* devil dog, Abaddon, walking toward the front porch. The dog moved slowly as if he was moving with caution.

Miss Margaret stood up from her chair. "I'm not sure what to do here, girls. Do you think he's dangerous?"

Sofia had her thoughts. "Miss Mary C. was going to shoot him in front of the store, but I was in the way and she couldn't do it. The dog ran away like he knew what was about to happen. That's when they found the baby and Mary C. went back to Mr. King's house."

Abaddon was at the bottom of the steps. Susan had her thoughts, too. "Come in the house. Just in case something's wrong with the dog. Please come inside."

Miss Margaret agreed. "I think that would be best. We don't know what he's capable of, but we do know something has happened today. Something awful. Inside girls."

Abaddon walked back out into the road when the four ladies walked into the house. Sofia looked out of the screen door. "Poor Abaddon. Mother, they're going to kill him as soon as they find him. They say this all started when he got hungry and killed some chickens to eat. He just kept on killing the animals around here. Then once he took the baby under that porch that was the end. I feel sorry for him."

Peggy was tired of Sofia's dramatics. "It's just a dog, a mean dog at that. You never know what those kinds of dogs will do. They change when you don't expect it. Jason said this would happen. Miss Mary C. didn't listen to him. Now, look. He was right."

Susan smiled at Peggy's comments. "Well, well, aren't we the cold hearted one today?"

Peggy did not care what her sister thought. "The dog's going to keep killing things. That baby was lucky this time. The next baby might not be so lucky."

Sofia ended the conversation about the dog. "Abaddon's gone. Should we tell some one we saw him?"

Miss Margaret thought Sofia had a good idea. "One of you girls go tell Mr. King. I think someone should know the poor creature's walking around."

Susan could not help herself. "Let Peggy go. Maybe she'll get lucky and run over the dog while she's driving."

Peggy did not care. "I'll go."

Sofia was afraid Susan was right and she did not want Peggy to run over the dog. "I'll go with you."

Stoddard Moore stood in his front yard surrounded by eight of the male Mayport citizens. Stoddard and his son Fabian made the count, ten. Each man was armed with a weapon of some kind. The weapon count was four shotguns, three pistols, two rifles, three machetes and four big hunting knives. They were preparing for a dog hunt. Four years in the military Special Forces had made Fabian Stoddard a confident and true leader.

"Don't take this dog lightly, gentlemen. He's already attacked a little boy on the dock. Make no mistake about it, this dog can kill you and he will, if you give him the opportunity. We'll hunt in pairs. Don't go off on your own. You'll only be asking for trouble. Please don't shoot your gun unless you are shooting at the dog. It'll just scare everyone and make us come running. Go ahead and divide up and let's go find that dog."

Peggy was at the wheel of the family station wagon. Sofia was with her. They were looking for someone to tell about seeing the killer hound. They drove to the front of Mr. King's house to see if anyone was there. Mary C.'s new Corvette was parked out front. Peggy stopped the car. Once again she did not like being there.

"Sofia, you go knock on the door and tell Miss Mary C. about Abaddon."

Sofia gave Peggy a smile. "That's right, if the ghosts are real let them get me, right?"

Peggy smiled, too. "That's about the size of it. I was just thinking the same thing myself."

"Very funny." Sofia got out of the car and walked up the steps to the front door. She knocked on the front door and waited for someone to answer. She looked back at Peggy and shook her head. The sound of the door, opening behind her, made her turn around. The door opened slowly and it only took Sofia a second to realize no one was standing there. Her throat went dry instantly. She was frozen with fear as the door continued to move until it was wide open. She could see the stairway to the upstairs directly in front of her. Peggy knew something was very wrong. Her heart raced as she watched her little sister standing in the doorway staring straight ahead. Sofia's legs were shaking at her knees. There was a noise from the upstairs. Sofia's heart actually hurt because it was pounding so hard. She wanted to call out for Mary C., but she had no voice.

Peggy was scared. She yelled from the car. "Come on, Sofia, let's go!" When Sofia did not turn or respond, Peggy got out of the car and stood at the driver's side door. She looked over the top of the station wagon. "Sofia, come on, this is not funny. You're really scaring me."

Sofia knew someone was standing at the top of the stairs. She could feel them. Sofia lifted her head slowly looking at one step at a time until her eyes could see the floor at the top. Her aching heart screamed in her beautiful chest when she saw a man standing tall at the top of the stairs. Some how in the midst of her fear Sofia found the strength to turn and run when she recognized the man looking down on her. It was Norman Bates, the Skeleton Man. He had finally settled in at John King's haunted house and Sofia was the unwilling recipient of his second appearance. Mathias actually saw Norman first.

Sofia made a great, *Mother May I,* jump from the porch. Peggy had the car moving before Sofia got into the front seat. Sofia pulled the car door open, as she ran along side and jumped in. It was as close to a stunt from a movie as you could get. The family station wagon's tires kicked up dirt and dust as Peggy buried the gas pedal to the floorboard.

Sofia was hysterical. "You were going to leave me! I can't believe you were going to leave me!"

Peggy yelled back and took her eyes off the road in front of her. "I thought you were getting in the car! I didn't know you hadn't opened the door yet! I'm sorry! I'm sorry! What was it?"

Sofia was still out of control. "Oh my God! Oh my God! Peggy, oh my God!"

"Stop saying, 'Oh my God'! What did you see in there?"

Sofia looked at Peggy with her ice blue eyes opened as wide as possible. "I saw the man who died at the Giant's Motel! I saw the Skeleton Man! I saw Norman Bates! Mr. King said he was coming! He's here. I saw him!"

Peggy looked out the front window of the car and realized they were approaching the store. She slammed on the brakes and the car stopped at the side of the building.

Margie had finished telling her story about Little Elmo, the dog and Mr. King finding the baby. She was her brazen self. She would never miss an opportunity to be with Jason sexually. They had moved to the back room of the store, Billy was lying on a blanket on the floor and Margie had already taken *the position.*

She was standing there with her pants down to her ankles and leaning forward with her hands on a table. Jason was in his normal position behind her. Margie left her shirt on because she knew they did not have much time and she would only have to pull up her pants if a customer entered the store. She looked back at Jason as he directed his manliness and stepped up to her. Margie had some instructions for Jason to follow.

"Don't forget, do it real hard. You can't stay inside me, though. You can do that when we do it at the tree. And I want to hold it when you pull out."

Jason took a deep breath. In his animalistic state he was not sure if he could remember all the instructions, but he really did not care. He knew one thing he was going to do. He was going to do it hard.

Sofia and Peggy sat in the station wagon outside the store. They were trying to get their wits about them. Peggy was trying to find an explanation. "Sofia, maybe when Mr. King told you about Norman, you had those thoughts in your mind and once you got to the house those thoughts came back."

Sofia was getting ready to respond when she saw Mr. King's new car turn the corner and head straight toward them. "It's Mr. King. We need to tell him about Norman and the dog."

Sofia jumped out of the car and waved her hand to get Mr. King's attention. He turned his car in her direction. Sofia saw that Mary C. was sitting in the front seat with Mr. King. Sofia continued waving her hand until the 1957 Chevy stopped next to her. Mr. King could see the distress on Sofia's beautiful face. He talked out the open window on the driver's side of the car.

"Sofia, what is it?"

She did not hesitate. "I saw him! I really saw him!"

Mr. King thought he understood. "You saw Abaddon?"

"Him, too."

"Where was he?"

"Which one?

"The dog."

"Oh, he was at my house. He went into the woods across the street."

Mary C. joined in. "That's where he attacked the horse. He might be stayin' in familiar places like you said."

Sofia was not finished. She did not really care about the dog. "Mr. King you were right about Norman."

Mr. King turned back to Sofia. "What did you say?"

"Norman Bates, the Skeleton Man, you were right."

"What do you mean, I was right?"

"About him coming to your house. I just saw him at the top of your stairs." Mr. King looked at Mary C. and then back at Sofia. He had no words, but Sofia still did. "We went to tell you about the seeing dog. I knocked on the front door and it opened by itself. I was really scared. I tried to run, but I couldn't. When I looked up the stairs there he was at the top looking down at me. Peggy yelled, I yelled and then I ran. I think he's settled in."

Jason moaned before he exploded and pulled away from his deep connection with Margie. She turned around quickly and grabbed Jason like she was holding a garden hose in her hand while his semen squirted in all directions. Margie was as wild as they came.

"Good grief, Jason, where you put all that stuff?"

Jason was embarrassed by Margie's playful and crude question, but he could not stop the flow she was referring to. She held him until it was over. She had one more instruction as she pulled up her pants.

"How about getting a towel out of the bathroom and wiping that stuff up off the floor? I'll get up front in case I get a customer."

Margie did not wait for Jason the respond to her request. She left him in the back room with his pants down and a mess to clean up. It was obvious Margie was in charge.

CHAPTER SEVEN

Mr. King was out of his car standing with Peggy and Sofia. Mary C. was still sitting in the car, but the door was open. She was listening. Peggy had joined the ghostly conversation.

"I told her it could have been that thing, you know when you tell someone something and it stays in their mind and they end up making it happen."

Mr. King smiled. He understood what Peggy was trying to say. "You mean, the power of suggestion?"

Peggy's eyes lit up. "That's it. That's what it was."

Mr. King looked at Sofia. "You think that's what it was?"

"I didn't make the door open. Peggy saw that, too." She looked at Peggy. "I know you saw the door open." Peggy nodded.

"Ladies, what we have here today is another ghost sighting at my house. There's no other explanation for it. It happens from time-to-time and today you were the lucky ones. You were at the right place at the right time."

Peggy had to comment. "Or the wrong time."

Mr. King smiled. "You can look at it either way. I prefer the right time, but I do understand folks thinkin' it's not good. I think it's good. I can't think of anyone I'd rather have walkin' my halls at night than Norman Bates. He'll always be a welcomed friend." He turned to Mary C. "I doubt Norman will be appearing again today, so let's go find that dog." He got back into the car and left the two sisters to ponder on what they had experienced at his haunted house.

Margie walked out of the store holding Billy with Jason walking behind her. She was all smiles. "I thought I heard voices out here. What are you two doing parked over here?"

Peggy looked at Jason and had her own question for Margie. "What are you doing?"

"I've been talking to Jason about the dog and the baby. Jason's a real hero again."

Sofia did not care that Jason was at the store with Margie. "We saw the dog at our house. I saw the ghost of Norman Bates at Mr. King's house. The ghosts are real. May I hold Billy?"

Margie handed Sofia the baby and looked at Peggy. "What's going on, Peggy?"

Peggy was ready to answer when she looked past Margie and saw two men walking up to the front of the store. Both men were carrying shotguns and had big hunting knives strapped to their waists. Fabian Moore was the first to talk.

"Excuse us. Anybody seen a big, ugly stray dog wonderin' around here?"

They all turned to see who was asking the question. Mr. King knew the two young men. "Fabian, Eli, I knew I'd be seein' y'all pretty soon."

Eli nodded. Fabian was the talker. "Nice to see you again, Mr. King." He stepped to Mr. King and shook his hand. "The family thanks you again for what you did today. Now, I need to find that damn dog!"

Margie, Peggy and Sofia stared at the handsome and muscular Fabian Moore. Fabian looked at the girls, but did not linger. He stepped to Jason and stuck out his hand.

"Good to see you too, Jason. It's been a long time."

Jason nodded as the two men shook hands. "I was fifteen when you left. That's almost eight years."

Fabian smiled. "I came back a couple of times, but didn't get to see you. I was sorry I missed you. You're looking good, though. How's that pretty mama of yours?"

Mary C. stepped out of the car and answered the question. "She's doin' just fine, you two handsome things. Eli, you look just like your daddy did when he was a younger man."

Eli smiled and put his head down. "Hey, Miss Mary C."

Fabian's face lit up when he saw Mary C. "Now, I'm embarrassed. Hey, Miss Mary C."

"Hey Fabian." Mary C. looked at the three girls. "He was the prettiest boy ever born in Mayport. His mama let us all know it everyday. But, she was right and we all knew it. We knew he would turn into a good lookin' man. We was right there, too."

Fabian Moore was tall, dark and more than handsome. He was a pretty man. His blue eyes ranked with Sofia's. His jet black hair was combed back on his head and he wore just enough Brill Cream to keep it slicked back and in place. His body was in perfect proportion for his height and weight. At six feet, three inches tall and two hundred twenty pounds, Fabian Moore was bad to the bone. Eli Sallas was a small knot of a man. His body was muscular and compact. He had his own unique look about him. The girls thought he was handsome, too.

After Mary C.'s comment, Fabian looked at Jason. "Why do you let her embarrass me like this, do somethin'."

Jason smiled and shook his head. "Now, you know better than that. You're on your own. If you wasn't so handsome none of this would happen. It's always been your fault."

Fabian remembered something special. "Uncle Bobby called it my curse. He told me one time it was possible to be too good looking. He said he had suffered with the same curse all his life."

Mary C. had to smile. "That was my fool brother, alright."

Fabian smiled at Mary C. "I was sick for days when I heard about Uncle Bobby. You couldn't help but love him. I know I did." He looked at Jason. "We used to have some great poker games with Uncle Bobby. I'll never forget 'em. I still play whenever I get the chance. I don't ever play without thinking about Uncle Bobby."

Mary C. had to tell Fabian how she felt. "You're really touchin' my heart, Fabian. I've been so wrapped up lately, I haven't thought about that crazy brother of mine. Thank you for making me stop and remember again."

The entire group was shocked over Mary C. heart wrenching moment. The usually quiet Peggy liked Fabian's handsome features and the way he carried himself. She wanted to talk to him. "We saw the dog near our house about fifteen minutes ago."

Sofia looked at Peggy. She did not want to have any part in killing the dog. "He's probably long gone by now, Peggy."

Mr. King made the introductions. "Fabian, Eli, these are three of Miss Margaret's daughters, Sofia, Peggy and Margie.

Fabian smiled at the three young women. "I knew who they were. No matter how long I was gone, I would never forget these ladies. I saw 'em each time I came home. Where's Susan, I thought y'all always ran together?" The three sisters were shocked with Fabian's flattering comment. "I've talked about you four to some of my old buddies. Nobody comes from a town with four beautiful sisters like you ladies. I know they didn't believe me, but I sure told 'em about y'all."

The sisters were speechless after such a compliment. No one had ever said anything like that to them as a group before. Mary C. had to jump in. "That's our Fabian, girls."

Margie just had sex with Jason, but she would have leaned over that table in the back of the store again for Fabian Moore if she had the opportunity. She wanted to tell him he could hunt for her any time he wanted. Sofia just had sex with Joe Croom, but she thought about sitting across Fabian Moore's lap for a brief moment. Peggy had a wild and disturbed vision of her in the woods on her knees in front of Fabian as he pulled the trigger of his shotgun and killed Abaddon. Miss Margaret raised some strange daughters. They were getting more insane everyday.

The massive hunt for Abaddon was in full force. Mr. King and Mary C. had gone back to Mr. King's house with Billy in case the dog returned there. Mr. King was also hoping to see Norman Bates. Margie still had an hour remaining on her shift at the store. Miss Margaret was supposed to relieve her. It was still a gray and gloomy day as the Northeaster continued to blow.

Sofia and Peggy went home to tell the new ghost story to Susan and their mother. They did not discuss Fabian Moore during the ride home. Jason had taken his mother's shotgun and joined Eli and Fabian. They were going to walk through the woods toward Miss

Margaret's house and see if they could find the dog. Two more
Mayport hunters, Wassie Franks and Joey Floyd, went to Mr. Leek's
dock where Little Elmo was attacked to see if Abaddon would return
to the scene of one of his crimes. Two other hunters, Fred Tillotson
and Rhodes Wylie, positioned themselves near Mr. Greenlaw's
fighting rooster pens, hoping Abaddon would come there looking
for his next meal. Mayport was a small town. Abaddon's time on
Earth was limited.

Stoddard Moore was not hunting with the others. He had stayed
home to be with his daughter, Theda. Stoddard was worried about
Duck Coolie's state of mind once they released him from jail. He
knew the crazy Coolie was unpredictable and was capable of
anything. He hated the fact his fifteen-year-old daughter had given
herself to such a man, but it was done. He could not change it.
Stoddard loved Theda and he would protect her and his grandson
from any future harm. As far as Stoddard was concerned, Duck
Coolie would not have anything to do with Theda or the baby's
future.

Rebecca Coolie had listened to her father's hateful plan to punish
the Moore family. Duck was close to being completely sober so he
was quiet and had been listening, too. Earnest Coolie was still
talking.

"We'll do this tonight." He looked at Duck. "I've changed my
mind about your little whore and the baby. We'll bring 'em here
and take care of 'em. I'd like to tell Stoddard they'll be livin' with
me right before he dies."

Duck was excited. "Thank ya Pa. She's a pretty thing. You'll
like her." He turned to his sister. "She can help you around here,
too. You can help her with the baby."

Rebecca did not respond. Earnest did. "You talkin' too much
again, boy. Just shut up and remember what you have to do."
Earnest turned to Rebecca. "Now, you go get cleaned up. When
you knock on that front door with your big titties showin' we want
all eyes on you. They won't see us comin'."

Jason, Eli and Fabian were walking on the narrow trail in the
wooded area that bordered Julia Street. Jason was comfortable with
his old friends. "This is were the dog attacked a black man and his

horse. The horse broke his leg and had to be shot. The man hit the dog in the eye with a bullwhip and tore his eye out."

Fabian interrupted. "This dog's got one eye?"

"He did until Chichemo and Margie put the eye back in his head."

Fabian and Eli stopped walking. Eli had to speak up. "My Uncle Chichemo put the dog's eye back in?

Fabian chimed in, too. "That girl, Margie, helped him? Why?"

Jason realized they didn't know about the dog. "I guess y'all don't know this is my mama's dog."

Rebecca was standing in the shower. They only had cold water, causing her huge nipples to pucker and stand straight up. With all three men at home she knew she had to hurry before they got the notion to take a peek through one of the cracked boards. She did not want to be part of her father's evil scheme, but she was too scared of his wrath to express her feelings. Her heart jumped behind her huge breasts when she heard Duck's nasty voice.

"That water's cold ain't it, Milkduds?" She turned to see Duck eyes through one of the cracks. She held her hands over her breasts.

"You get out of here, you nasty pig. Leave me alone."

Bucket's voice made her blood run colder then it already was. "We just want to be sure you're getting' clean like Pa said. We thought you might need some help washin' them big titties."

Rebecca was scared. She had never had them gang up on her like that. It was more than sad that she was afraid to call her father for help, because he could easily join the tormentors. She was more afraid than she had ever been when Bucket pulled the door to the shower open and stared at her with lust in his eyes. Duck stood behind him. They liked to see the fear in her eyes. Earnest Coolie's voice was her unlikely salvation.

"Bucket, Duck, y'all quit teasin' her and get in here. We got things to do."

Bucket smiled and reached out to touch Rebecca, but she moved away. "Later little sister. Comin' Pa." Duck grinned at her as he followed Bucket.

Rebecca knew not to stay in the shower. She stepped out and ran dripping wet to her bedroom. There was no lock on her door, but she did slide her dresser in front of the door so she would have a warning before someone entered the room. She knew it would not keep her strong brothers out if they wanted to come in, but it was the best she could do. At least she would hear them and have a few seconds to prepare to defend herself. She dried off her body and hurried to get dressed. If she got ready like her father said she would go up in the front of the house and perhaps they would leave her alone.

Jason, Fabian and Eli were sitting in the woods. Fabian wanted to know about the dog. Jason had told them the story about the attempt to take his son, the deaths that took place, the devil man, devil dogs, the fire, the Punjabi priest, Hawk's brutal death and his mother keeping the dog. The two young men were captivated by the story of evil, bravery and death. Fabian had to speak up when Jason stopped talking.

"I don't know what to say. I feel like I've been beaten with a stick. I'm so sorry all this happened to y'all. I heard you had a son. That must feel different. I'd like to see him when all this is over. I don't know if I've ever seen a real oak baby before."

Jason was surprised with Fabian's unexpected oak baby comment. "You just saw him at the store. He was in the blanket they were passing around."

Fabian stood up. "That was your son? I'm sorry. I was just preoccupied with those sisters. They're some unbelievable women. All of 'em. Come on, let's find that damn dog." Fabian put his arm around Jason's shoulder. "Now, tell me more about Miss Margaret's daughters. I hear you're the one to talk to. The youngest is sure the prettiest, but there's somethin' about that Margie. She has that look in her eyes. I think she's a man pleaser. I can't believe I left you here with all four of 'em." Fabian laughed as they continued to walk on the narrow trail.

Mr. King was sitting in his living room with the shades pulled down and surrounded by flickering candles. He knew how to create the proper atmosphere for those who walked in the spirit world. He was looking for Norman Bates, but would welcome any of his ghostly houseguests who wanted to join him. Mr. King had a habit of speaking out loud when he was alone.

"Norman, I'm sorry I wasn't here when you came through again. You really scared the hell out of Sofia, but I'm sure she's one of the believers, now. She'll tell that story for years to come. I'm not sure why you chose her, but I guess you ain't got any control over who's around when you materialize." A voice interrupted Mr. King's one-sided conversation. It was Mary C.

"John, you ain't tryin' to talk to that Skeleton Man, are ya? You got it like night time in here." She walked into the room. "You and me might just be the craziest of 'em all. That's probably why we ended up together here. We really do understand each other. You think there's something wrong with us?"

Mr. King wanted to be honest and say, *I think there's something wrong with you, but not me,* but he kept that thought to himself.

"I told you before, we're all different and we all have our odd and strange moments, some of us more than others. I'm sittin' here alone in my own house. It don't hurt one soul if I want to talk to a ghost or not. It's my business and my odd moment. We're all entitled to be what we want. I'm the master of a haunted house. That's what I am, that's what I want. Now, you're welcome to sit with me and try to get in touch with the other side. I wish we had the carousel." Mary C. sat down in the dark with the master of Mayport's haunted house.

Miss Margaret and three of her daughters were sitting on the front porch. Sofia and Peggy had finished telling their story about Norman Bates and meeting Fabian and Eli. Miss Margaret knew the two young men.

"I haven't seen that Fabian for years. He went off to the military and that was it. If he came back I sure didn't see him. Is he still handsome?"

Peggy had her answer. "Yes ma'am he sure is." Sofia looked at Peggy. Miss Margaret nodded.

"Fabian was the prettiest baby boy I ever saw. He was too pretty to be a boy. We all knew he was going to be a handsome man. It was his destiny."

Peggy turned and whispered to Susan. "I think I know where Sofia gets her dramatic moments."

Miss Margaret was on her way down memory lane. "Fabian's father, Stoddard, was a handsome man in his day, too. His mother was a beautiful young woman. They say a bleeding ulcer took her life, but some say it was cancer. Her passing left Stoddard to raise

Theda and Fabian. I don't know how dear little Theda got mixed up with that awful Duck Coolie. It's a sin and a crime. I don't know how this happened." The girls were quiet as they listened to their mother's Mayport story. "Did y'all say Eli Sallas was with him?"

It was Sofia's turn to have the answer and a question. "Yes ma'am. You know him, too."

"My yes. He's always been so quiet. He and Jason were the quietest boys in town. He's a well-mannered young man. Jason, Fabian and Eli used to run around together all the time. I guess things change when people start to grow up. Fabian was two years older than Jason. He left for the service when he was seventeen. It was before all that awful stuff happened to Jason. If Fabian had been here it might have been different. He seemed to be the one who took care of Jason. He was older, but he liked Jason. It's nice to hear they're getting the opportunity to see each other again. It's sad that it's under these circumstances. You know girls, folks used to say if oak babies were real, Fabian Moore was definitely one of the best. We used to tease his mother about having sexual relations under the oak tree."

All three daughters had open mouth syndrome after their mother's, way out of character, comment and recollection. Peggy was the first to speak. "You teased a friend about having an oak baby?"

"We all did. He was so beautiful. It was funny to think someone actually had an oak baby. We knew it wasn't real, but it was fun to tease her. After a while she just told people she did. That was even funnier. It sure embarrassed her husband, Stoddard. He didn't joke around too much. He was always real serious about things. Mary C. called him a 'rock head'. That was funny, too. I had never heard that before. It was her way of saying someone was hard-headed. Mary C. always came up with the craziest names for people."

Peggy looked at her two attentive sisters and then back at Miss Margaret. "Mother, you're sure full of surprises lately."

Eli was walking about ten yards behind Jason and Fabian as they scanned the woods on both sides of the narrow trail. He felt the call of nature and stopped to relieve his full kidneys. Fabian talked as he and Jason kept walking.

"Remember the time we were playin' poker with David Pack on his boat and Uncle Bobby caught Scooter cheatin'? He made me and you throw Scooter in the river. Scooter floated all the way down to the ferry slip before he swam to the shore. If he ever played cards again I'll bet he never cheated." They laughed as they walked.

Eli was finishing his private business when he heard a noise. He turned his head and looked into the thick palmetto fans to his left. When the bad feeling overcame Eli, it was too late. The devil dog blasted through the palmetto fans like a black cannon ball being shot at ground level. The collision knocked the breath out of Eli's lungs as he fell to the ground. Abaddon clamped his sharp teeth and powerful jaws down three times before Eli could yell. The first bite was on Eli's side, tearing skin, muscle and the material of his shirt at the same time. The second and third bites came when Eli was on the ground. One was to his face under his eye on the cheekbone. The third and deepest bite was on Eli's throat. Abaddon's canine teeth punctured Eli's jugular vein in three places, causing an instant gushing of blood. Fabian heard a noise and turned back to see they had lost sight of Eli.

"Eli, where are ya?" Abaddon continued to rip away at the wounded Eli. The vicious attack was ending. Fabian heard the dog growl. "Eli!"

Jason and Fabian ran back to find him. They backtracked about twenty yards when they saw Eli lying face down covered with blood on the ground in the middle of the narrow trail. Fabian got to their wounded friend first and turned him over. Eli was choking.

Fabian saw the bites marks and gashes on Eli's face and throat. He put his hand on the bleeding puncture wounds, but the blood continued to flow between his fingers. Fabian looked into Eli's empty eyes. His friend died in his arms.

Mary C. and Mr. King sat in the dark living room with the candlelight bouncing off the walls. Mary C. tried not to look at James Thorns skull, sitting above them on the mantle over the fireplace. The flickering candlelight seemed to flash in the empty eye sockets of the white, shiny skull. Norman Bates did not reveal his ghostly remains to either one of them. Mary C. had an observation.

"John, you of all people should know that ghosts don't ever show up when you want 'em to. I think there's a ghost code that says don't appear when they're lookin' for ya, wait 'til they ain't expectin' ya."

Mr. King had to smile at Mary C.'s humorous ghost appearing philosophy. "I know, I know, but I always think I can help 'em get through. I guess I'm hopin' once I do it for 'em it will be easier the next time. You're right though; they come when you least expect it. It must be the ghost's creed."

Sofia put her hand over her mouth to keep from screaming. Miss Margaret saw the scared look on her youngest daughter's face. She turned to look into the direction that had Sofia's attention. Miss Margaret put her hand over her mouth, also when she saw Fabian Moore walking out of the woods across from the house carrying the limp dead body of his good friend. Jason was walking behind, carrying the guns. Fabian was carrying the heaviest load.

Miss Margaret was the first to respond, making the other two daughters turn to see the men walking toward the house. "Dear Lord, what has happened now?"

Fabian stopped in the front yard and lay Eli's body down on the ground. He knelt down next to his bloody and mutilated friend. Miss Margaret hurried to help. The three daughters followed their mother. The four ladies stood over Eli's body. Fabian was calm and collected as he looked up.

"Miss Margaret, we don't need a doctor. Eli's dead. I don't know what I'm going to tell his family. I asked him to help me kill a crazy dog and now he's dead. This was not supposed to happen!" He looked up at Jason. "This was not supposed to happen!"

Mary C. left Mr. King alone in the haunted house still waiting for any ghost to appear. She was sitting on the front porch in one of the wicker chairs holding her wide-awake grandson. She touched his hair. "You miss Miss Margaret's rockin' chair, don't ya? I'm buyin' you one tomorrow." Billy smiled as if he understood what his grandmother was saying. "Oh, you like me buyin' you a new rockin' chair, don't ya?"

A police car pulled up into Mr. King's front yard. Mary C. recognized Officers Boos and Short when the car stopped and they both got out of the car. Officer Short was the talker.

"Miss Mary C., can we talk to you a minute?"

"Don't look like I got much of a choice."

"You always have a choice, we just hope it's the right one."

Mary C. could not resist. "We sure had some excitement on our little trip down South, didn't we? I went down there to get my grandson. Y'all went down there to get Tom Green. I got my grandson right here with me." She looked toward the police car. "Y'all got ol' black Tom in the back of that police car?"

Officer Short ignored her sarcasm. "You don't know anything about a man named Junior Pane or a man they called Moochee, do ya?"

"I know they work on Vona's dock, but I don't hang around with 'em."

"You didn't see those two on the road or at that motel, did ya?

Mary C. shook her head. Officer Short had more. "Do you know Zeke Shackleford?"

"Of course I do. Is there anybody around here that don't know that name? You know damn good and well, Hawk killed his son and then they fought at Bill's on the beach. What a damn fight that was."

"Did you see him down there?"

"Down where?"

"In Gibsonton. At that motel."

"No. I ain't seen nobody. Y'all need to take care of the citizens here in Mayport since y'all came way out here."

Officers Boos and Short did not understand. "What's happened, now?"

Mary C. smiled. "Well, there's this army of dog hunters runnin' all over town with loaded guns and big knives. Somebody's gonna get killed and when they do, you two remember I'm sittin' right on this porch rockin' my grandson. I don't want you two to get like my ol' friend Mr. Butler and start blamin' me for any dead body that shows up."

The two officers were concerned with Mary C.'s information. Officer Boos walked to the car and looked back. "Let's talk to her later. We need to take a look at these hunters before her predictions come true."

Officer Boos turned the police car onto the road next to Mr. King's house. He had to slam on the breaks as Miss Margaret's family station wagon stopped in front of the police car. Miss Margaret was driving, Jason was sitting up front on the passenger's side and Fabian was in the back seat with Eli's body. When the car came to a complete stop, Jason jumped out. Officer Short got out of the police car. Jason talked first.

"The dog killed Eli. He's in the back seat." Officer Short looked at the family station wagon, then at his partner, then at Mary C. She was still sitting in the wicker chair on the porch.

Earnest Coolie was sitting at the wooden picnic table in his junkyard. His two nasty sons were sitting with him.

"When it gets dark we're gonna rain hell down on that high falootin' Stoddard Moore and that hat wearin' boy of his. Once that sister of yours gets their attention and they let her in the house, they ain't gonna know what hit 'em. I knew it would come to this one day. It was just a matter of time. He's been lookin' down his nose at me ever since we got here. I've had hate in my heart since the day I met him. All I wanted was a chance to work on one of his boats. Hell, he had three shrimp boats and one snapper boat. Didn't think I'd be dependable enough. That son-of-a-bitch never even gave me a chance. He never talked to me again. Even when he'd see me around, he still never talked to me. Yes siree, I've been waitin' for this day to come." He looked toward the shack they called home. "Becky, get out here and let's see what ya look like."

Duck and Bucket looked toward the shack waiting for their sister to walk out. Earnest Coolie did not want to wait. "Hurry up, girl. You're a big part of this tonight. Get on out here."

Rebecca stepped out into the dirt in front of the door. She wore a red silk, tight fitting, short skirt that stopped half way down her thighs. Her legs were perfect. The white halter-top that tied under her huge breasts was at least two sizes to small. It was obvious the top was to be worn with out a brazier underneath. She was barefoot, but she held a pair of red high heels in her hand. Her two brothers stared like the idiots they were. Earnest Coolie got up and walked over to her.

"Damn girl, you look just like ya mama did when I first saw her. You got bigger titties, but the rest of ya looks just like her. When ya get them shoes on you'll look even better." He stepped closer and pulled her halter-top open wider so more of her eight-inch cleavage would show. She felt his fingers touch her as he opened the blouse, but she did not flinch. "Now, they'll sure as hell be lookin' at you. You know what to do, don't ya?" She nodded her head. "Then say it. Tell me what you're gonna do."

Mr. King, Mary C., Jason and Billy sat on the porch of the haunted house. An ambulance was taking Eli's body away. Miss Margaret had gone back to her house to get Susan to relieve Margie at the store. The two police officers took Fabian home and went to tell Eli's family about his horrible and untimely death.

Mary C. had an interesting observation. "You know they're gonna say it happened 'cause Jason was with 'em." Jason looked at his mother. "Well you know they are, son."

Mr. King looked at Mary C. "Who's gonna say that?"

"Those two policeman. Mr. Butler brainwashed 'em. They're after me, too."

"What makes you think somethin' like that?"

"You didn't see the looks on their faces when they saw Jason in that car with Eli."

Mr. King knew it was time to change the subject. "This has been another wild day around here. Some say it's in the sulfur water. It might be makin' us all crazy."

Mary C. smiled at Mr. King's attempt to add a little Mayport humor to the conversation. "Okay John, we can change the subject. But, even though Fabian's gonna tell 'em what happened they'll come here to question Jason. You mark my words."

CHAPTER EIGHT

Jason sat alone on Mr. King's front porch with the mist of the Northeaster touching his face. He knew the sun was going down on the Fort George side of the St. John's River, but the heavy cloud cover from the Northeaster kept the sun covered.

Susan looked out the front window of the store. There was still a little daylight, but she knew darkness would soon take Mayport. With the wind and rain it would most likely be a slow and boring night in the store. She would pass the time thinking about the events of the last week and especially that day.

Margie walked into the kitchen where Miss Margaret was snapping green beans. "Mother, may I use the car?"

Miss Margaret snapped one of the beans. "You and your sister's used to play that sometimes out front. I'd sit on that porch and watch you. Where did those little girls go?"

Margie wasn't sure what her mother meant. "What did we play?"

Miss Margaret snapped another bean. "Mother, may I. You know, the game. When you said mother may I use the car. I thought of you girls playing the game. It was a lovely memory. Why do you need the car, dear? You seem tired and the weather is dreadful. I don't want to be worried. In the last week, we've had enough excitement to last a lifetime. Where do you need to go?"

Margie was hoping to get the car without getting the third degree from her mother. Miss Margaret was right about the trouble that had surrounded them for the last week. Her good advice for Margie to stay home fell on Margie's deaf ears. The oldest was becoming the best liar of all her daughters.

"Miss Mary C. asked me to come by and see her when I got off work, but I forgot with all the excitement. I just thought about it when I was taking a bath. I think she wants to go out and she going to ask me to take care of Billy."

Miss Margaret snapped another bean. "And you're going to stay at Mr. King's house with Billy?"

"If she wants me to keep him, I'll bring him back here."

Miss Margaret smiled. She was far too gullible. "Go get that little rascal."

Theda was in bed with her son next to her. Stoddard Moore and his son Fabian sat on their front porch. A group of the dog hunters walked up into the yard. Wassie Franks stepped up to the porch. "We gonna call it a night. This darkness favors the dog, not us. He's probably layin' low with this wind and rain. We need to do the same. We'll find him in the mornin'. I'm goin' over to the see Eli's family. He was my God child." Wassie turned and walked away.

The Coolie's were waiting for night to fall. The right time for their evil plan had arrived and Earnest Coolie's three offspring had their instructions and were prepared to do grave harm to the Moore family. Earnest Coolie and Rebecca were in a truck and the two Coolie sons were in a rusty 1952 Buick. They were on their way to Mayport.

Stoddard Moore stood next to his son. "Maybe we should sell this house and move the boats to Fort Myers or Key West or even Texas. A fresh start for us all."

Fabian looked up at his father. "That might be a good idea for you and Theda. She don't need to stay here with Duck lurkin' around. He's not gonna just let this go, ya know. Theda needs to be able to take care of her baby without bein' scared to go outside. We won't be so lucky if Duck gets his hands on the boy. I think you and Theda should get out of here for a little while. You can think about leaving permanently later. Go on down to Fort Myers and see Uncle Mel. He'd love that. Y'all can talk about movin' the boats down there. He's got room on that big dock of his. He's been askin' you to join him for years. It might be time to do that."

Stoddard Moore nodded his head. "I'm gonna go in a tell Theda to get ready. We'll leave in the morning."

Fabian stood up. "I'm gonna ride over to Eli's and see if they need anything."

Stoddard Moore had a fatherly thought for his son. "Fabian, this was not your fault. I blame Mary C. for keepin' that awful dog. Everybody knows she's crazy. Whenever she's involved somebody dies. God just didn't give her Theda's baby." Stoddard went into the house. Fabian went to Eli's.

Mary C. walked out onto Mr. King's front porch. Jason was still sitting in the misty night. "You're gonna get sick, sittin' out here like this. I don't need you getting' sick. We got too much to do."

"I'm fine, Mama. It feels good out here. I like the way it looks and feels when a Northeaster blows through."

"Don't start actin' like John. He sits out here all hours of the night in all kinds of weather. You ain't lookin' for the new spook Norman, are ya?"

Jason had to smile at his mother's rare attempt to make a joke. He liked it. He liked being on the porch alone with her. Jason always liked it when it was just the two of them. The sight of car lights took both their attention as a truck and a 1952 Buick rolled past the house. Mary C. recognized the truck.

"Big trouble just hit town. That's Earnest Coolie's truck. I saw him when I was out at Miss Carolyn's. That other car's followin' him. Somethin' bad's comin'. I can feel it." She put her hand on Jason's shoulder. "Maybe we oughta ride out there and tell Fabian the Coolie's are in town. He needs to know that."

Jason had been waiting to talk to his mother. "I'll go out there, Mama. I need to see how Fabian's doin'. Mama, Chichemo's gone. He said to tell you he was sorry. He was probably goin' to Texas. That man, Beanie, didn't like it when I made him get off the boat, but Chichemo told him to leave. I think they went together."

"When those two get together it always ends up no good. They'll be back. They stay away longer each time, but they always come back. I guess you want to run the boat and start shrimpin' again?"

Jason nodded. "The boat should be shrimpin'. I know I ain't no Chichemo, but I can do it."

"We don't need the money, son."

"That don't make no difference. The money won't last forever and I need to be workin' and takin' care of you and Billy. The *Mary C.* ain't made for stayin' at the dock."

Mary C. smiled at Jason's convection about the status of the boat. "You've got to get somebody with some experience to go with you." Jason looked at his mother with a half smile. She knew he was thinking about her condition for him to go shrimping. "What is it, Jason? That was a strange little smile on your face."

"Fabian wants to work on the boat with me."

Mary C. shook her head. "Oh no, Tweetle Dumb and Tweetle Dumber. Let's talk about this later. Go on out there and tell Fabian about the Coolies. Let me make a list of a few things I need you to get from the store."

Fabian Moore was driving past the sand hill and the oak tree when he saw Miss Margaret's family station wagon parked close to the grape arbor. He was concerned and wondered why the car would be park there in the dark on such a stormy night. He pulled up next to the station wagon and got out of his car. Fabian looked into the empty station wagon. He turned away from the car and looked up. He could see there was somebody at the top of the sand hill. His curiosity was raging inside him. He wondered which one of the daughters was visiting the oak tree. Fabian had to take a look.

Earnest Coolie stopped his truck in a wooded area near Stoddard Moore's house. He reached over to his daughter, grabbed the front of her shirt and ripped it open, completely exposing both her huge bare breasts. She was surprised and held the shirt closed with her hands.

"That's the way you go to that door, with both of 'em showin', nipples and all. You hear me? I want who ever opens that door to be thinkin' about nothin' but you. I said, 'do you hear me'?"

"Yes, I hear you." Rebecca looked out the front window of the truck and saw car light flash in the woods on the far side of the house. Earnest Coolie saw then, too.

"Your brothers are in place. Let's get this thing done."

When Fabian reached the top of the sand hill he saw Margie sitting on her favorite limb. She had just started her body rubbing sexual ritual with the oak tree. Margie did not care if a Northeaster was blowing or not. Her back was to Fabian as he approached the limb. Margie realized she was not alone. It scared her at first, but when she turned to see Fabian, for some reason, her fear left her. She smiled and continued rubbing her body on the limb. Margie was insane.

"You think being an oak baby made you come to the tree tonight?"

Fabian was smart. He could deal with everything and was ready for anything. "I was called "oak baby" for years. I get a funny feelin' when I'm near here. You a believer?"

"I'm gonna have the next oak baby, if I can ever get Jason up here at midnight. He's already got one oak baby. Miss Mary C. wants me to have the next one."

Fabian knew Margie was talking crazy but he was attracted to her from the first time he saw her. He was not going to let this opportunity pass him by.

"That feels good to you, huh?" Margie pushed her hips and slowly humped the tree. She liked him watching her. "Don't waste all your energy up there. It ain't midnight and I ain't Jason, but I think you're unbelievable. You can practice with me if you want. Somethin' like that interest you?"

Margie stopped moving. "Pretty sure of yourself, aren't you?"

"Oh, no ma'am. I'm not sure at all. I just asked if you might be interested. Either you are or you're not. It's pretty simple. I am sure of one thing, though."

"I'm listening."

"Being with a stranger under this tree in the middle of a Northeaster would be the most exciting thing I've ever done. It would be something to remember for the rest of my life. I've never been with a woman like you."

Jason drove his Uncle Bobby's truck to the front of Miss Margaret's store. He stopped at the store first, hoping to see Sofia. Jason entered the store, ringing the bell as he walked in. Susan was the working sister at the moment. She was the sister whom had spent the least amount of time with Jason. She still wanted to be with him, but the opportunities had not been as numerous for her as they had been for her three sisters. Susan was more reserved and did not take the chances the others did. She was still glad to see Jason.

"Well, well, I know you didn't come here to see me."

Jason knew when to lie. "I didn't come to see any one person, but it's nice seeing you. We don't get to talk very much, do we?"

Susan was smart. "Jason, you don't talk to anybody very much." Jason had always liked her red hair and the line of freckles that crossed her little nose.

Stoddard Moore turned to his front door when he heard a woman's voice on the front porch. She was screaming. "Help me, please! Help me!"

Stoddard grabbed the shotgun he had leaning against the wall next to the front door. He looked out the window of the door and saw a woman wet from the rain with her clothes ripped, exposing her breasts, nipples and all. When he opened the door a scared and panicking Rebecca "Milkduds" Coolie fell into his arms.

"Please help me, mister!"

When she fell forward, Stoddard found himself holding one of her oversized bare breasts in his hand. The shotgun was in his other hand. "I was out with a new boy friend and he tried to rape me! I got away and saw your light!"

She was as close to being naked as a woman could get. Her wet and clinging clothes revealed more of her body. She threw her arms around Stoddard and he put the shotgun down on the floor. Rebecca stepped back so he could get a better look at her. Stoddard Moore had never seen or touched such huge and beautiful breasts. Even with the dramatic situation at hand, he wanted to touch them again, but he just stared. She did nothing to hide herself. Like the way her father planned it, Milkduds had Stoddard's complete attention.

It was too late when Stoddard Moore realized there was someone else in his house. His peripheral vision had failed him as he concentrated on Rebecca's incredible female attributes. Stoddard Moore had no idea the burning sensation he was feeling was Earnest Coolie slitting his throat. He turned as shock took his body. He fell against the wall. The last thing Stoddard Moore would see was Duck Coolie opening the door to the bedroom where his daughter

Theda and his grandson were sleeping. Stoddard was dead before he hit the wooden floor of his living room. Rebecca Coolie covered her body with her torn shirt. Earnest Coolie wiped Stoddard's blood off of his big hunting knife and slid it back into the leather sheath strapped to his waist. He turned to his daughter.

"Check his pockets for money and get his watch."

Theda screamed when Duck pulled her up out of her bed. She was dressed in a thin, short, white, cotton nightshirt. Bucket picked up the baby. Theda fought Duck until he hit her with the back of his hand. The fight was over as he carried her out of the house and into the woods where the car was parked. Earnest took the baby from Bucket.

"Becky can hold the baby 'til we get home. You don't know nothin' bout holdin' no baby. Take a look around. If you see anything worth takin', take it. Don't be long."

Bucket handed Rebecca the baby. She walked out of the house toward the truck parked in the woods. Duck was putting Theda into the car. She was scared, but conscious. Her nightshirt revealed her firm breasts as the wet material pressed against her bare skin.

"Please don't hurt me, Duck! Don't hurt my baby, please!"

Duck Coolie was crazy. "Your baby? Our baby. You think I'd hurt my own son? What kinda man ya think I am?"

Theda was just a child. She was petrified. "Please don't hurt me, Duck. I wanted you to see the baby. They wouldn't let me. Please don't hurt me."

"I told you I ain't that kinda man. I wouldn't hurt the mother of my child. We're gonna raise him together. He's gonna need and mama and a daddy. His mama won't run off like mine did. I'm sorry 'bout ya daddy. I didn't like him much, but him dyin' was 'tween him and my pa." He leaned toward Theda and kissed her on the cheek and squeezed one of her breasts. He smelled awful, but she was too traumatized to react to the odor. Duck Coolie was more than crazy.

Duck could not see the truck in the woods with the rain and wind hitting his windshield. Bucket jumped into the car with Duck and Theda. She was in the middle. Bucket's flow of adrenalin took him to another dimension. He gave a wild and frightening Rebel yell. "Yeeeha! Damn that was great!" He looked at his brother through wild eyes. "Don't ya just love that blood rush?" He gave the same wild expression to a horrified Theda Moore. "Welcome to the family, girl. Duck said you was a looker." He stared at her breasts.

Duck smiled. "I told ya, she had pretty titties didn't I? They ain't that big, but they're big enough and they're pretty."

Bucket could not take his eyes of Theda's breasts. He directed his nasty question to his crazy brother. "Can I touch 'em without ya getting' mad?" Theda's heart raced even harder than before.

Duck started the car and gave a proud smiled. "Don't squeeze 'em too hard."

Rebecca Coolie sat in the truck holding the baby. She could see her father walking in the rain toward them. He opened the driver's side door, but did not get in. Earnest Coolie had his own flow of excessive adrenaline.

"Damn, that felt good, girl. And you done good. That bastard's always been a dirty old man. I knew he'd be lookin' at you, when I cut him."

There was a noise behind Earnest Coolie. He knew the sound of a growling dog. Rebecca heard it, too. She saw the fear and pain in her father's evil eyes when the devil dog, Abaddon, sunk his sharp teeth into the back of his leg. The powerful dog pulled him to the ground. The dog's second bite was on the inside soft part of Earnest's thigh. Earnest Coolie screamed like a child as each snap of Abaddon's jaws opened another gash somewhere on his body. Earnest tried to roll away from the wild dog. He managed to roll under the truck. Abaddon had to release him for a second, but began to crawl under the truck to get another bite. Earnest screamed in pain.

"Open your door! Open the door!"

Rebecca opened the passenger's side door and slid over behind the wheel with the baby. Earnest crawled out from under the truck on the passenger's side. He jumped in the truck and slammed the door. Abaddon came from under the truck and jumped up at the closed window, cracking the glass. Rebecca screamed. The dog was gone. She looked at her injured and bleeding father.

"Pa, you alright?" His pain was too great. He had no words. "What was that?"

Earnest grimaced, but still had no words. Rebecca laid the baby on the seat between them. She started the truck and drove out of the woods. She looked for the dog, but he was gone.

Margie stood under the oak tree with Fabian Moore. She had taken all her clothes off, even her shoes. Fabian gazed at her naked body. Her skin was glistening with the misty rain from the Northeaster. Fabian had followed her lead and was completely naked. Margie looked at his wet muscular body. She turned away from him, bent her body forward and put her hands on the oak tree. She was in her favorite position and gave her usual instructions.

"Please do it as hard as you can. Don't stay inside me. When you pull out I want to hold it."

The muscles in Fabian's legs actually quivered after Margie's instructions. He had never heard a woman talk like that before. He was pleasantly surprised over her aggressiveness. His lust and total excitement was obvious. He had no problem with her forward and unlady-like requests. As he stepped to her, Margie went up on her toes. Her calf, hamstring and butt muscles all flexed at the same time. It was an incredible vision for Fabian's lustful eyes. He pushed his hips toward her and his manliness slid inside her with one thrust. The heat took Fabian's breath away. It was far more than he had ever felt before. Margie commanded his full attention.

"Do it hard, now!" Fabian got to the business at hand. He should have been home protecting his father, sister and new nephew. Margie was becoming more and more like Mary C. everyday.

Duck drove the 1953 Buick past the Little Jetties. Bucket had been feeling and squeezing Theda's breasts for at least a mile of riding. He worked his hand under her nightshirt and even sucked on her nipples. Duck could hardly keep his eyes on the road. It excited him to watch his brother touching his woman. They were both nasty and crazy.

The rain was not as heavy as it was earlier, but the wind was still carrying a misty rain. Rebecca kept looking at her injured father as she drove the truck out of Mayport.

"You're really bleedin' bad, Pa. You need a doctor."

Earnest Coolie gritted his teeth and spoke through his agony. "I can't go to a doctor. We gotta get back to the house and then take Duck's woman and the baby out to your Aunt Annie in Black

Hammock. Nobody'll look for 'em out there. You can doctor me up when we'get home."

Perhaps it was because her father seemed weak and vulnerable in his present condition, but Rebecca found a small amount of courage when she looked down at the baby.

"I thought we was gonna take Duck's son. I didn't know you was gonna kill nobody."

Earnest Coolie grimaced again. "Now, ya know."

Jason was in the back room of the store kissing Susan's full lips. She was still completely dressed, but she allowed him to touch her breasts. Jason reached down and rubbed her between her legs. She moved his hand away.

"If you do that I won't be able to stop. I'm scared to do that here. I'll come to the boat or meet you anywhere, but not here. I'm sorry Jason, I'm just too scared."

Susan left Jason standing in the room and went to the front of the store. Jason took a deep breath and followed the sister that, for the time being, got away. Susan's refusal to perform at any risk excited Jason even more. He said the words before he thought of what he was saying.

"Meet me on the boat when you get off."

Susan smiled. "I'll be there at ten o'clock."

Duck stopped the Buick in front of their wooden shack. Bucket got out and took Theda with him. Theda had not said another word during her abusive ride to the junkyard. The dirt in the yard had turned to mud from the rain. Theda's bare feet were covered in the black muck by the time she got into the house. Her nightshirt was soaking wet and completely see through.

Bucket was still riding mentally high from the killing and the lustful ride home. He pushed Theda to Rebecca's bedroom and onto the bed. With one strong grab and tear Bucket Coolie ripped Theda's nightshirt completely off her body. Theda was so petrified; she had no scream inside her. She thought her heart was going to rip open like her nightshirt. Bucket dove on top of her and his body weight took her breath away as he pinned her to the mattress. As soon as she felt his weight pressing her down, he was gone. Duck grabbed the back of Bucket's long greasy hair and pulled him off Theda. Duck was mad at his brother.

"You must be crazy." He threw Bucket to the floor. "You can't have her first. You know that ain't fair."

Bucket got off the floor with rage in his eyes. He took an aggressive step toward Duck, but stopped when Duck held up a big black pistol and pointed it at his forehead.

"I know I can't whip ya, Bucket. But, I will shoot ya. You gotta calm down. I knew this was gonna happen if I let you touch her. I try to do somethin' nice for you and you get crazy. It ain't fair Bucket, it just ain't fair."

Rebecca got out of the truck and ran around to the passenger's side to help her murdering father make his way to the house. She left the baby on the front seat. Earnest continued to make his painful faces as he moved slowly, getting out of the truck. He leaned on his daughter all the way through the mud until they reached the front of the house. He grabbed one of the support posts to steady himself while Rebecca opened the door.

There were noises coming from the back of the house. Rebecca assisted her father until he fell down onto a small couch with torn cushions. "I'll get somethin' to clean those cuts, Pa."

Rebecca walked to the back of the house. She realized the noises were coming from her bedroom. The door was closed. She pushed the door open slowly and saw both her nasty brothers in the bed with Theda. Rebecca's heart raced at the awful sight. Bucket and Duck were both completely naked. She could hardly see Theda. Theda was on her knees with Bucket behind her and Duck kneeling at her head. Duck looked up when the door opened. "Come on Milkduds, join the fun!"

Rebecca was too horrified to throw up, but she wanted to, so the burning and sour feeling in her stomach would go away. She heard Theda Moore make a painful noise. Rebecca found that moment of courage again. "Pa's hurt bad. A big dog bit him bad. We gotta get him to a doctor."

The two animals jumped out of the bed and ran naked to the front of the house. Theda lay in the fetal position in the middle of the muddy bed. Rebecca did not follow her brothers. She closed the bedroom door and walked to the bed.

Earnest Coolie was still lying on the couch. He looked up when his son's stepped to him. "What the hell are you two fools doin' now? Get some clothes on."

Duck was the quickest liar of the two. "We was in the shower tryin' to get cleaned up before we head out to Black Hammock."

Earnest was in intense pain, but he was still upset about his two naked sons. "When did you two queers start takin' a shower together?"

Duck was still the talker. He smiled. "We ain't queer, Pa. We was just hurryin', that's all. We knew you'd be ready to go as soon as you got here. What happened to ya, Pa?" The subject had changed.

"A big dog come after me and I couldn't fight him off. I thought he was gonna kill me. I rolled under the truck and got away long enough to get in the truck. Becky's gonna get somethin' to stop the bleedin'. I'll get some help when we get to your aunt's house. Now, get some clothes on and tell ya sister to get her ass in here before I bleed to death."

The two brothers walked back to the bedroom. Duck pushed Bucket and they both smiled at their father not knowing about what they had done to Theda. Bucket spoke for the first time. "That dog sure put an ass whippin' on Pa, didn't he?"

Duck smiled again. "Sure did." He opened the bedroom door. He was still naked. "Pa needs ya Milkduds."

There was no one in the room. There was no one in the bed. Both evil siblings looked up at the window at the same time. It was wide open. The two abused women were gone. Bucket moved to the window and looked outside. He saw no one. Duck ran to the front of the house. The sound of the truck engine told all three men in the house something was happening.

Duck ran past Earnest on the couch. "Who is it, Duck?" Duck was out the door before he had time to answer. Bucket ran past the couch. "What's the matter, Bucket?"

"They runnin', Pa. They runnin'." Bucket ran out the front door to see his naked brother hanging on the outside of the driver's door of the truck. He was reaching into the window and trying to stop Rebecca from driving off.

Duck stood on the side running board of the truck holding on to the side view mirror with his left hand and reaching into the truck with his right hand. At first he was trying to reach the key and turn off the engine, but the truck started moving faster. He hit his sister in the face with his closed fist, hoping it would make her stop the moving truck. Duck had forgotten his younger sister could fight like a man.

Rebecca threw her right hand as hard as any man. Her closed fist and clinched knuckles hit Duck on the bridge of his nose, causing an instant of painful blindness. He did manage to hold on to the mirror. Duck also realized the truck had driven onto the oyster shell road that led to Mayport Road. The speed of the truck had increased drastically.

Rebecca threw a second fist full of knuckles, hitting Duck on the front of his mouth causing his two top front teeth to go through his upper lip. The two hard punches Duck had taken were no comparison to the amount of pain and damage he endured when he was thrown from the moving truck and his naked body hit the oyster shell road at forty miles an hour.

When Duck hit the road his body did not land and stop, it rolled and tumbled for at least twenty yards. The sharp oyster shells that formed the road took small chunks of flesh out of his exposed and naked body. Not just one or two, but maybe fifty or more chunks of his flesh.

Duck knew when he hit the ground his attempt to use his arms to break the fall had actually broken both his arms. His right arm broke at the elbow and his left arm broke at the wrist. Duck's femur bone under his thigh muscle had a compound fracture and the jagged top of the splintered bone was sticking out of the skin. Duck Coolie passed out from the shock and the pain as the Mayport Northeaster blew across his severely damaged naked body. Duck did not see the headlights of the Buick as it approached him on the oyster shell road. Bucket was far too late to save his evil brother and partner.

The truck was speeding down Mayport Road. Rebecca was visibly shaking from the trauma of the ordeal she had faced. She was scared and had no idea what to do next. Theda spoke for the first time.

"Thank you."

Even in Rebecca's confused and frightened state she was still realistic. "Don't thank me yet. You don't know 'em. They'll come after us. We're probably closer to bein' dead than we know."

Theda turned and looked out the back window of the truck. "I'd rather be dead."

"Well, you're with the right person, cause I'd rather be dead, too. So we got nothin' to loose, do we?" The baby made a noise. Theda and Rebecca looked down at the infant. Rebecca looked back at the road. "Well, maybe you have something to loose."

Theda picked up her baby and held him to her body. Her upper body was wrapped in the muddy sheet off the bed.

Rebecca kept her eyes on the road. "I didn't know they were gonna kill ya daddy."

Theda did not react to Rebecca's statement. She knew they had to get away. "We have to find my brother. We'll be safe with him."

Rebecca did not trust one man to protect them from her family. "We need to fine a policeman with a gun and the authority to protect us. And that might not be enough."

Fabian and Margie sat in the sand beneath the oak tree. They were both still wet and naked. Fabian had followed all of Margie's sexual instructions to the tee. He had never been with such an uninhibited and aggressive woman. Margie knew she had been more than Fabian expected or could handle. She liked that. She wanted to challenge his earlier words. "Was that exciting enough for you? Will it be a lifetime memory?"

"It's etched in stone in my heart, my head and it's on my soul. You have no equal. I just hope it was as exciting for you. If it wasn't I apologize and please don't tell me. I couldn't handle the truth." Fabian was a smart young man.

Margie smiled at his humble comment. "It was exciting, but maybe it's because we were at the tree. Didn't you feel something different here?"

Fabian had to admit he did feel something. "I felt something, but I thought that was because of you."

Margie smiled again. "It's the tree. We need to get dressed and go. We'll both be sick from this weather."

Jason stood on the front porch of Fabian's house. The door was open and Jason's heart raced in his chest when he saw Stoddard

Moore's dead body lying face down on the floor. A huge pool of thick blood surrounded his body. Jason wanted to run away and pretend he had not gone there. There was a noise behind him. He turned to see what other horror was waiting to be discovered. Jason's heart screamed in his chest when he saw the devil dog, Abaddon, standing only a few feet away at the bottom of the steps.

The killer hound growled and showed his teeth. Jason knew the dog hated him and he hated the dog. Jason also knew that without a weapon he was no match for the dog's power and killer instinct. Jason was sure the dog would not stare at him very long. He grabbed a small table and threw it at Abaddon, giving Jason the time he needed to run into the house and close the door. Jason had a better chance of survival inside the house with Stoddard Moore's dead body than he did outside with the killer canine.

Jason heard Abaddon walking back and forth of the porch for about a minute. Then Jason heard a car engine. He looked out the window and saw Fabian's car rolling up to the house. Fabian jumped out of the car with his shotgun and began shooting. Jason knew Fabian saw the dog. Jason ran out onto the porch as Fabian walked toward him. "It was that damn dog. He was standin' on the porch. You didn't see him?"

"I saw him."

Fabian stepped up on the porch. "I can't believe I missed the bastard. You think we should go after him in the dark?"

"No. You gotta stay here. Somethin' awful's happened."

Jason's words stopped Fabian's excited rambling. "What is it?" Fabian looked past Jason and into the house. He saw his father's body on the floor. He ran into the house.

Mary C. looked out the front window of John King's haunted house. John sat in one of the chairs reading the paper. "John, it's gonna rain and blow all night, ain't it?"

"That's what a Northeaster's supposed to do. It's the Northeaster rule."

"Me and Miss Carolyn went to the beach and watched the foam tumble."

John King gave Mary C. a strange look over his reading classes. "That's nice."

Mary C. did not notice the "are you crazy" tone of his reply. "I wish Jason would come on back. I don't like the feelin' I've been gettin' tonight. When I saw the Coolies it hit me and it ain't lifted yet."

As soon as those words left Mary C.'s mouth Earnest Coolie's truck went speeding by on the road in front of Mr. King's house.

"John, there goes Coolie's truck again. Goin' fast toward Stoddard's place. I didn't see 'em goin' out, but they must'a left and now they're back again. I sent Jason out there to tell Fabian they was here. I don't like this John. I don't like it one bit."

Mr. King put the paper down. "Let's ride out there. You'll feel better if we do."

CHAPTER NINE

Jason was still standing on the porch when he saw the light of the truck speeding toward him. He stepped into the house. Fabian was kneeling next to his father. Jason picked up Fabian's shotgun and pulled the pump handle down loading a shell into the firing chamber.

"Somebody's comin'."

Fabian stood up and took the gun from Jason. He walked out onto the front porch as the truck slid on the wet grass and stopped at the porch. Fabian raised the gun and pointed it at the passenger's side window. The windows were wet and fogged up. The door opened and Fabian recognized his sister's voice.

"Don't shoot, Fabian, it's me Theda." Fabian lowered the gun as Theda ran to his arms still wrapped in the mud-covered sheet. "Oh, I'm so glad you're alright! They killed daddy. They took the baby. They raped me and did awful things to me." She buried her face in her brother's chest. "She saved me and we got away." Theda pointed to the truck where Rebecca was still sitting behind the steering wheel.

Fabian was trying to absorb the horror and tragedy that was unfolding in front of him. He stepped to the truck. "Come on out of there!"

Rebecca was scared. "You ain't gonna shoot me, are ya? I ain't had nothin' to do with your daddy bein' killed."

Theda grabbed Fabian's arm. "She helped me get away. She fought with Duck. She saved me and the baby. Please don't hurt her, Fabian. She wants to die and I don't want her to."

"Get out of the truck. I'm not gonna hurt you."

Rebecca stepped out of the truck. She was still wearing the torn blouse. Her huge breasts were still visible. She did not care. Even with all the awful things that had happened, Jason and Fabian had to stop and take a long look at Rebecca's body as she walked toward the porch. She was a showstopper. Fabian did not know who she was, but Jason did.

"You're the daughter, ain't ya?"

"Yes, I am. I'm really scared, too. I'm scared of y'all and my family. I had to stop 'em from doin' what they was doin' and what they was gonna do. What ever happens to me happens. When I saw the baby and her." She looked at Theda. "I had to get 'em away. I didn't think it out, I just did it."

Fabian was trying to conduct himself in a rational manner, but he was losing the battle. "Where are they, now?"

Rebecca had her scary thoughts. "I thought they'd be right behind us. I'm lookin' for 'em any minute."

With her comment, a set of car headlights scared them all. Theda grabbed the baby out of the truck, took Rebecca's hand and ran into the house, pulling Rebecca as she ran. They ran past Stoddard's body and side stepped the pool of blood.

Fabian lifted his shotgun preparing to defend them all. Jason ran into the house to get another gun. Fabian did not recognize Mr. King's 1957 Chevy. He pointed the gun at the moving vehicle. Jason stepped out onto the porch carrying another rifle. He saw the car.

"Don't shoot, Fabian, it's Mr. King." Fabian lowered the gun for the second time. He wanted to shoot somebody. The Chevy stopped. Billy was sleeping on the front seat of the car. Mary C. and Mr. King got out at the same time. Mary C. was first to speak.

"Jason, what's wrong?"

Fabian answered. "The Coolie's killed my daddy. They took Theda and the baby." Mary C. did not change her facial expression.

Jason had to speak up. "We got Theda and the baby back. The Coolie girl helped 'em get away. Mr. Moore's inside."

Mr. King went into the house to see to his friend Stoddard. Mary C. turned to Fabian. "Where's the Coolies, now?"

Fabian came to life. "That's what I was findin' out when y'all came up. We thought you might be them." He looked at Jason. "Get the girl. If I go get her, I might just kill her."

Mary C. nodded to Jason. He went into the house. Mary C. stepped to Fabian. His head was down. "I'm sorry, Fabian, but this ain't no time for huggin' and feelin' sorry. What's done is done. What's to come is the most important thing, now."

Jason walked out of the house with Rebecca. She had covered her upper body with a small blanket she had taken off the couch. Her pretty, but dirty face, showed her fear. Fabian was ready. "I'm only gonna ask you one time. Where are they?"

Rebecca's mouth was dry. She knew not to hesitate with a man like Fabian Moore. She would answer any and all the questions. She had gone that far and she could not turn back. Rebecca was proud she saved the baby and Theda. "Pa's hurt bad. Before he left here a big dog got hold of him. He's at the house, but he's hurt. Duck tried to stop us and got throwed from the truck. We was movin' pretty fast, I don't know what happened after that. Bucket's probably tryin' to get the other two where they can come to get us. I know they'll be comin' for me. After what I've done, I'll never get a good night's sleep. Hell, I never got one anyway."

Fabian looked at Jason. Jason nodded. "I'll go with ya."

Fabian walked back into the house. Mary C. stood with Rebecca. Jason stood with his mother and checked the rifle he was holding to be sure it was fully loaded. Mary C. looked at Rebecca.

"I heard you was a pretty girl, but I ain't never seen you close up like this. They was right about you, underneath all that dirt you are pretty." Rebecca had no response. Mary C. did not care. "I don't think I've ever seen a woman with a body like yours. We've all got some kind of gift. That body is definitely your gift."

Fabian walked out of the house dressed in his combat uniform, Green Beret and all. He was a striking and menacing figure of a man. He had a holstered pistol, and a huge serrated combat knife strapped to his waist. His pump action shotgun was reloaded and would be his weapon of choice. Rebecca got chills when the Green Beret moved past her. Fabian said nothing to the others as he walked to his car. Jason followed him and got in on the passenger's side.

Rebecca looked at Mary C. "Duck's gonna be scared when he sees that hat."

Mary C. walked to the window of the car as Fabian turned the key and stated the engine. "I'll make you two boys French toast in the mornin'." She was more than insane.

Bucket Coolie had been trying to get his brother, Duck, up off the road and into the back seat of the car. Bucket had put on a pair of stained skivvy underwear. Duck gave out a blood-curdling scream of pain each time Bucket tried to move him.

"I can't leave ya here and go get help. We got to get you in the car, go get Pa, and get both of y'all some help."

Duck tried to explain, but the pain was so intense he became frustrated and was helpless. "My leg's broke bad. I can't move without it stickin' me. I need a amba'lance. They can give me somethin' for the pain and then lift me up."

Bucket shook his head. "We can't do that. They gonna want to know what happened."

"We ain't gotta tell 'em the truth. We'll say I fell off the back of the truck. Just go get help, Bucket."

"I'll go back and get some clothes. I'll see what Pa wants to do. You can't be naked when somebody comes to help."

Duck was pitiful. "Tell Pa I'm really hurt bad. He never thinks we're really hurt."

Duck laid his head down on the shell-covered road. He tried to hold perfectly still. Any movement brought on excruciating pain. There was an old blanket on the floorboard of the car, but Bucket did not look for anything to cover his brother from the wind and rain. He got into the car and drove back to the shack.

Mr. King was on the phone calling the police when Rebecca entered the house. Mary C. sat in the car with Billy still sleeping in the front seat. Rebecca walked to the back of the house where she had left Theda and the baby. She knew Theda was her only friend. Mr. King hung up the phone. He walked outside to his car.

"Police are on the way. Don't tell me those boys went after the Coolies. Let the police handle 'em."

Mary C. shook her head. "That ain't the way, John and you know it. To many things can go wrong when the law shows up. People get away with awful things all the time. These Coolies are just the ones who get away with this kinda evil and killin'. No John, the boys are doin' the right thing."

"Mary C., just twenty minutes ago you were worried about Jason. You remember the bad feelin' you had? Well, this was it. There was somethin' wrong. Your feelin' was right. Don't you think the boys are in danger, goin' to face the Coolies alone?"

"They'll be back. I promised 'em French toast." John King knew the subject matter was closed. He had no response for Mary C.'s French toast comment.

Margie drove up to the store and blew the horn. Susan stepped to the screen door. Margie leaned over in the front seat and rolled down the passenger's side window.

"Why don't you just close up, now?   Nobody's coming out in this weather. Mother will understand. If she gets mad, so what."

Mary C. walked out onto the front porch waiting for the police car to arrive. Mr. King was talking to Theda about what happened. He really wanted to get a good look at Rebecca. He had never seen her before and he was not disappointed in what he saw. The talk about her was true. She had the most incredible body ever put on the Earth. She allowed the blanket to fall off her shoulders. Her huge breasts were in full view.

Bucket walked into the shack. Earnest Coolie was still lying on the couch. He opened his eyes when Bucket opened the door.

"What the hell's goin' on? I'm dyin' here. Did ya catch 'em? Bucket was scared to give his violent father the bad news. "I asked you what's goin' on. We gotta get out of here." Bucket would add mental pain to his father's physical pain.

"They got away, Pa. Becky took the truck and the girl and baby with her. Duck tried to stop 'em. He held on to the truck all the way to the shell road, but fell before he could stop 'em."

"Where's Duck, now?"

Bucket took a deep breath. "He's layin' in the middle of the road, Pa. Duck's hurt bad."

Earnest Coolie exploded with unreasonable anger. "He's hurt bad? Hell, I'm the one's hurt bad! What do ya mean, he's layin' in the road?"

"I can't move him, Pa. His leg's broke. Both arms is broke. He's bleedin' all over. I ain't foolin and he ain't actin', Duck's hurt bad. He said to get a amba'lance and they could get him up."

Earnest rolled off the couch in obvious great pain. He was able to kneel down next to the couch. "We gotta get him up and in that car. Ain't nobody out and about 'cause of the storm, but somebody's gonna see him sooner or later." Earnest struggled to his feet. Bucket reached to help him.

"Get you hands off me! I've been sufferin' all this time and you ain't done one thing to help. Now, you wanted help me up. Get some damn clothes on ya idiot."

Bucket backed away as his father slowly moved to the kitchen sink. Bucket got dressed and got some clothes for Duck while Earnest washed his face in the sink and cleaned the blood off of his arms.

"Get the car started. Let's get your brother and then we'll lay low in Black Hammock. Ain't nobody gonna find us there. Hell with that girl and the baby. I got what I wanted. We'll deal with that Judas sister of yours later." Bucket walked past him. "Why you got them other clothes?"

"Duck was naked when he left, remember?"

"Oh yeah, y'all was takin' a shower together. You must think I'm a fool, boy. Y'all was screwin' that little split-tail whore. Ya couldn't wait 'til it was all over. Ya greedy bastards. What the hell's wrong with you two? You act so stupid all the time."

"I'm sorry Pa. I tried to wait. But she was wantin' me bad. I'm just weak when I know the woman wants me. Then when she said she wanted us both, well what could we do?"

Earnest nodded his head at his eldest son. "I guess you're right, boy. I'd a done the same thing. Let's go get your brother."

Fabian and Jason were already out to Mayport Road. Jason knew the turn off to the oyster shell road leading to the Coolie junkyard. He had been there one time when he was younger. Uncle Bobby was looking for a tire rim for an old car he was trying to fix up. Jason knew they would soon reach the turn off. The rain had stopped but the wind was at its strongest thus far. Jason saw the shell road.

"Right up here, Fabian. Right at the end of the ditch."

Fabian slowed down the car and turned off Mayport Road onto the oyster shell road. He pressed the brake, stopping the car. Fabian's Special Forces training were about to be ignited. He turned to Jason

"I don't know if they'll be lookin' for us or not. We're goin' in blind. Hell, they might not even be there. We should go in ready to kill anything that moves. If we hesitate it could mean the difference in walking out of there or being carried out. If these boys are as mean as folk say, they won't go out easy. We'll have to adjust as we go. I'm glad you're with me. Two oak babies can't lose." Jason smiled and shook his head. He never really cared about the oak baby talk.

Fabian drove slowly down the shell road. The vegetation on both sides of the road was thick and moving with the wind. "How far down the road, ya think?"

"It's a pretty good ways. It's closer to the water and the marsh. There's a little wooden bridge before we get there, I do remember that."

There was a sharp turn in the road ahead and Fabian could not see what was on the other side of the curve. As the car turned into the curve he slammed on the brakes when he saw Duck's naked body lying in the middle of the road.

"Holy shit, what's that?"

Jason saw Duck, too. "It's a naked man."

Fabian was a smart man. "You stay in the truck and cover me. I'll see what's goin' on." Fabian got out of the truck and walked slowly to the body. He watched the thick woods around him.

"You alive mister?"

Fabian did not recognize Duck Coolie. Duck was in such shock and pain he did not hear the car drive up. He opened his eyes and could only see Fabian's shiny black combat boots. Fabian saw the serious compound fracture of Duck's leg. Fabian did not think of the story Theda told about Duck being thrown from the truck.

Duck Coolie was hallucinating and still staring at the boots. "I knew you'd come back. Where'd ya get them boots?" He strained to look up. Duck saw Fabian's Green Beret. "Damn Bucket, where'd ya get that silly hat? Fabian knew the name Bucket. He looked back at the truck.

"Ain't one of the Coolie's named Bucket?"

Jason stepped out of the car. "The oldest one. The other one's called Duck."

Fabian realized whom he had found. "I met this one the night when he came to the house to get Theda and the baby. This is Duck. This is the bastard that took my fifteen-year-old sister and had his way with her."

Duck Coolie had no idea he was making his final introduction. "That's me, I'm Duck, I'm Duck Coolie."

Before Jason could turn to look at his friend, Fabian drew his big combat knife and took a backhand slicing motion at Duck's throat. The cut almost took Duck's entire head off. Only a piece of the skin on the back of Duck's neck kept his head from falling off onto the shell road. The death slice scared Jason for a moment and his heart pounded against his chest. Fabian grabbed Duck's broken leg and pulled him off the road into the thick brush that bordered the road. Duck's body would be hard to find unless the flock of local buzzards gave his whereabouts away. Jason and Fabian got back into the car.

Bucket Coolie was waiting in the car for his father. He could hear the sound of a police siren out on the main road. He could tell it was passing by and going on down Mayport Road. It was louder for Fabian and Jason as the police car passed the oyster shell road. Fabian took a deep breath.

"They're goin' out to the house to get daddy. There's two of these bastards left. Let's finish this thing."

Fabian pushed down the gas pedal and the car started moving again slowly on the shell road. They rolled about fifty yards when the Coolie's Buick appeared about fifty yards in front of them. The Buick stopped and began to back up. Fabian knew whom he and Jason found.

"That's them!" Fabian hit the gas pedal and the car jumped like a stallion. "Run you bastards! Run!"

It took all Fabian's driving skills to keep the car on the wet oyster shell road. It was not a road made for a high-speed chase. Bucket

Coolie even had more problems trying to back up at such a speed. He did have a big enough lead to reach the house before Fabian could catch up with them. When Bucket stopped the car he jumped out and ran into the house, leaving his injured father in the car. Bucket wasn't actually deserting his father, but he was going to get another gun so his father could defend himself. Bucket was carrying his gun.

Earnest Coolie pushed the car door open and pulled his torn body out of the car, supporting himself with the open door. His eyes widened with ultimate fear when he saw Fabian's car coming right toward him. His legs would not move fast enough for him to get out of the way as the front right bumper of Fabian's car slammed into the open door. Earnest Coolie heard hundreds of his bones breaking as the door blasted into his already injured body.

The door bounced away from him and he fell to the ground next to the car. He held his bloody hand up in a very late motion of surrender. The car pulled up next to his broken body. This time the driver's side was facing him. He looked up to see Fabian's Green Beret covered head in the window.

"I'm glad you're still alive Mr. Coolie. I wanted you to know who I was." Earnest Coolie could not respond. He was dying. "I'm Fabian Moore. I'm revenging the death of my father. I thought you might like to know that." Fabian knew Earnest Coolie was looking at his Green Beret before he closed his eyes and died.

Bucket ran out of the house shooting his gun. A number of bullets hit Fabian's car so he and Jason ducked down. Fabian hit the gas pedal to get some distance between him and Bucket's attack. Bucket stood in the open, firing at the car as it moved away. The car was out of sight. Bucket ran back into the house for more bullets.

The police car pulled up to the front of Stoddard Moore's house. Officers Boos and Short were on duty again. Mr. King met them on the front porch and gave them the story he had been told so they would have some idea of what was going on. He did not mention Jason and Fabian. Officer Boos looked at Mary C. as Mr. King showed them Stoddard's body. She had to say something.

"I just got here, fellas. This ain't my work."

Officer Boos went to the back room to talk to Theda and Rebecca while Officer Short went back to the car to call for an ambulance to transport Mr. Moore's body. Officer Boos stepped into the small bedroom. He was taken aback when he saw Rebecca Coolie sitting in a chair next to the bed. She was showing enough of her body to get anyone's attention. He slowly turned his head away from Miss Coolie and looked at Theda.

"I know you've been through a lot tonight. Mr. King told me what he knew, but I really need to hear from you two ladies."

Theda had been preparing herself for that moment over the last hour. "Mr. Coolie and his sons came here to get me and the baby. They killed my daddy and took me and my baby to their house. That big, mean dog bit Mr. Coolie before he got into the truck. When they got me out there, Duck and Bucket raped me. When they left me alone, Becky helped me and the baby get away. We came back here to tell my brother, but he ain't here. He's still lookin' for that dog. Miss Mary C. and Mr. King came by and they called you."

Officer Boos was impressed with the smoothness of her story. She never quivered one time while she told it. Even after being kidnapped, raped, rescued and seeing her father lying dead in the living room, Theda told the perfect story. He looked at Rebecca.

"Were you here when they killed Mr. Moore?"

Theda answered. "No sir, I didn't see her 'til we got to the house."

Rebecca's heart raced after Theda's protective lie. She shook her head as she looked into Theda's eyes.

"No sir. I didn't know they was comin' here. I just do all the cookin' and cleanin'. I ain't killed nobody."

Officer Boos wanted to say, '*You're killin' me right now*'. *Cover those things up*, but that was only what he wanted to say.

Bucket Coolie was standing behind the wall in the front of the house when he heard the car coming back. The engine was roaring, so he knew it was moving fast. He fired two shots at the car, as it seemed to fly by. It disappeared into the junkyard, but he heard it turning around for another pass. He waited, but heard the engine die down. Bucket looked out the window to see the car moving slowly in front of the house. The car stopped directly in front. Bucket knew he couldn't hit anyone inside so he would save his bullets until he had a better shot.

He was shaking and afraid. "Come on, show ya self. Who the hell are ya, anyway? You ain't that queer hat wearin' son of 'ol Stoddard Moore now, are ya? Like Duck said, we got hats, too." Bucket looked to his right and his blood ran cold instantly when he saw the Green Beret hanging over the electric meter attached to a post. His eyes widened with fear. He looked just like his father right before the car slammed the door into his body.

Bucket was also like Stoddard Moore. When he realized he was not alone, it was too late. Before Bucket could turn to see Fabian standing behind him, Fabian used the huge combat knife to chop off Bucket's right hand. The gun and his hand fell to the dirt. There was a burning sensation in Bucket's handless arm. He staggered to the door of the house. Fabian walked over and took his hat off the pole. He put it back on his head as he walked back to a trembling Bucket Coolie. Jason got out of the car and stood there waiting for Fabian to end it all. Bucket held his bloody stump against his chest as if it was more comfortable that way. Fabian looked at Jason.

"We need to go, Fabian." With Jason's words Fabian drove the combat knife into Bucket's groin. As he pulled the knife out, the serrated top edges of the blade tore chunks of skin and muscle. Bucket screamed in pain as he fell to the ground. Fabian pulled out his pistol and put two bullets in the back of Bucket's head. It was over.

The ambulance was driving away from the Moore house. Mr. King got into his car. Officer Boos watched Mary C. walk toward the car first. The policeman was curious. "Where's Jason, tonight? Ain't that his truck?"

Mary C. stopped at Mr. King's car. She was way too smart to make a mistake. "John, I'm gonna stay with Theda a little longer. I'll see ya later. If ya get sleepy just lock up. I've got my key." She turned to Officer Boos. "That's my brother's truck, but since he's dead, me and Jason use it. Jason's out with Fabian huntin' that crazy dog. I expected 'em back by now. I hope ain't nothin' happened to 'em. I don't like 'em huntin' that wild dog in the dark like this. I'll probably be the one that has to tell Fabian about his daddy when he gets here."

Officer Boos was leery of the beautiful Mary C. "I'm sure you'll be just fine."

Rebecca was still sitting in the bedroom with Theda. Theda was holding her baby. Rebecca was grateful to her new and unlikely friend. "No one's ever spoke up for me like you did tonight. I won't ever forget that."

Theda smiled. She was mature far beyond her fifteen years. "Well, that works both ways. No one has ever saved my life like you did. What you did makes us blood sisters forever. Let's not talk about killin' ourselves no more."

Rebecca Coolie was not sure if she could agree to that, but she would keep her thoughts of suicide to herself.

Jason and Fabian took the bodies of Earnest and Bucket Coolie and threw them into the low marsh area on the other side of the junkyard. There was a good possibility the Coolies would never be found. They threw the guns away, too. Fabian also knew he had to get rid of his car. The damage to his car would bring a police investigation against him. Fabian parked his car in the middle of the junked cars already scattered in the woods around Earnest Coolie's shack. He took off the license plate and threw it into the water of the marsh. Jason and Fabian walked to the end of Mayport Road in the middle of a Northeaster.

Jason sat at a table in Silver's bar and package store. Fabian was talking to his sister Theda on the pay phone. "We need somebody to ride out to Silver's and pick us up." Mary C. was standing in the room with Theda.

"I'm scared to leave the house."

"Don't be. Nobody can hurt us again."

Mary C. stepped to Theda. "Is that Fabian?"

"Yes ma'am". Theda handed the phone to Mary C.

"You two alright?"

"We're just fine. I had to get rid of the car. We're at Silver's. We need a ride."

Three police cars went roaring by Silver's. Jason and Fabian knew they were on their way to the Coolie's junkyard. Mary C. was in Uncle Bobby's truck headed to the end of Mayport Road.

Susan had closed the store early and ridden home with Margie. Miss Margaret was sleeping when they got home so they would not have to explain about the early closing. Sofia had gone to bed at the same time her mother did and Peggy was reading in her room.

Susan took a shower, hoping Margie would join the other family members and retire to her room. Susan wanted to take the station wagon and go see if Jason was waiting for her on the boat. She had no idea he had been in a gun battle with the Coolies and now he was at Silver's bar and package store waiting for a ride.

Mary C. walked into Silver's at the end of Mayport Road. Jason and Fabian were still sitting at the table. Mary C. looked at the bartender, Joey Andrew. "Hey Joey, a double Jack Black and coke." She walked to the table.

Joey Andrew liked looking at Mary C. "You ain't been in here in a long time. The wind blew you this way?"

Mary C. smiled as she sat down at the table. "You might say that. I came to get these two stranded wet puppies. Ain't they both the cutest things?

Joey smiled as he mixed her drink. "I was just thinkin' about how cute they was. I didn't recognize your boy at first. He's grown into quite a man. I saw Fabian a few days ago, so I knew him. They seemed to be havin' a private conversation over there so I ain't bothered 'em none. It's always good to see you, though. When you gonna let me buy ya dinner?"

Mary C. smiled as Joey placed the Jack Black and coke on the table in front of her. "You sure you want to take a grandmother to dinner?"

"If Gramma looks like you, I do."

Mary C. sipped the drink and put it back down on the table. "I'll give your invitation serious consideration. But, I've heard about you and you might be too wild for me."

"Well, what ever you say, but I don't think anybody's too wild for you. Just let me know when you get hungry."

Joey walked back to the bar. Jason and Fabian were waiting for Mary C. to end her sexual sparing match with another male suitor. Mary C. knew they were waiting.

"Other than bein' wet, you boys look pretty good." She looked at Fabian. "You know the police will be goin' out there?"

"Yes ma'am. We heard the sirens a little while ago. I don't think they'll find anything, but they might. We'll have to wait and see. I'd like to get back to Theda and the baby."

Mary C. drank the rest of her drink with one swallow. "What's the tab, Joey?"

"That one's on the house. Hope to see ya later."

Susan got her wish, or at least she thought she did. Margie was not downstairs when Susan finished her shower. Susan was even more excited when she saw that Margie's bedroom door was closed. Susan moved quietly to her room and got dressed. Jason and the shrimp boat were her destinations.

Jason was at the wheel of Uncle Bobby's truck. Mary C. sat in the middle and Fabian was at the passenger's side window. Mary C. understood about the silence that filled the cab of the truck. She was happy to see that Jason and Fabian were safe. That's all she needed to know.

Three police cars were parked in the Coolie junkyard. Six officers were looking for the Coolie family. Officers Boos and Short were standing at the front door. Paul Short had an observation.

"Something bad went on here. And I don't think it was too long ago. Maybe a few hours, maybe less."

Another officer walked out of the shack. "There's nobody here. They left in a hurry. They didn't take anything with 'em, that's for sure. They didn't have much to take, but what they had's still here. Somebody was bleeding on the couch, but there's no sign of a struggle, not in the house anyway. I think the bleeder was just layin' there."

Officer Boos looked out into the yard in front of the house. "Some car's really tore through the mud."

Another officer was standing next to Earnest Coolie's Buick. "There's blood on this door and even more in the mud. Something hit this door really hard and it looks like somebody was standing next to it, when it happened." Officer Boos looked at Officer Short.

"Well, I know it's late, but I think a ride out to Mayport is definitely in order here, don't you?"

Officer Short had a different idea. "Can't this wait until morning? It's almost midnight, David. The Coolie's are either gone or dead. The Moore girl's back safe at home with her baby. The Coolie girl's her new friend. Mary C. and that dog are out there somewhere. Can't we just go home?"

Susan opened the front door of the house and stepped quietly out onto the front porch. She held her set of keys to the family station wagon in her hand. Susan was excited about meeting Jason at the boat. She closed the front door and turn to the walk down the front steps. Her heart jumped in her chest when she saw the family station wagon was gone. Sister Margie was not in her room at all.

Margie pulled up to Mr. Leek's dock in the station wagon. She got out of the car and walked on the narrow wooden dock that ran along the outside of the fish house. The misty rain had stirred up again. She moved slowly on the wet slippery wood of the dock. When she reached the boat, Margie jumped down from the dock and onto the deck. The wheelhouse of the *Mary C.* was locked. Margie knocked on the wheelhouse door, but Jason was not there.

Uncle Bobby's truck rolled into the front yard at Fabian's house. The ride back to Mayport was fast and quiet. Mary C. leaned over and kissed Fabian on his cheek.

"Go take care of your sister and your nephew. They need you."

Fabian looked at Jason. "Thank's for everything, Jason." Jason nodded. Fabian got out of the truck and walked to his house. Jason pushed the gas pedal and Uncle Bobby's truck headed to Mr. King's haunted house.

Margie opened the driver's side door of the family station wagon. She was disappointed Jason was not on the boat. She started the engine and turned on the headlights. Her heart jumped when the lights revealed her sister Susan standing in front of the car. Susan walked to the passenger's side and got into the car. Susan was not very happy with her older sister.

"I knew you were over here. You're so greedy. You're greedy with the car, greedy with Jason, greedy with everything."

Margie did not care what Susan said or thought. "And what exactly are you doing here?"

"I came to see Jason. He asked me to meet him. But, I guess now that big sister's been here he won't need me."

"He's not there, Susan. I'm really sorry I messed up your little rendezvous. If I had known I would have brought you with me."

"Oh sure, both of us."

Margie turned the car engine off. "Why not. We both like him. And I know he'd love it."

Susan was shocked at her sister's suggestion. "Are you serious? What makes you think he'd do that? You wouldn't do that. You're just saying that to see my reactions."

"Trust me, he'd love it. I've been thinking about it for a while now, but I didn't know if I should ask you. I keep having dreams about people watching me. I think I'd like you to watch me and then I'd watch you. It would be pretty wild. It would be better than strangers watching us."

Uncle Bobby's truck stopped in front of John King's haunted house. Mary C. had some after midnight instructions for Jason.

"I'll get Billy to bed. You go check on the boat. If Beanie's still around town and drinkin' no tellin' what he'll do. If ya think you should stay on the boat, I'll see ya in the mornin'. You had a hell-of-a day, didn't ya, son?" Jason nodded and waited for Mary C. to get into the house with Billy before he drove off.

Fabian, Theda and Rebecca were sitting in the front room of the house. The paramedics in the ambulance had cleaned up the pool of blood in the doorway. Theda was talking.

"Fabian, she has no place to go. I told her she can stay here as long as she wants. She saved me and my baby. She's his Aunt Becky and she's welcome here. It's my house, too"

Rebecca looked at Theda. "Thank you for what you're trying to do, but this ain't such a good idea." She looked at Fabian. "I don't blame you at all. How can you trust me after my family did this awful thing to you? I would feel the same if I was in your place. What if I just sleep in the truck until daylight? I really don't know where to go tonight, but maybe by mornin' I'll know. If my Pa catches me, I'm dead anyway, or even worse. There is a worse than dead, ya know?"

Fabian knew she did not have to worry about any of her family looking for her. Rebecca had a question for him. "You and Jason went after my Pa, didn't ya?"

"They were gone." Fabian stood up. "You can stay." He walked out onto the front porch and looked out into the darkness. The clouds of the Northeaster covered the moon. He saw something moving across the front yard. It was Abaddon, the devil dog. He was on the move. Fabian took a deep breath and spoke out loud. "You're next dog, you're next."

Margie was backing the family station wagon away from Mr. Leek's fish house when a set of headlights flashed in her rearview mirror. She knew it was Uncle Bobby's truck. Her heart raced in her lustful chest. She looked at Susan. "Time to make a decision."

Fabian walked back into the house. Theda was going into her father's bedroom with the baby. "I'll sleep in daddy's room, so Rebecca can stay in mine. Thank you, Fabian. I love you. It's just us three, now."

He hugged his little sister. "You do mean me, you and little Sam, don't ya?"

"Of course."

Jason could not believe what was happening. Margie asked him to take her and Susan to the boat. She said they had a surprise for him. Susan walked with them, but did not say a word. When Jason unlocked the door to the wheelhouse Margie led the way with him, then Susan following her. Margie went to the small bunk and turned back to Jason. Her suggestion sent chills down Jason's back.

"I want Susan to watch us and then I want to watch you and her." Margie started undressing. She was naked before her words had time to settle in Jason's head. Susan's heart was racing as she stood there with her naked sister. Margie was crazy.

"Susan, you've seen me naked before. I've seen you. We've both seen Jason and he's seen us. This is really the perfect situation for all three of us. Now, get undressed so Jason will, too."

Jason looked at Susan. She smiled and took off her clothes. Jason was standing on the boat with two naked sisters. He took off his clothes.

Abaddon, the devil dog, walked around the outside of John King's haunted house. He was looking for an opening to get under the house so he could get out of the wind and rain. Mr. King had closed all the holes with plywood. The frustrated dog moved to the corner of the house where the baby was found. He sniffed the ground and could still smell the infant.

Margie changed her mind and let Susan go first. Susan was kneeling down in the bunk with Jason behind her. Margie moaned with pleasure each time Susan moaned. Jason paid no attention to Margie. His full concentration was on pleasing Susan. Margie had told Jason not to stay inside Susan when he exploded. She also asked him to let her hold "it" when he pulled out. Margie did yell, "Harder!" one time during Jason's sexual attack on her sister.

The haunted house was quiet. Mr. King was in a deep sleep. Mary C. was in her bed, but still awake, thinking about building a Jim Walter Home out near Miss Carolyn. Miss Margaret's house was quiet, also. She had no idea two of her daughters were having sexual relations with the man who ran away with her beloved, Sofia.

When Jason pulled out of Susan, Margie grabbed him and watched his explosion. Susan looked, too. She had never done such a thing. She liked it.

The two wild sisters took turns orally stimulating Jason until he recovered. It was Margie's suggestion. When he was ready she climbed into the bunk and took her favorite and usual position. Jason moved in behind her. She did not have to give him any instructions. Susan was the spectator. She liked that, too.

CHAPTER TEN

The sun was rising out of the Atlantic Ocean once again. The story of the baby, the buzzards and the dog would be told in the future as one of the better Mayport stories. The brutal death of Stoddard Moore would be another tragedy to add to the others. The story of the revenge killing of the three Coolie men would never be told, because only Jason and Fabian knew the truth and they would never mention it again. The wind and misty rain from the Northeaster had lifted and there would be patches of blue in the sky throughout the day.

Fabian was already out of his bed. He would take care of his father's funeral arrangements and then take care of the devil dog. He was hoping one of the other dog hunters would find and kill the dog before he had to start hunting. He walked out of his room and was not thinking about their houseguest, Rebecca Coolie, when he opened the door to the bathroom. Fabian's eyes fell upon the most incredible sight he had ever seen, that morning or any other morning. Rebecca "Milkduds" Coolie was standing there completely naked. She was preparing to step into a bathtub full of hot water. Her back was to Fabian at first. Rebecca's back was flawless, with no marks of any kind. Her butt cheeks were round and hard with no dimples or rippled skin. He could not look away.

Rebecca turned and gave him a full frontal view of her perfect body. Fabian's throat went dry when she did not cover herself or flinch in any way. His blood rushed to fill his manhood. Her breasts were like two footballs with nipples coming out of her chest. They were huge, but stood firm, pointing in his direction. Rebecca's waist was small with rounded hips below and full hard thighs. She was big boned, but solid, with no fat pockets to be seen. If Fabian had scanned all the way down to her feet he would have seen she had perfect feet, too. His eyes just did not get that far down.

Rebecca had no embarrassment or shame in her eyes. She liked the way Fabian was looking at her and he liked the way she was allowing him to do so. There was an unspoken mutual agreement as they both stood there. It was a first for them both. Fabian's head moved up as he took in her beauty a second time. His eyes reached her eyes. Her face matched her body. She was a beautiful woman. Fabian came out of his Milkdud trance when Rebecca smiled. It was a stupid thing to say after he had stood there so long, but it was all he had.

"Oh, I'm sorry. I didn't think anyone was in here."

Rebecca smiled again and just stood there. "I didn't think to lock the door. It was my fault. I always get up early. I ain't took no real bathtub bath in years. We only had a cold shower at home. I'm lookin' forward to soakin' in this hot water."

It was a strange stand off. Fabian did not want to turn away and Rebecca did not want him to. She was enjoying the way he followed her ever curve with his eyes. It was the first time a man other than her father and brothers had looked at her naked. Fabian found some more words.

"After your bath we need to talk."

Rebecca finally stepped into the bathtub and eased her body down into the hot water. "You can sit and talk to me now, if me takin' a bath don't bother ya."

Rebecca did not have to make the invitation again. Fabian sat on the closed toilet seat while Rebecca lathered the soap on her shoulders. She even looked better with wet hair. Fabian had a question. "Why you let me sit and watch you like this?"

"I like the way you look at me. I want you to see me. I want you to look all you want. There's something behind your eyes. It comes out when you look at me. Your eyes become more than eyes. They fill up with your soul. If it bothers you, I won't do it again. I was just hopin' you'd like it."

"So I'll let you stay?"

Rebecca smiled. "You can look at me when ever you want, if you let me stay or not. But, you were gonna let me stay before you saw me like this. Now, you have even more reasons to let me stay. You were doing it out of the goodness of your heart and now you have two good reasons."

Fabian was speechless, but what Rebecca said next was every man's fantasy. "I'll take care of this house for you. I'll cook, clean and be sure Theda and the baby are cared for. My body will be here for your pleasure whenever you want me. I just want to stay here with you and Theda. I'll make no demands on you if you have other women. I'm supposed to be here for you. I knew, when you came back last night, you had already killed my family. You didn't know it, but you saved me from a life no woman should have to suffer through. I'll always be yours, whether you let me stay or not."

Fabian did not know what to say. It was like a dream, but for some reason he knew it was real. He actually felt sad that she would be so desperate. "You can stay. Let's take it one day at a time."

Fabian found the courage to leave the temptress in her first bathtub bath in years. He could not help but think about Rebecca's proposal and proposition, as well as her unbelievable body. He wanted to wait for her to go back to the bedroom so he could take her up on her offer of uninhibited pleasure.

Fabian heard the bathroom door open and he heard her walking to the bedroom. He looked down the hall and could see that his houseguest did not close the bedroom door. Fabian knew the open door was another open invitation. He was helpless. He walked to the bedroom door and looked in.

Rebecca was standing there drying her hair with the single towel she wrapped around her body to walk down the hall. She was completely naked as she looked toward the door. Again, she did not flinch when she saw Fabian staring at her. Fabian had his thoughts together.

"I wanted to look at you, again. If that's alright?"

Rebecca tossed the towel onto a chair. "Of course it is. I meant everything I said to you. Would you rather do more, right now, then just look at me?"

Fabian was captivated by the daughter of the man who killed his father. He was mesmerized by the daughter of the man he killed only hours before. Fabian stepped into the small bedroom and closed the door. It was the beginning of the most outrageous alliance one could conceive of. It was Mayport and it was insane.

Jason woke up with a naked sister on each side of him. They were all jammed into the small bunk. He could not believe they had spent the entire night with him. Margie had orchestrated the sexual threesome. Jason knew they had to get up and go home or to the store. When he woke them Susan jumped out of the bunk.

"Oh God! Margie, get up! We've got to go! Oh God!"

Margie looked up with droopy eyes at her panic stricken sister. "Calm down."

Susan was unable to do so. "Calm down! How can you say that? We've got the car. Don't you think Mother will see the car's gone?"

Jason put on his pants and walked into the wheelhouse. His heart jumped when the ferry horn blew, disturbing the quiet morning air. He knew the big carrier was crossing from Mayport to the Fort George side of the river. It also told him it was six thirty in the morning. Susan was getting dressed. Margie sat up in the bunk.

"I'm supposed to open the store." She got out of the bed and began dressing, too. "You can drive me to the store and then go on home. Tell Mother we both woke up early and you drove me over so y'all could have the car. It's no big deal, unless you make it one."

Mathias walked out of the fish house and onto the dock as the sexual tag team was climbing up off the boat and onto the dock. Jason assisted each morning beauty until they were standing on the dock. Jason was relieved they were leaving. Margie and Susan hurried through the fish house and out to the family station wagon. Jason looked up at Mathias. Mr. Leek's trusted dockworker smiled at Jason and moved his thick eyebrows up and down. Jason returned the smile and went back into the wheelhouse. The family station wagon rolled away with Susan at the wheel. Margie had the perfect plan. She always did.

Fabian had never experienced the sexual prowess of a woman like Rebecca Coolie. At eighteen, she knew everything there was to know about pleasing a man. She was physically, mentally and sexually superior. The fact that her body was perfect only added to her appeal. She allowed Fabian to do what ever he wanted, but she actually did more to him than he did to her. Fabian needed to remember about taking care of his father's funeral.

Mr. John King sat on his front porch drinking his first morning cup of coffee. He was curious when he saw the family station wagon coming toward the store from the wrong direction. He watched the car stop in front of the store and Margie jumped out. The car pulled away as Margie unlocked the door and opened the store. Mr. King saw movement to his left. He looked down to see Abaddon at the foot of the steps. The ugly dog was still on guard duty. Mr. King knew he was in grave danger with the unpredictable canine so close. The dog did not growl or show his teeth, but Mr. King was still scared. A voice took Mr. King's attention away from the dog. It was Mary C. at the door.

"Mornin', John. At least that storm's gone."

"Get the shotgun, Mary C." She looked past Mr. King to see Abaddon standing there. She turned slowly and reached behind the door. Mary C. should have waited to pull down the pump handle. When Abaddon heard the sound of the shotgun shell dropping into the chamber the dog bolted away from his guard post. The devil dog had heard that deadly sound before.

Mary C. jumped into her fire engine red Corvette, shotgun and all. She looked back at Mr. King. "Check on Billy for me, please."

Mr. King had no choice as the red Corvette took off. Mary C. would be the first one to hunt the dog that day. She forgot about making French toast for Jason and Fabian. The other dog hunters were all at their homes. They were frustrated with not being able to locate and corner the elusive hound from hell. The Northeaster had hampered the search, but they knew the clear weather would assist them when they took up the hunt again.

Fabian was lying on the bed looking up at Rebecca's naked body. She was sitting across him with her knees at his sides. She had drained him of all his body fluids and his sexual energy. "Do you want me to do more or should I get dressed before Theda gets up?"

Fabian actually whispered his answer. He was a sexually fatigued man. "Go ahead and get dressed. I really have a lot to get done today."

Rebecca moved off the bed and began dressing. "Theda gave me these clothes. I'm sure they're going to be a little tight, but I'll do the best I can with 'em."

Fabian smiled. "You and Theda can go shopping later today when I get back. You need some clothes of your own."

Miss Margaret was in the kitchen preparing breakfast. Sofia walked into the room. "Bacon always smells so good. Good morning, Mother."

"Good morning, Sofia." They both turned to see Susan walk into the kitchen. Susan was relieved with her mother's uninformed comment. "I didn't know you were up. I thought you were still sleeping. You're not going to wear that same blouse you had on yesterday, are you?"

Susan was ready. "No ma'am. I just threw it on to take Margie to the store. We were both up early and she asked me to take her."

Miss Margaret was entirely too trusting. "You two must have still been charged up from all the excitement yesterday. I had a pretty restless night myself, but I finally fell asleep sometime in the early morning. I'm glad to see Margie's becoming more responsible in her old age."

Sofia looked at Susan. She knew the story was weak. Susan changed the subject. "I'm going to take a shower then I'd love some of that bacon with toast."

Fabian was dressed and getting ready to go and talk to the police about where they took his father's body. He was sorry in his heart he did not go with his father, but his need to find and punish the Coolies overshadowed any other of his responsibilities at the time. He wanted to stay clear of the question asking police, but he thought it would be smart to make him self available. It would make them think he had nothing to hide.

Fabian saw Theda walking from her father's bedroom to the bathroom. Rebecca walked into the kitchen wearing a tight t-shirt over her huge braless breasts. She looked as good with the shirt on as she did with it off, maybe even better by the way her bare breasts and nipples pushed the shirt outward. She wore one of Theda's wrap around skirts that adjusted to any set of hips. It was short, showing off her legs. Rebecca's bare feet only added to the enticing sexual vision she was purposely creating. Fabian had to smile when she walked into the kitchen.

"I made us some coffee." He pointed to the stove.

Rebecca smiled. No one had ever made her coffee before. "I should be making your breakfast."

Theda joined them in the kitchen. "Let me make breakfast for you two. I'd like to serve my two heroes. If Jason was here I'd have all three of my heroes."

Mr. Leek stood with Jason on the stern of the *Mary C.* Jason had told him about his plan to shrimp with Fabian. Mr. Leek had a question. "You think you two know enough to make a livin' on this boat? Ya know Fabian's been gone a long time. He was just a boy when he went shrimping with Stoddard."

"It won't hurt us to try. The boat's just sitting here, now. She should be out there and not sitting at the dock. She's a workin' boat."

"You sound like your Uncle Bobby. He loved this boat."

Jason smiled. He liked thinking about Uncle Bobby. "That's why I have to get her back out there."

Al Leek nodded and smiled. "That's a good reason, son. I hope it works out for y'all. You know Fabian's got a lot on his mind right now with Theda, the baby and his daddy's funeral. And don't forget that dog runnin' all over. He probably won't be able to join you 'til the funeral's over."

Jason had not thought about all the weight on Fabian's shoulders. He wanted to wait for his good friend, but he also wanted to start shrimping again as soon as possible.

Two Moores and one Coolie sat at the kitchen table. Theda had prepared a great breakfast. Rebecca looked at Fabian with an *I'm yours* look in her eyes. She knew she would do anything to stay with Theda and Fabian. Fabian was the talker at the moment.

"I've gotta make daddy's funeral arrangements and meet with the police." Rebecca's heart raced behind her huge breasts as Fabian continued. "If it don't take all day, I'll be back to hunt down that dog." He reached in his pant's pocket and pulled out a roll of money. He gave Theda half the roll. Her eyes lit up. "Y'all two go shoppin' today and get some new clothes." He looked at Theda. "You'll need a black dress for the funeral." He looked at Rebecca. "You drive, don't ya?" Rebecca nodded her head. "Y'all can take daddy's car."

Mary C. drove out to her property, hoping to see the dog near her burned house. She rode past Mr. Greenlaw's fighting rooster cages, but Abaddon was not there. The eight o'clock sun was beginning to dry up the moisture left by the Northeaster. Mary C. was riding past the Croom house when she saw Joe Croom walking to her old Ford Falcon. She had to stop. Joe was getting into the car when Mary C. stopped her Corvette next to him. "Mornin' Joe. How's Betsy runnin'?"

Joe was excited to see her and his face revealed his high level of excitement. "Hey, Miss Mary C. She's doin' great. No problems at all. I just gave her an oil change."

"You can do that kinda stuff?"

Joe smiled. "Daddy had me sittin' under the hood of a car watchin' him before I could hardly walk. He's always said a man that can fix his own car will save a lot of money."

"You're daddy's right, Joe. Maybe he ain't such a rock head after all."

"No ma'am, he's a rock head like you said." Mary C. had to laugh at the young man's sense of humor. She liked Joe Croom a lot. Mary C. knew a potential real man when she saw one. She was the expert on real men.

"You ain't seen that big dog, have ya?"

"No ma'am. I didn't even see him yesterday. I don't think I've ever seen him. I've heard talk, but I ain't seem him."

"If you do, be careful. He ain't no regular dog. If you get the chance to put him down, do it. Don't think about it, just do it. Where ya headed so early?"

"Just for a ride. I was gonna stop at the store and see what sister's workin'."

Mary C. was curious. "Is there a certain one you want to be workin'?"

"No ma'am. It don't make no difference to me. I like 'em all. I guess if I had to pick one, I'd pick Sofia." Joe Croom had his own style.

Mary C. nodded. "She is the prettiest, but they're all pretty girls."

The police patrol car rolled up to Mr. King's house. Officers Boos and Short were always on official business. Mr. King sat in one of his porch chairs holding Billy in his arms. Officer Boos did not get out of the car. He rolled down the driver's side window

"Mornin' Mr. King. They got you babysittin'?"

"I'm a natural. What can I do for you gentlemen this mornin'?"

"Jason wouldn't be around, would he?"

"He stayed on the boat last night. Yesterday was mixed with sadness and jubilation at the same time. Y'all find the Coolies?"

"No sir. They were long gone. Either they ran away or somebody made sure they were gone. Somethin' went on out at the junkyard, but we can't seem to put it together. We were hopin' Jason and Fabian would be able to shed some light on the whole thing."

Mr. King looked up as a car came toward the house. "You can talk to Fabian right now. Fabian drove his car up behind the police car and got out.

"Mornin' Mr. King."

"Mornin' Fabian. You're just the man we need."

Fabian looked at the police car. "I need to see them, too."

The two officers got out of the patrol car and met Fabian at Mr. King's steps. Mr. King was glad they had all stopped there. He would have the first hand information if the questioning took place on his front porch and it looked like that was exactly what was going to happen. Fabian was first.

"I'm glad I saw y'all. I was headed to the station. Is my daddy still there or did y'all move him to the funeral home?"

Officer Boos had his own questions, but he would answer Fabian's first. "No, he's still in the coroner's lab. They'll move him before noon. You doin' all right?"

"Yes sir, I'm fine." Fabian was smart. He knew what was coming. He decided to beat them to the punch. "Please tell me you arrested the Coolies."

"I wish I could. We can't find them. They left before we could get out there. We were hopin' you might be able to help us."

"Hell, I wish I could. If I found 'em, you'd be puttin' me in jail."

"Well, let's hope you don't find 'em, then."

It was time for Officer Short to take over. "When we were out at your house last night they said you were still huntin' for that dog. You find him?"

"That ain't just a dog, mister. It's a devil dog. Jason told me about how that evil creature came about."

"You must be pretty upset with Mary C. for keepin' that crazy dog."

"I'm never gonna be upset with Miss Mary C. She's like a second mama to me. You can't ever be mad at your mama." Fabian looked past the officers and saw Uncle Bobby's truck rolling up. "There's my brother, now."

Officer Short turned to see the truck stop next to the patrol car. "Good. We need to talk to him, too."

Jason joined the King house morning porch group. "Mornin' Mr. King, Fabian."

They both said good morning to Jason. Jason did not greet the police officers, but they did not care. Officer Boos was the talker, now. "Jason, we'd like to ask you a few questions."

Jason looked at Fabian. "Go ahead."

"What did you do last night after you heard Mr. Moore was killed?"

"Me and Fabian didn't hear about it 'til late. We was huntin' that dog, but it got too dark. The storm forced us in. Huntin' a dog like that in the dark gave him the upper hand."

Both officers knew something was strange. They had never heard Jason say so many words at one time since they started patrolling the area. It was surely well thought out and rehearsed. Fabian wanted to join in the conversation.

"Look. If I could have killed those three last night, I would have, but I didn't. If I get the chance, I will. I'm goin' to go make sure my father has a proper burial. If you have any more questions you'll have to arrest me." He looked at Jason. "Talk to me before I go." Jason walked with Fabian to his car. The police officers nodded to Mr. King, got into the patrol car and left. Fabian had to tell Jason about Rebecca "Milkduds" Coolie.

Joe Croom drove up to Miss Margaret's store in his blue Ford Falcon. Margie turned to the door when she heard the bell. Within the last four days she had sexual relations with Jason, Fabian and

Joe. She had also used the carousel for another tumble with Jason
and the night at the tree with at least fifty men. Joe was surprised to
see her. She gave the greeting.

"Good morning. May I help you with something?" Miss
Margaret would have been very proud of her eldest.

"I just stop by to see if you were here. You doin' okay?"

"I'm fine. Did you really come by to see me?" She stepped to
him and kissed him. "Or are you looking for Sofia?"

"I'm lookin' for you, Margie. It ain't that easy to get you out of
my head. I've tried, but it ain't workin'."

Margie liked him saying that to her. It gave her the control she
loved. "You want to go in the back? We can't take off our clothes.
We'll have to hurry."

Joe did not care if he took his clothes off or not. He was smart.
"You mean it?"

She took his hand. "Just do it hard like you did before."

Fabian was still telling Jason about the sexual breakfast he had
with his houseguest. He was so wrapped up in the details and
wasn't thinking about tending to his father. Jason felt obligated to
his friend so he shared his sister tag team match he took part in on
the small bunk on the shrimp boat. Fabian was the first person
Jason had ever shared such information with. He was glad to have a
friend he could talk to and trust.

Susan was in her bedroom drying her hair from her morning
shower. Sofia walked into the room. "What's going on with you
and Margie? She's up to something with getting you up early to
take her to the store."

"She might be up to something, but all I did was take her to the
store. I couldn't sleep. She asked me to take her. I did."

Margie was standing with her hands on the table in the back of
the store. Her pants were at her ankles with one foot free. It would
allow her to spread her legs, but also make it quick and easy for her
to pull up her pants if she had to hurry back to the front of the store.
Joe was behind her. It was much more comfortable than the night
under the oak tree. He already knew what Margie wanted, but he
still listened to her giving her patented instructions.

"We have to hurry. I like it when it's fast and hard. Don't stay
in me. I want to hold it when you pull out."

Mr. King had gone back into his house when the police left. Fabian and Jason were still talking about their great sexual fortune. Jason looked toward the store and saw his mother's Falcon. He knew it now belonged to Joe Croom. Fabian saw it, too.

"That's your mama's old car over there."

"Yeah, she gave it to Joe Croom when she got her new one. He needed a car and she gave it to him."

"That's your mama. She's always done crazy unexpected stuff. She wouldn't be Mary C. if she didn't do things like that." Fabian smiled and had another thought. "I wonder what sister's takin' care of the store? That Margie's wild. Between her and Rebecca, I've got my hands full. I'm not complainin', mind ya, but I'm not real sure I can handle both of 'em. I might need you to take some of the pressure off me." Fabian smiled and gave Jason a little push. "I'm gonna go see who's at the store."

Jason nodded. "I'm gonna check on Billy."

Fabian looked up at Mr. King's front door. "You have a son and y'all are livin' at the haunted house. How in world did that happen?" Fabian knew Jason would not answer his question. He turned away as Jason went into the house to take care of Billy.

Mary C. stopped her Corvette in front of Miss Margaret's house and blew the horn. Miss Margaret stepped out onto her front porch. Mary C. yelled from the car. "Y'all ain't seen that crazy dog, have ya?"

Miss Margaret shook her head. "Not since yesterday. I thought all those men would have blown poor Abaddon to pieces by now. I can't believe he's been able to avoid all those determined hunters."

Mary C. had the answer. "They think they're huntin' a dumb dog. He's much more than a dog."

Miss Margaret did not like Mary C.'s crazy talk, but she knew when to be quiet. Mary C. had more. "Just be careful. He might feel safe here and come back. Don't be fooled if he comes around and seems tame. He's not at all." Mary C. drove away, leaving Miss Margaret on the porch with the scary thoughts.

The bell on the door sounded causing Margie's heart to jump. Fabian Moore walked into the store. Margie pushed Joe away as he exploded on the floor. She pulled up her pants.

"Stay back here. Clean that up. Go out the back." Margie left Joe to clean up his mess.

Margie walked to the front of the store. Fabian was at the cold drink box pulling out a bottle of Yoo-Hoo chocolate drink. He turned to Margie. "I was hoping you were here."

Margie smiled. "I'm so sorry about your father. That was horrible for you and your sister. It was so wonderful when they found the baby, but then that awful thing happen to your father. You doing okay?"

"I'm fine, Margie. You okay? You look a little flushed."

"I'm surprised to see you. I didn't think I'd see you this soon. I know you've got a lot on your mind. I didn't want to interfere."

Fabian grabbed Margie and kissed her. Margie returned the passionate kiss. Joe Croom went out the back door of the store and hurried to the Falcon parked in front. He started the car and drove away as Margie pulled Fabian to the back room. The floor was wet, but Joe Croom was gone. Margie pulled down her pants and took her position at the table. Fabian was smart, too.

"I know the drill and I know we have to hurry. Don't worry, just enjoy yourself." Fabian would pump Margie so hard she would actually scream one time during the encounter. Within the last twenty-four hours Margie had been sexually active with Fabian under the oak tree, Jason on the boat with her sister watching, Joe Croom in the back of the store and now with Fabian again. She had also used the carousel for two sexual dreams. Margie was well on her way toward insane nymphomaniac status.

Joe Croom was driving past the sand hill with Margie's bare butt fresh on his mind. He had a memory flashback as he looked up at the huge oak tree. His pleasurable thoughts were short lived when he saw his twin brothers, Chuck and Buck, running down the sand hill with looks of horror and fear on their faces. It only took seconds for Joe to see why his little brothers were running for their lives. The killer devil dog was chasing them.

Abaddon was about twenty yards behind the two scared boys. They were side-by-side as the dog was quickly closing in on them. Joe could only yell.

"Run! Keep runnin'! Don't stop!" Joe reached over and opened the passenger door of the Falcon, hoping the boys would make it to the car before the dog took one of them down. Joe jumped out of the car and left the driver side door open, too. He started running toward his brothers. "Get in the car!"

Chuck fell a step behind Buck. It was just enough for Abaddon to catch up with Chuck and gave Buck the time to get to the car. Buck passed Joe as Joe tried to get to the fallen Chuck. Abaddon was tearing at Chuck's pant's leg as the boy screamed in pain and terror. When Joe reached his brother he kicked the wild dog, causing the hound to release his death grip on Chuck's pants. Abaddon turned his evil intentions to Joe Croom as Chuck got to his feet and ran to the car. Without a weapon Joe Croom did not have a prayer against the killer instinct of the powerful canine. The twins sat in the blue Ford Falcon and could do nothing as they watched Abaddon tearing at their brother. They screamed and cried and beat on the dashboard. They hid their eyes so they could not see. They held their hands over their ears to block out the sound of the growling dog and Joe's painful screams.

The dog's sharp teeth and powerful jaws were doing severe damage to Joe's arms and legs. Joe did all he could to keep the

dog's teeth away from his throat. He also fought to stay on his feet.
Joe knew if the dog got him down in the sand he would die with his
little brothers watching. Joe was becoming fatigued from the fight
and the wounds. The dog seemed to be getting stronger. Joe tried to
use what strength he had left to get back to the car, but he was too
far away. Joe Croom saw that his brothers were safe in the car as
Abaddon jumped on his back, knocking him down in the sand.

Joe felt the dog's sharp teeth sink into the back of his neck. He
had no more fight left in his young strong body. Joe heard his
brothers scream. There was a deafening sound that seemed to close
his eardrums. Joe felt burning pain on his left side, butt cheek and
leg. He heard the dog give a painful yelp and the weight of the dog
was no longer on Joe's back. He rolled over onto his back and
watched Abaddon walking away slowly. There was movement in
Joe's peripheral vision. Chuck and Buck knelt down next to their
bleeding and torn brother. Joe was still protecting his brothers. He
whispered. "Run! Get back in the car!" The two boys looked up as
Mary C. stood above them holding her favorite shotgun.

Mary C.'s heart raced in her chest, as she looked at the damage
her dog had done to her new young friend. "You two boys get your
brother to my car. I think some of the pellets hit him when I shot the
dog." She dropped to one knee and got her face close to Joe's face.
"I'll get you to a hospital. I gotta finish off the dog first."

Mary C. stood up while Chuck and Buck used all their double
strength to try and pick up Joe and carry him to the Corvette. They
had to drag him through the soft sand.

Mary C. walked to the fatally wounded devil dog. The bleeding
dog stood there as she pulled the pump handle and loaded another
shell. Abaddon looked up at Mary C. as she raised the gun to her
shoulder and aimed it at his oversized head.

"I'm glad I'm the one who gets to kill you, but I hope me and
you ain't killed that wonderful young man over there." Mary C.
pulled the trigger, scattering Abaddon's huge head all over the white
sand of the sand hill.

Margie and Fabian had completed their back of the store sexual
encounter. They were standing at the front counter when the red
Corvette actually slid up to the front of the store. Mary C. held the
horn down. She had sent the twins home to tell their mother and

father about the dog attacking Joe and that she was taking him to the Beaches Hospital. Margie opened the screen door of the store. Mary C. yelled to her. "Joe's hurt. I need somethin' to stop the bleedin' 'til I can get him to the hospital. He won't make it if he keeps bleedin' like this."

Margie's stomach went sour when she saw the critical condition of her friend and one of her new lovers. Fabian stepped to the car as Margie ran back into the store. His throat went dry when he saw the damage the brave young man had endured. Mary C. was the talker.

"The dog got him. I was too late to help him."

Fabian's eyes lit up. "Where's the dog?"

"He's dead. I was supposed to be the one to put him down, but it wasn't soon enough. It wasn't 'spose to be like this." Fabian understood. He said the same thing when the dog killed Eli.

Margie ran out of the store with gauze; roll bandages and Kotex feminine napkins. She moved to the passenger's side to render first aid to her friend. "If you put these against the cuts and wrap these around them it will stop the bleeding." She placed one of the wide Kotex napkins and pressed it against one of the deeper bleeding gashes on Joe's right arm. Then she wrapped the bandages around his arm to keep the Kotex tight against the wound. She covered four serious areas in the same way as Mary C. and Fabian watched her work. The worst of the bites was the one on the back of his neck. When she was finished she looked at Mary C.

"I hope that does it."

Mary C. smiled. "You're a woman of action, Margie and I love you."

Mary C. pushed down the gas pedal with her foot. Mr. King was stepping out onto his front porch as the red rocket went flying by his house. He knew something was terribly wrong. He turned to see Fabian walking back from the store. Fabian would tell Mr. King what he knew.

A police car was rounding the curve at the Little Jetties headed toward Mayport when the red Corvette passed it going in the opposite direction. Officer Boos was at the wheel. He looked at his partner Paul Short, when the red car flew passed them at a high rate of speed. He turned on his siren and turned the car around so he could catch the speeding Corvette. The police car did not catch up to Mary C. until she had driven all the way to the end of Mayport Road. David Boos pulled the patrol car up next to the Corvette while Mary C. stopped the car before she turned onto Atlantic Boulevard. Mary C. looked at Officer Short on the passenger's side. She pointed to Joe Croom in the seat next to her.

"He's hurt bad, I'm takin' him to the hospital!"

Paul Short's eyes lit up when he saw the blood on young Joe Croom. "We'll lead you in."

The police car pulled out onto Atlantic Boulevard with red lights flashing and the red Corvette following behind. The ride to the Beaches Hospital was fast, but it still took twenty minutes. Young Joe Croom had lost a great deal of blood in the sand beneath the oak tree and during the long ride. He was unconscious when they reached the emergency entrance. Mary C. did not like the expressions on the faces of the emergency staff when they took Joe's limp body out of the Corvette. The two officers and Mary C. followed the emergency medical team into the hospital.

Sofia was on her way to the store to take over for Margie. She was driving the green family station wagon and still had about fifteen minutes before she was supposed to begin her shift. Sofia passed the store and drove toward Joe Croom's house. She was hoping to see her new, intimate friend. She drove up to the house and saw two ladies standing in the yard. The twins, Chuck and Buck, were swinging on an old car tire swing hanging from a pecan tree next to the house. The brother they called Pee Wee was sitting on the porch crying. She stopped the station wagon and stepped out of the car.

"I was wondering if Joe was home." One of the ladies walked to the car. Sofia could see the solemn look on the woman's face.

"You're one of Miss Margaret's girls ain't ya?"

"Yes ma'am. I'm Sofia."

"I thought that was you. My, my, I heard you had become a pretty woman now, but I didn't think you was this pretty. Me and your mama go way back. You had the best baby shower I ever went to. I'm Joe's Aunt Wilda."

Sofia looked at Pee Wee. "Is Pee Wee all right? He's such a nice boy. I'm sorry he's sad."

Aunt Wilda looked back at Pee Wee and then at Sofia. "They took Joe to the hospital. He's hurt bad. That wild dog attacked him and the twins at the sand hill. Joe saved the twins from the dog, but he couldn't get away. I don't know all the details. His mama and daddy's gone to the hospital. We're waitin' to hear."

Sofia's mind went blank when Aunt Wilda said, "He's hurt bad." She did not hear the rest of the statement. Aunt Wilda could see the shock in Sofia's beautiful face. "You all right, sweetie?" Sofia nodded her head and got back into the car. She went to relieve Margie.

Mary C. was sitting in the emergency waiting room when Big Joe Croom and his wife Stella walked in. Stella saw Mary C. and walked to her.

"Where's my son?"

Mary C. looked up, but stayed seated. "They took him in there." She pointed to a set of swinging double doors. "I didn't go back there. You'll have to ask 'em." Stella walked past Mary C. and went through the double doors. Mary C. looked at Big Joe.

"The dog was killin' him. I shot the dog, but I'm sure some of the pellets hit Joe, too. I was too far away when the dog first got to him. If I waited to get closer before I shot, the dog would have killed him before I got there." Big Joe nodded and went to find his wife.

Sofia walked into the store. Margie met her at the door and had all the gruesome details about Abaddon mauling Joe Croom. Margie had no idea Sofia had been sexually active with the handsome young man. Sofia had no idea Margie had been sexually active with Joe Croom only minutes before the dog attacked him. Sofia listened to Margie as she told of how Mary C. brought Joe to the store so Margie could help stop his wounds from bleeding.

Mr. King and Jason walked into the hospital waiting room. Jason was carrying Billy in his arms. "Mama, you all right. You ain't hurt are ya?"

"My heart's hurtin'."

Neither Jason, nor Mr. King had ever heard Mary C. make such a statement. To have her say her cold, hard heart could feel pain was far out of character. They both sat down and remained quiet. If there were to be a conversation, Mary C. would be the one who initiated it. They were only silent for a few seconds.

"When I shot the dog the first time I hit Joe on his side. I don't know what I'll do if that kills him."

Mr. King responded. "That might be what saves him. Let's think the best."

Mary C. shook her head. "I ain't had much practice at thinkin' that way."

"I know you and Jason ain't had a good hand dealt your way in a long time, if ever, but the dog didn't hurt the baby, you probably saved Joe and ya got plenty of money. It just might be time to start lookin' for the best."

Mary C. smiled at Mr. King and then looked at Jason and Billy. "Is he a silver tongued devil or what?"

The double doors opened and Big Joe Croom walked into the room. A doctor was with him. When Big Joe's eyes met Mary C.'s eyes he could not look at her. Mary C. knew something was wrong. The doctor stepped to Mary C.

"You brought the young man in, ma'am?"

"Yes."

"I'm sorry. He had lost too much blood. We couldn't save him."

The pain in Mary C.'s body was so intense she actually thought her heart had split into two pieces in side her chest. She was instantly sick to her stomach. Her face went pale as she looked at Jason. He had never seen her look so helpless. Mary C.'s body started shaking. She turned back to the doctor. Her voice cracked when she spoke.

"What killed him?"

The doctor was surprised at the question. He hesitated, but did answer. "The bite on the back of his neck was the worst of the wounds. That was probably the fatal injury. Why did you ask that question?"

Mary C. tried to swallow, but her mouth and throat were dry. "When I shot the dog, some of the pellets hit Joe on his side. I was worried about that."

"Oh, now I understand. The wounds to his side were minor, not fatal. We did count six small punctures on his side and his hip, but they had nothing to do with his death. He died because he lost too much blood from the dog bites."

Stella Croom came through the double doors yelling at Mary C. "She killed my son. She just had to keep that evil dog. Everything and everybody she touches dies. She's a menace to society; always has been. All he talked about for the last few days was you and that damn car. Don't you have enough lives to ruin without adding my son to the list? When do you think you'll finally realize what you're doing? You sleep with the devil. When will you leave Mayport and set us all free from your reign of terror?   It ain't the oak tree, it ain't the King house, it ain't the old Spanish graveyard, it ain't the Indian mounds, it's you, Mary C. You are the evil in Mayport. You need to be burned at the stake like the witch you are." Stella looked at her husband. "You don't need to be out here with her. You need to be with your name sake." She turned and went back through the double doors. Her husband followed her.

Mary C.'s facial expression did not change while Stella Croom was chastising her. She turned to Mr. King. "Let's go find Hank's room and see if we can talk to him about Miss Stark's necklace."

Sofia was sitting on a chair at the store. Margie had told her about how badly hurt Joe Croom was when Mary C. brought him to the store. Sofia was sick to her stomach. She surprised Margie with her next comment.

"I really like Joe. He's the first person to make me look away from Jason. He was different. I'm different."

Margie wasn't sure if Sofia had given herself to Joe Croom, or was it just more drama from her little sister.

"Well, just how different are you?"

Sofia was serious. "You know how we have all changed. Some of us more than others. Those are your words. How can I ever be the same? Too much has happened in a short amount of time."

"I thought we were not going to talk about it any more."

Sofia had been thinking about all the sadness around them. "What's wrong with this place? Have you thought about all the awful things that have happened in the past year? No wonder everybody's crazy. We can't help it. We all need to go away for good. People move to live other places all the time, why can't we?"

"You're not going any where. None of us are. We belong here. We're creating the next page of Mayport history. Folks will tell stories about us when we're dead and gone. We're part of some great Mayport stories."

Sofia shook her beautiful head. "Who are you? What did you do with my older sister?"

Mary C. and Jason waited for Mr. King to talk to the young woman at the information desk. "Excuse me ma'am, could you tell us what room Hank Haygood's in? We're close friends and would like to see him."

The young woman looked in a logbook in front of her and then she looked up at Mr. King. "Well, he's in room 61, but he is still in critical condition and only family members are allowed in the room and that's for only five minutes at a time. He's only responded a few times. Mr. Haygood is very sedated."

Mary C. stepped up to the desk. "I'm his sister and I come a long way to see him. Do I get a pass from you or somebody else?"

The young woman looked at Mr. King. He nodded in agreement with Mary C. "We'll stay out of the room if that's the rules, but please let her go in to see him."

Stella Croom sat next to her dead son. Joe Croom Sr. stood behind her. She held her son's cold hand. "I'm so angry, Joe. I hate her. How can we live through this? I don't want to hear, 'it was his time' or 'he's in a better place'. I don't want to hear, 'it was God's will'. I want to be angry. I want to hate her. I want something awful to happen to her and her son."

Joe Croom had to stop his angry wife. "Stella, I know how hard this is gonna be for all of us. You can't say those things out loud. You're not yourself."

She was unreasonable. "Of course I'm not myself! A wild animal has just killed our son. Our beautiful son." She took a deep breath. "The person who caused his death is sitting out in the waiting room. We're just one more family to add to her evil spells of death. You need to start thinkin' about what you're gonna do about it. Someone has to stop her." Stella Croom clinched her teeth. "It needs to end, now! If you're not man enough to do it, I'll find somebody who is."

Jason and Mr. King sat outside the room in chairs near the nurse's station. Jason still held Billy in his arms. Mary C. stood next to Hank's hospital bed. He appeared to be sleeping. His right eye was swollen shut, his face was bruised and his lips were cut and also swollen. He opened his left eye when Mary C. touched his hand. Mary C. whispered. "Hey, Hank." Hank nodded his head. "Who did this?" He closed his left eye and took a painful deep breath. Mary C. could see he was in pain. She whispered, "Are you able to talk?"

Hank whispered, too. "It hurts a little, but they got me pretty doped up."

Mary C. had the necklace on her mind. "Did ya see 'em? Did ya know 'em?" A chill ran through Mary C.'s body when Hank nodded his head. She looked toward the door to see if they were alone, then back at Hank. Mary C. took her own deep breath. "Did they take the necklace?"

Hank's one good eye popped open. Mary C. knew her last question surprised him. She needed to explain. "Bill told us about you findin' the necklace. We've been tryin' to get here to talk to you, but so much has been happenin' that we couldn't get here. You bein' beat and robbed was just the beginin' of all the trouble. Who did this to ya, Hank?" Mary C. could see Hank did not like the fact she knew about the necklace. "Don't be mad at Bill. He's just worried about you and he talked to me and John about what you told him. If you know who took the necklace, we can get it back before they sell it or leave with it. It's pretty important to John. You know how he is about history and doin' the right thing. If you know who took it, we'll go get it back. If you wait to long it could be lost again and this time forever."

Even with Joe Croom's brutal death still burning in her stomach, Mary C. still had her usual cold heart. "You know Hank, if you was to die from all this and take what you know to the grave, nobody would ever see the necklace again. You need to tell me."

Hank's eye widened to its fullest again. He whispered again. "You are one of a kind, Mary C. There ain't none like ya." Mary C. touched Hank's swollen face. He decided to talk to her. "I did somethin' real stupid. I thought I was past such foolishness, but I ain't." Mary C. remained quiet. She would not interrupt her father's old friend and she would allow him to take his time. "I had the necklace in the car with me. I was scared to leave it at the cottage.

Every time I'd take a break at work, I'd go out to the car and look at it. I really didn't know what to do about it. I was scared."

"Well, it almost got ya killed." Hank closed his left eye and seemed to drift away from the influence of the drugs in his system. "Talk to me, Hank! Stay with me!"

Hank opened his left eye. "I'm tryin'. I just want to sleep."

"You can sleep after you tell me who took the necklace. While you're sleepin', I'll go get it back for ya."

Hank kept his eyes closed, but he did continue talking. "I just wanted to see them titties. I told her I wouldn't touch 'em, I just wanted to look at 'em." Hank Haywood closed his one good eye and fell deeply into a drug induced painless sleep. There was a voice coming from behind Mary C. A nurse had joined her in the room.

"Excuse me, ma'am, but he needs to sleep. You've been in here longer than we're supposed to allow. You'll have to go now." Mary C. had all the information she was going to get at the moment, or perhaps at all.

Fabian finally found his way to the funeral home to see his father's body and make arrangements for the funeral service. The police had delivered the body earlier that morning. He had good intentions when he first got ready to go find his father, but two unbelievable women and his weakness for the flesh had sidetracked him from his original purpose.

Theda and Rebecca were twenty-five miles away from Mayport, shopping for clothes at May Cohen's in downtown Jacksonville. Theda left her baby, Sam, with one of her relatives. Fabian would make the funeral arrangements for his father and get back to Mayport as fast as he could just in case there was more sexual excitement waiting for him. Fabian had lost his father and also held his dying friend, Eli, in his arms. He killed the three Coolie men, had sex with Margie under the oak tree and at the store and had more sex with Rebecca Coolie. It was enough to send anyone over the edge to insanity. It was becoming a common trait for the citizens of Mayport.

Mary C. stood in the hospital parking lot next to her red Corvette. Mr. King, Jason and Billy were with her. Mr. King was interested in Hank's condition and what he might have said.

"How's Hank doin'?"

"He don't look too good. He's been beat up pretty bad. He said he did have the necklace." Mr. King's eyes lit up. He knew Mary C. had more. "He nodded his head when I asked him if he knew who robbed him."

Mr. King was excited. "Then he knows 'em."

"Maybe he does, but he didn't tell me. He started talkin' crazy from the painkillers and then he fell asleep. The nurse came in and made me leave. We do know one thing. Miss Stark's necklace was found and then it was stolen."

Mary C. could see the disappointment on Mr. King's face. "That's it? He didn't say anything else?"

"Well, if you must know, he did say he wanted to see my tits or somethin' like that. He was talkin' crazy."

Margie left Sofia at the store. She drove home in the family station wagon so she could tell her mother about Abaddon's vicious attack on Joe Croom. Miss Margaret was sweeping off the front porch when Margie drove up. She stepped out of the car and walked to the steps.

"Oh Mother, something awful has happened!"

CHAPTER ELEVEN

Mary C. was driving her new red Corvette down the beach toward Bill's Hideaway. She needed a hard Jack Black and coke. Mr. King, Jason and Billy were on their way back to Mayport. Miss Margaret sat alone in one of her porch rocking chairs. She was saddened by Margie's story about young Joe Croom. Margie had gone into the house to take a shower. She was going to go to the hospital and see about her new young lover, Joe Croom.

Mary C. stopped her red Corvette next to the steps of Bill's Hideaway. She sat in the car for a few minutes trying to get her thoughts together. Her involvement in Joe Croom's unexpected death weighed heavily on her mind and cold heart.

Mr. King sat in one of his front porch chairs. He watched Miss Margaret's station wagon roll past his house. He could see there was only one person in the car, but he had no idea which member of the family was driving. Jason was lying in the bed next to Billy. He was tired and fell asleep along with his son.

Theda and Rebecca were on their way home from the shopping trip. Rebecca was driving and she turned the car off of Atlantic Boulevard onto Mayport Road. They passed Silver's bar and package store to the left. The road to the Coolie junkyard was also to the left of the main road. Rebecca had a request.

"Do you think it would be okay if we went by my house so I can get a few of my things? I'm sure nobody's out there."

Theda did not like the idea of returning to the awful place where she was raped and held against her will. "I'd be too scared. You can take me home and come back if you really want to."

Rebecca nodded her head as they passed the shell road that led to her house. "You sure Fabian won't mind me using the car?"

"You need to get your things. He won't mind at all. Just be careful."

Mary C. walked to the bar in Bill's Hideaway. She knew Joe Croom would not be the bartender. She was surprised to see Bill, the owner, behind the bar. He was surprised to see Mary C.

"Hey Mary C., I didn't expect to see you out this way."

"I didn't expect to see you behind the bar."

"I guess not. Joe didn't come in. I didn't have anybody else, so I'm it. He's probably got the night off and I just didn't schedule anybody. He's a good kid. He wouldn't miss work. I'm sure he's off and I didn't remember. I'll fix the schedule next time. Can't make anything fancy, just easy mixed drinks and I can draw some beer. What can I get for ya?"

Mary C. was shocked that Bill had no idea about his nephew's death. She knew the sad and horrible news would be too much for Bill to handle. She did not want to be the messenger, but she also knew she had to tell him.

"Don't fix me anything yet, Bill. I need to tell you somethin'."

Bill could see the seriousness of her tone. "What is it, Mary C.? What's wrong?"

"Joe didn't have the night off. He's supposed to be here."

"He is? Well now, that ain't like him. Why ain't he here?"

Mary C.'s stomach burned. She took a deep breath. "Bill, nobody's told you what happened?"

"Told me what? I just got here. I went fishin' early this mornin' and just got back. When I saw we didn't have a bartender, I showered in the back and here I am. I always keep some clean clothes here for emergencies. What's goin' on?"

"Joe was attacked by my wild dog at the sand hill. I had to shoot the dog and then take Joe to the hospital."

Bill's eyes popped wide open. "It was a good thing you were there. How's Joe doin'? I hear that was a big, mean dog."

Mary C. reluctantly let the awful words pass through her lips. "Joe's dead, Bill. He bled to death from the dog bites."

Joe Croom Sr. walked into his house. He would tell his other three sons that their brother was dead. Stella Croom did not go home with him. She would stay with her firstborn as long as she could. Mary C. was an expert at creating new enemies. Stella Croom was the latest.

Bill sat with Mary C. listening to her story about shooting the dog and trying to save Joe's life. She also told him about Stella Croom's reaction to Mary C.'s participation in Joe's untimely death. Bill was shocked at the awful story.

"I need to go find Stella. She may not be able to handle something like this. She had a special relationship with Joe. He was one of the bright spots in her life." He hesitated and then continued. "I know you would have never hurt Joe. People become victims of circumstances. You seem to be that victim more than others. I need to get one of the waitresses to tend bar so I can go."

As Bill stood up, Mary C. thought about her strange meeting with Hank. "When I was at the hospital I went to see Hank."

Bill's eyes lit up. "How is he?"

"He looks bad. He's all busted up. Pretty doped up, too."

He knew it was not the time, but Bill had to ask. "Did you ask him about the necklace?"

"He said he had it. At first he said he knew who robbed him. I was waiting for him to tell me, but he fell asleep before he did. He was talkin' crazy before he conked out."

Bill wanted to go console his sister, but he also wanted to know about Hank. "What kinda crazy things did he say?"

Mary C. took a deep breath. "Well, it's just stupid stuff. He said something about seein' my titties, or somebody's titties."

Bill's eyes widened again. "Hank does like women's breasts. He was beside himself the other night when that Coolie girl came into the bar. He couldn't keep his eyes off of her. I got tickled at him when he said he wished he was a younger man. He said he'd pay to see her breasts. He even said he wouldn't touch 'em, he just wanted to see 'em. It was funny."

It was time for Mary C.'s eyes to light up. She remembered Hank's words. "That's what he said to me. He said, 'He just wanted to see 'em. He wouldn't touch 'em.' He wasn't talkin' about me, he was talkin' about that girl." Mary C. had a question for Bill. "What else do you remember?"

"Well, she was alone, pretty dressed up and showin' off those breasts. She sat at the bar, but didn't drink anything. Hank talked to her for a while, but I was in and out and didn't pay much attention. When she left is when he talked about her."

"You think he met her later?"

"I don't think so. He might have run into her on the beach when he got off, but I don't think so."

Mary C. had another thought. "This has some possibilities, Bill. Them Coolies would be able to do somethin' to Hank. Them's some mean boys. That daddy of theirs is just as bad. If Hank told that girl about the necklace or showed it to her to see her tits, she could have told her daddy. All this really fits together. What do we do next?"

Mary C.'s reasoning had taken Bill's thoughts away from his grieving sister. He had to get back to his responsibility as a brother and uncle. "This is crazy. I've got to see my sister. We've got to talk to Hank again."

Mary C. had another thought. "Or, that girl."

Rebecca stopped the car in front of Theda's house. "I'm gonna go back and get my things if you think it's okay with me taken the car. I won't be long. I'll be right back. I don't want to stay out there no longer than I have to."

Theda picked up the bags of new clothes off of the back seat of the car. "It'll be fine, just hurry and please be careful. I'll take this stuff inside. See ya in a little while."

The red Corvette was on the move again. Mary C. would go home first to talk to John King about her conversation with Bill. Bill was on his way to the hospital.

Rebecca Coolie drove down the shell road leading to the junkyard. She passed a group of black turkey buzzards on the side of the road. She had no idea the nasty birds were feasting on her brother, Duck. The buzzards around Mayport were the best fed of all the local animals.

Fabian drove up to the front of his house. His sister, Theda was sitting on the porch with her son in her arms. He noticed right away his father's car was not parked in the yard. He rolled the driver's side window down. "Where's daddy's car?"

Theda was quick to answer. "Rebecca wanted to go back out to her house to get a few of her things. I didn't want to go, so she brought me home and went back. She'll be right back." Theda was surprised when Fabian turned his car around and the tires of the car threw dirt and grass into the air as he drove away.

Rebecca stopped the car in front of her shack house. She was uneasy as she looked around the yard. Her heart raced in her chest when she thought about the possibility her family members were waiting for her to return. Rebecca Coolie was afraid as she slowly stepped out of the car and walked to the small porch entrance to the shack. She pushed open the front door and stepped into the front of the house. She almost fainted when a man's voice cut through the silence.

"We knew someone would show up sooner or later." Rebecca was frozen with pure fear as her eyes focused on a man sitting in one of the chairs in the front room. Her body quivered as he continued. "You're the hero daughter who saved the Moore girl and her baby." Rebecca Coolie realized the man was one of the police officers she had seen the night before. She was afraid and did not respond.

"I'm Officer Boos of the Atlantic Beach Police Department. I saw you at the Moore house last night I was waiting for y'all to return. Where's your father and brothers?"

Rebecca's was sick to her stomach. She tried to calm herself so she could answer the policeman. "I know you won't believe me, but I really don't know where they are."

Officer Boos stood up from the chair. He looked directly at Rebecca's huge breasts that were packed into a pull over t-shirt that was two sizes too small. The stress and fear running through her body caused her nipples to stand at attention. It was impossible for any man to look away from her incredible female assets. Officer Boos heard about Rebecca Coolie's body, but he had not had the pleasure of seeing it close up and in person. It was a true treat, even under the current circumstances. He pulled his eyes away from the breast-full trance.

"You might be telling the truth about not knowing where they are, but you do know something. Do we talk here or do I take you to the station? We already know something went on here. We think somebody got hurt or even killed. You need to tell me what you know."

Rebecca sat down in one of the chairs and crossed her legs. She gave Officer Boos another good look at another of her female attributes. He stood over her. Officer Boos knew Miss Coolie was not wearing anything under the tight skirt. He found the strength to continue his questioning. "What do you know, Miss Coolie? What can you tell me? Give me something I can use."

Miss Coolie took a deep breath making her already over-sized breasts look even bigger. "You already know my father killed Mr. Moore. My brother brought Theda and the baby here. I helped 'em escape. I didn't want anything to do with no killin' and no baby stealin'. My family's gone. I don't know where they are, honest. I'm scared of what my daddy might do if he finds me."

"You came back here. You must not be too scared."

"I didn't think they'd be here, with you after 'em and all. They know when the heats on. They know how to hurt folks, but they also know when it's time to run."

"Sounds like you done some runnin' before."

"That's why I'm here talkin' to you. I ain't runnin' no more. I want to have my own life and I ain't never gonna be with those three again. I ain't done nothin' wrong. When they did bad things I might have been wrong for keepin' quiet about it, but I wasn't sure who to trust so I didn't tell. If that's a crime then I'm guilty of bein' too scared to tell. I'm eighteen years old, mister. I've been scared for all eighteen years. I want to have my own life."

Officer Boos felt sad for the young woman, but he knew she could tell him much more than she was telling. "It's good you're gonna change your life. You did the right thing when you helped Miss Moore and the baby. I still think you have an idea where your father and brothers have gone."

"They probably went across the river to my aunt's house. She's my daddy's sister and as mean as a woman could ever be. She lives

out on Black Hammock Island. We've stayed out there when we
was on the run before. Her name is Annie Coolie. She ain't never
married. She's more of a man than a woman. She lays with other
women. I hated it when we had to stay out there. I always had to
sleep with her. You can't miss her place. It's at the far end of the
inland. There's one road in and out. Aunt Annie lets some nasty
people stay at her place. It's like a gathering of thieves and
criminals. Sometimes it looks like an army's set up camp out there.
Then other times it's just Aunt Annie and what ever woman she's
sleepin' with at the time. It's a real good hidin' place for folks on
the run."

Officer Boos was shocked at the amount of information the
young woman was willing to supply. He realized she was actually
trying to cooperate with him. "I know of the area, but I've never
been out there."

Rebecca Coolie smiled. "Ain't no lawman ever gone out there.
That's why it's a good hidin' place. There's stories about the old
days and how when the law tried to take a criminal off the island,
the lawmen was never heard from again. This supposedly happened
a number of times ending any interference from the law. I guess
you'll be the first one in a long time to go out there."

"If I do, it won't be alone. I can get an army, too."

Rebecca nodded her pretty head. "I'm sure you can. Now, can I
get my things? I need to get back."

Officer Boos nodded his head. "Go ahead. Get what ya need."

Rebecca walked to her bedroom in the back of the house.

Officer Boos watched Rebecca walk away. The noise of a car
engine took his attention from her. Officer Boos walked to the front
door to see his partner, Officer Paul Short, had returned to pick him
up. Officer Boos stepped out onto the porch as Paul Short got out of
the patrol car. He looked at the car parked near the shack.

"Got a visitor?"

Officer Boos nodded again. "Miss Coolie, herself. She came
bouncing right in. And I do mean bouncing." He gave a rare smile
at his clever description of Miss Coolie's entrance. "She came back
to get her things so she could go back to stay with the Moore
family."

Rebecca stepped up behind Officer Boos. She was carrying an old Navy duffle bag and two paper grocery bags filled with her personal items. She looked at Officer Short. He looked directly at her huge bouncing breasts.

"Milkduds" Coolie was accustom to all the men she met looking at her breasts before they actually looked into her eyes. Some men never did let their eyes work their way to her beautiful face. Men had talked to her and never looked away from her breasts. She moved off the porch and walked to the car.

Officer Boos had to make a mandate. "You know we can take you to the station? We still need to talk about your role in all this. I think you know more than you've told me, but you were helpful."

She looked back at the two police officers. "I've told you what I know, but I'm going to stay out at the Moore house. If you need me I'm easy to find. Can I go now?"

Officer Boos looked at Officer Short and then back at Rebecca Coolie. "You can go. If you see him, tell Fabian Moore we'd like to talk to him, too." Rebecca got into the car and drove away.

Officer Boos turned to Officer Short to discuss Rebecca's information with his partner. "Paul, you ever been out to Black Hammock Island?"

Paul Short's eyes lit up, but before he could answer the question the sound of another car took his attention away from the conversation. Both police officers turned to see Fabian Moore drive his car up to the Coolie shack. The car stopped and Fabian stepped out. He remained standing at the opened car door.

Officer Boos did not like Fabian Moore. "You know they say a criminal always returns to the scene of his crime?"

Fabian smiled. "I'm not sure why you said that to me, but I ain't never been out here before. I was lookin' for Rebecca. I wanted to be sure she was safe."

"She was here. She got her things and we let her go back to your house. Miss Coolie promised to stay put and talk to us later. I hope you'll encourage her to do so and I hope you'll do the same."

Fabian looked at Officer Boos. "She ain't done nothin' wrong. She ain't part of the killin' and what ever else they did. As for me, I ain't goin' no where."

"She knows about a lot of criminal activity. I could arrest her, you know?"

"You can talk to her any time you want. Don't you think she's been through enough? I'll be sure she stays here. I'll guarantee it."

Officer Boos looked at Officer Short. "Mr. Moore has just guaranteed that Miss Coolie won't leave the area and be available for more questioning if we need her." He looked at Fabian Moore. "What makes you so sure?"

"Because she'll do anything I tell her to do, that's why. Anything. You ought'a see her naked. She's unbelievable. I need to get on back home. Theda's cookin' supper and Rebecca's probably takin' another shower. My daddy won't rest 'til those Coolies are buried with him. I hope you two find 'em. If ya do, kill 'em all."

Mary C. was sitting in John King's living room telling John what she and Bill had talked about. As usual, Mr. King was all ears when it came to any talk about Miss Stark's necklace and the big breasted, Rebecca "Milkduds" Coolie. He had a comment.

"So you think Hank was talkin' 'bout that Coolie girl when he said he wanted to see your titties?"

"I think so."

"You think the Coolies took the necklace?"

"If that girl went home and told 'em. They went to Hank's and took it."

"If this is true. We might not ever find it. With all this stuff goin' on with the Coolies, they're probably long gone with the necklace. I think Stoddard's killin' was somethin' they didn't plan on when they first took the necklace. They're on the run now, but they've got the necklace. It sure is interesting that the girl's still here, living at Stoddard's house. This is pretty crazy stuff."

Bill stood at the nurse's station of the emergency room of the hospital. "I'm trying to find my sister. My nephew was brought in after a dog attacked him. He died here. Can you tell me where they are?"

The young nurse was sad. "I'm sorry about your nephew. They have already taken him to the funeral home. I signed them out. His mother went with them. She insisted and the driver did not want her to cause a scene here at the hospital. We all felt so sad for her. They called her husband to meet them at the funeral home. They were hoping he would be able to reason with her."

"Thank you. Maybe I can go over there and help her." Bill walked away from the desk toward the exit door. He turned back to the nurse. "You couldn't tell me where Hank Haywood's room is, could ya? He's a good friend and I should stop in while I'm here."

The young nurse had the same sad look on her face. "I'm sorry sir, but Mr. Haywood expired about an hour ago."

Officer Paul Short drove his police car away from the Coolie junkyard. He looked out the front windshield, but he talked to his partner. "Why ya think the Moore boy had to say all that stuff about her takin' a shower and her doin' what ever he said?"

Officer Boos had the answer. "Because he's one big wise-ass, that's why. He likes playin' with us. He knows plenty. Let's get out of here."

Margie stood at the nurse's station in the hospital. She had just been told that Joe Croom had died from the dog attack. She sat down in one of the chairs near the wall because her quivering legs would not hold her up. Margie was sick to her stomach. She was in the middle of another Mayport tragedy.

Officer Short drove the police car away from the Coolie shack toward the narrow shell road. Officer Boos wanted to share his information. He asked his question again. "Paul, you ever been out to Black Hammock Island?"

Officer Short's eyes lit up. "No, and I don't want to go."

"You heard all the stories, too?"

"Since I joined the force. You're not tellin' me the Coolies are hidin' out on Black Hammock, now are ya?"

"It seems a female relative of theirs is pretty much in control of what happens out there. No tellin' what we might find if we showed up unannounced."

Officer Short ended the conversation when he had to stop the car because another group of buzzards hopped out into the road in front of the moving vehicle. Officer Boos looked to his right and saw an abnormal number of the big, black birds in the woods next to the road.

"Stop here for a minute, Paul. When there's this many of these damn birds you can bet they're eatin' somethin' big. Last time I saw this many buzzards in the woods they were eatin' Mr. Butler for breakfast. And I never will forget all those birds on Mr. King's house. I had no idea we had so many buzzards around here. Where the hell are they comin' from?"

Officer Boos rolled down the passenger's side window, pulled his pistol out of its holster and fired his gun into the air directly above the mass of black buzzards. The flock of nasty birds seemed to explode into the air as they all took flight, leaving the deteriorating carcass of Duck Coolie. Officers Boos and Short would find one of the three dead Coolies.

Bill was on his way to the funeral home to see if he could assist his sister in her time of need. He wanted to talk to Mary C. and Mr. King and let them know Hank Haygood was dead. He knew Mr. King did not have a phone so he would have to talk to them after he went to see his sister, Stella.

The red Corvette rolled into Fabian Moore's front yard. Mary C. and Mr. King were looking for Rebecca "Milkduds" Coolie. As they got out of the car Fabian drove his car into the yard behind them. Theda Moore stepped out onto the front porch when she heard the cars drive up. Fabian looked around the yard and did not see his father's car. He looked at Theda.

"Where is she?"

"She ain't got back yet." Mary C. and Mr. King stepped toward the porch as Fabian did the same. "Hey, Miss Mary C., Mr. King." He was close to his sister. "I went out to her place and she had just left. Those two cops were out there snoopin' around and askin' questions. She's had more than enough time to get back here."

Mary C. was interested. "Fabian, what's goin' on?"

He took a deep breath. "I'm not sure, maybe nothin'. I just need to calm down and think. It looks like our guest has taken off with my father's car. She was supposed to go out to her house and get her things. It seems she did that, but she didn't come back here. I hate to think she's run off, but there's a possibility she's gone."

Mary C. looked at Mr. King. She knew they would not share the information about Miss Stark's necklace with Fabian and his sister. She had to give Fabian a false reason for them being there.

"We just wanted to see if you two needed anything. I don't feel like we've helped you very much."

"We're fine. Daddy's funeral's set for Tuesday at ten o'clock at the Presbyterian Church. The burial will be right after the ceremony at the Mayport Cemetery. Everybody's goin' over to Aunt Wilda's house to eat and complete the day."

Mary C. nodded. "We'll go by Wilda's and see what she needs for Tuesday." Mr. King nodded his head, too. Mary C. turned to Theda. "You and the baby doin' all right?"

"Yes ma'am. He's a good baby. He's sleepin' as usual."

"They are good when they sleep. We'll see y'all on Tuesday."

Margie walked up the steps to her front porch and into the house. Miss Margaret was walking down the inside stairs. She turned as Margie walked into the house. "Oh Margie, I didn't hear you drive up. You need to take Peggy over to the store and pick up Sofia. How's the Croom boy doing?" The sad look on Margie's face told Miss Margaret something was terribly wrong. "Oh dear God, what is it?"

"He's dead. He bled to death from the dog bites. I tried to stop the bleeding, but I guess I didn't."

Miss Margaret's eyes filled with tears for her daughter. "Oh Margie, you did all you could. How much death can we take around here?" She stepped to Margie and held her. Margie hugged her mother and cried. Peggy walked from the kitchen and joined them.

"What's wrong?"

Miss Margaret did the talking. "Joe Croom died after the dog attacked him."

Peggy's face showed her sadness and surprise. She hugged Margie, too. Miss Margaret looked at Peggy.

"I'll drive you to the store and pick up Sofia. Margie, you stay here and try to relax. You do know none of this is your fault?"

Margie nodded, but did not say anything. She moved away from the other two and walked up the stairs toward her bedroom.

Fabian and Theda were sitting in their living room. Theda was defending Rebecca Coolie. "She'll come back, I just know it."

Fabian was not so sure. "Then, where is she? She's had plenty of time to get here. I didn't see her on the road on the way back, so she didn't have any car trouble. Now, that I think about it, I should have passed her on the way out there. When she left her place she must have turned right on Mayport Road. I think she's gone and she's got daddy's car. If she had money she can gas that thing up and no tellin' where she is by now. I was a damn fool. You were, too."

The sound of a car engine ended the conversation and they both moved quickly to the front door. Theda smiled when she saw her daddy's car roll into the front yard.

"I told ya." They both stepped out onto the front porch. Fabian jumped off the porch to meet Rebecca as the car stopped rolling. He was angry. He grabbed her arm as she stepped out of the car.

"Where the hell you been?"

"You're hurtin' my arm. What's wrong?"

"What's wrong? We thought you ran off. That's what's wrong." He released her arm.

Rebecca looked at Theda who was still standing on the porch. "I wouldn't run off like that. I wouldn't steal your car. Y'all have been so kind to me. No one has ever treated me like you have. I'm sorry I worried you. I got some money I had saved and hidden in my room. I went and bought some groceries, so I would be doin' my share here." Fabian looked into the back seat of the car and saw the bags of groceries. She continued. "I guess I took so long because I ain't never been able to ride around Atlantic Beach by myself. I ain't never been in none of the stores. I just drove around and looked at the pretty houses. I even saw the pier in Jacksonville Beach. I'd sure like to go fishin' on that thing one day." She looked at Fabian. "I'm sorry I worried you. I just lost track of the time. It was the first time I ever felt free. I would never hurt you or Theda."

Fabian was calmer and a little embarrassed, but just a little. "I'm sorry I hurt your arm. I should have given you the time to explain. I've just got so much on my mind. I won't ever hurt you, either."

Rebecca's smile of forgiveness and acceptance told Fabian he had a companion for life, if that's what he wanted. Rebecca turned and opened the back door of the four-door car. "I'll get the groceries."

Fabian stepped to the door behind her. "We'll both get 'em." He looked into the backseat. "Look at all this stuff."

Miss Margaret and Peggy walked into the store. Sofia was assisting a customer. Miss Margaret knew the lady with Sofia at the counter. "Miss Carolyn, what brings you out this way?"

Miss Carolyn's face lit up when she turned to see Miss Margaret. "Miss Margaret, I was hopin' I'd see that pretty face today. I already got to see this beautiful daughter of yours. She looks like an angel." Miss Carolyn looked at Peggy. "And here's another one. You girls know I hear about y'all all the time. Everyone talks about how beautiful all of you are. What a blessing to be able to move people with your beauty." She looked at Miss Margaret. "How blessed you are and how proud you must be."

Sofia and Peggy loved the way Miss Carolyn talked. They had heard her name before, but never met her. The girls could tell their mother was happy to see her friend from the past.

"Ever since you moved out on Mayport Road we don't get to see you very much. I miss you."

"Oh darlin', I miss you, too. I'm not sure why I just stay out there. I just love my house and I am workin' ya know? Actually, I've been out here a lot lately, but just to work. I'm waitin' tables for Mr. Willie Strickland. I've been workin' there about three weeks. I'm headed to work, now."

Miss Margaret was surprised. "I had no idea. I haven't eaten there in over a year. You know I've always been a home cooker."

"And a wonderful cook, too." She looked at the two girls. "If I cooked like your mother, I'd be cookin' at home, too."

Peggy had a thought. "I guess you've had gopher stew with her?"

"I'm sorry to say darlin', but I've had my share of gopher stew. Not 'cause I wanted to eat it, but because that's all we had. I never liked it, though. I never ate none of your mama's before, but I do know if your mama cooked it, it was the best."

The two girls looked at their mother. Miss Margaret was all smiles. Then her face changed when she thought about the bad news she needed to share with Sofia. She took a deep breath.

"We've just gotten some more sad news." She looked at Sofia. "Joe Croom died at the hospital."

Miss Margaret could see Sofia's face change color as she digested her mother's comment. Miss Carolyn made the sign of the cross. "Lord have mercy on us." She knew the name, but did not know what had happened. "I haven't seen anyone from the Croom family in years. What happened?"

Miss Margaret took a deep breath. "A wild dog attacked him at the sand hill. It seems he bled to death from the dog bites."

"Oh dear God, what an awful thing. His mother must be out of her mind with grief." The group in the store had no idea Sofia was also going out of her mind as well.

Susan walked down the upstairs hallway and passed Margie's bedroom. She was taking a shower when the other members of her family were talking about the latest awful tragedy. She saw her sister lying on the bed. Susan wanted to discuss their tag team of sex with Jason on the shrimp boat.

"Margie, you sleepin'?"

Margie's head was down into the pillow, but she did answer her sister. "No."

"Where is everybody?"

Margie kept her head buried in the pillow. "Mother took Peggy to the store."

"You sick again?"

"Kind'a."

"What's wrong?"

Margie rolled over onto her back and looked at her sister through tear filled, bloodshot eyes. "The dog killed Joe Croom."

Miss Margaret and Sofia were driving home. Miss Carolyn had gone to Strickland's Restaurant and Peggy was tending the store. Susan sat on the edge of Margie's bed.

"Another person's dead, another Mayport person, another friend of ours. Don't you think that's scary?"

Margie took a deep breath. "It's more than scary. We used to talk about the people that died around here always seemed to have something to do with Miss Mary C. and Jason. Now, it's people who have something to do with us."

Susan's eyes lit up. "That's too creepy. Why you think that's happening?"

"I don't know, but I'm trying not to be scared. I'm trying not to think about it, but I can't help it. What if one of us dies? All the death is sure close to us. It seems it's just a matter of time."

Susan did not want to think about such things. "Stop it, you're really scaring me. If you say something it will come true. I heard

Mother and Miss Mary C. talking one time about 'speaking the word'."

"What's that mean?"

"I think it means if a person speaks of something like somebody dying before it actually happens, it can make it happen. You say it, it comes true."

Margie did not like her sister's interpretation of the "speaking the word" concept. "Now you're scaring me. I don't want my words to be the cause of someone's death."

"I'm just telling you what they said. I didn't say I believed it."

The two sisters heard the front door open and close downstairs. Miss Margaret and Sofia had returned. Susan left Margie's bedroom and walked down the stairs to see her mother. Sofia was walking up the stairs. Susan saw a strange look on Sofia's beautiful face. It was a look she had never seen before.

"Sofia, are you all right?"

Sofia walked past Susan and did not even look at her. Sofia walked up the stairs and into her bedroom. Miss Margaret joined Susan to the foot of the stairs.

"This awful thing with Joe Croom has just added to Sofia's sadness. She's too sensitive to handle all this."

Susan wanted to tell her mother how Sofia had much more to be sad about, but she did not. "You're right Mother, she's always been too sensitive. I'm so sad for Joe's family."

Peggy was excited when the customer bell on the door rang and Jason walked into the store. "Well, well, what a nice surprise. Did you hear about Joe Croom?"

Jason knew Peggy had not given him the proper Miss Margaret greeting, but he knew the daughters had been very lax lately with the way they greeted him. "I know about Joe. Mama took him to the hospital. The dog's dead. Mama finally killed him."

Peggy nodded, but did not respond. Jason turned toward the cold drink box. "I was cravin' a Nehi for some reason."

Peggy was glad he changed the subject of their conversation. "We've got all flavors." Jason walked to the box, opened it and pulled out a strawberry Nehi soda. The icy cold water dripped off the bottle as he walked to the counter.

"Here, give it to me. I'll open it for you." Jason handed Peggy the full bottle and she pulled out the silver bottle opener that was tied to a white string at the end of the counter. She popped the cap off the bottle and handed it to Jason. "There you go."

Jason handed her a dollar bill and she gave him his change. Peggy was very excited to be alone with Jason. After she had listened to Margie, Peggy decided she was never going to pass up an opportunity to be with him. She had to express her thoughts.

"Come in the back with me for a minute. Bring your drink." She turned and walked into the back storeroom. Jason had been back there many times. He followed her and closed the door.

Peggy moved Jason to a chair and he sat down. She hurried to unbuckle his belt, unsnap his pants and pull the zipper down. She reached under his skivvies and pulled out the "thing" she was digging for. Peggy held "it" in her hand. She used her other hand to take the bottle of strawberry Nehi away from Jason. She surprised Jason when she took a big drink of the cold red soda and then handed him the bottle. When he took the bottle, Peggy moved her head down to his lap and inserted his exposed manliness into her mouth. It gave Jason a jolt when his flesh slid into her mouth and he could feel that Peggy had not swallowed the cold red liquid from the bottle. It was a new and exciting feeling for them both. Peggy sucked on Jason until he exploded and added his hot fluid to the cold. Peggy moved her head away from Jason's lap and wiped away some of the red liquid from the edge of her mouth. She smiled at a most satisfied Jason.

"Pretty neat, huh?" Jason could only nod his head. He had no words. "My cousin Peggy told me about that. I'm sure you remember my cousin, don't you? They call her Older Peggy because there's two Peggies in the family. She's always got something new to tell me about. She's the reason I let you have me the first time. Like I said then, 'If she wanted you, I wanted you, too.' She was so excited for me when I told her we did it. She's my favorite relative."

As Peggy was walking down memory lane, Jason was taking his own little trip to the past and the time Older Peggy shared her huge boat bed with him. He thought perhaps he should pay Older Peggy a visit to see if she still walked around the house in her panties and bra. The bell on the door sounded, ending another sexual encounter in the storeroom. Peggy was calm, cool and collected. "Just stay back here. If you have to, go out the back. That was fun, thanks." Peggy was fully dressed and walked to the front. Jason listened to hear who had walked in.

When Peggy made the official greeting he knew it was a customer and not a member of her family. He would wait for the customer to leave and then go to the front of the store. He looked down and started to fix his pants. He wondered if he should thank Peggy for the red stain she had left on him. He hoped it was going to wash off. He decided to go out the back door. The customer left and Peggy walked back into the storeroom, hoping to see Jason again. He was gone.

Mary C. sat with Mr. King on the front porch. They had no idea Rebecca Coolie had returned to the Moore house. They also had no idea Hank Haygood was dead and any information he had was gone with him. Mr. King was talking.

"We've got to talk to Hank again to be sure it was the Coolies. Hell, they might all be gone, gone with the necklace. They knew they was leavin' and ol' Earnest decided to kill Stoddard out of revenge. No tellin' where they are by now."

Mary C. knew more than John did. "I need to talk to Jason first. He can tell us if the Coolies are gone or not. I knew him and Fabian wouldn't say anything, but I think they know what happened to the three Coolies. We already know the girl was still here until today. I think Jason's got the answer about the three men." There was a noise to their right. Mr. King and Mary C. looked in that direction. Mary C. smiled. "Speakin' of the devil. Here's that good lookin' son of mine, right now. You must'a felt your mama needed ya."

The only thing Jason needed at that particular moment was to get to some soap and water. Red was a good color for his mother's car, but not for his privates. Mary C. was serious.

"Sit down, Jason, so we can talk." Jason knew he would have to wait until he talked to his mother before he might have to take some Babo cleanser to his stained organ. He sat down with his mother and Mr. King.

Mary C. wasted no time. She was a woman of action. "We think the Coolies beat up Hank and took Miss Stark's necklace. Are the Coolies dead or did they get away?"

Jason did not want to betray Fabian, but he knew he had to answer his mother's question. Mary C. sensed his thoughts. "I know y'all went out there. I know why. Hell, I told ya to go. If they got away then fine, but if they didn't, well then we've got one hell of a situation on our hands. I can go ask Fabian, but I'd rather talk to you. I understand when more people know about somethin' the more chance there is for them to tell others about it. That ain't the way it is with us, John included. This is too important. Anything you say will stay on this porch."

Mr. King nodded his head. He was all ears when he realized Jason was going to answer Mary C.'s question. Jason took a deep breath.

"We went out there to find 'em. We found one of 'em, the one they called Duck, layin' out on the shell road naked and all busted up. He was hurt pretty bad. His leg was broke and he was bleedin' from hundreds of little cuts and gashes on his body. It didn't take Fabian but a few seconds to realize who it was. He killed Duck first." Mr. King looked at Mary C. She did not respond. She knew Jason had more to tell. "When we got to the junkyard Fabian killed the other two. We took their bodies out to the marsh near the waterway. We left Duck's body on the side of the road in the woods. They're all dead."

Mary C. looked at Mr. King. "The necklace is still here. Either it's out there or the girl's got it."

Mr. King reminded Mary C. "She might be gone with it."

Mary C. smiled. "I think a girl like that might be pretty easy to find. She probably don't know nobody or have nowhere to go. She's easy to describe. I think we can find her if we really try." Mary C. looked at Mr. King. "You feel like takin' a ride out to the Coolie place?"

Susan walked back into Margie's bedroom. Margie was sitting at her dressing mirror. "Can we talk about something else?"

Margie looked at her sister. "Why, do you want to go find Jason with me?"

Susan smiled and sat down on the bed. "Margie, I do. I really do. That was great. I can't stop thinking about it. It was so neat watching you. And when I knew you were watching me, I was so excited. And I liked it when Jason looked so excited, too. How did you know that felt so good?"

"It was the dreams from the carousel. I like people watching me and I like watching them. I thought it would be safer if I did it with you."

Susan was puzzled. "Safer? Why did it have to be safer?"

Margie wanted to tell of her dream-like sexual experiences with the midget and the black Amazon Woman. She told her sister about the possibility she had participated in two threesomes with the strange couple and one foursome when Jason was added to the sexual mixture. She also shared the dream about the men lining up to have sex with her under the oak tree.

Billy was sleeping. Mary C. and John King were in Mr. King's Chevy and on their way to the Coolie junkyard. Jason was in the bathroom washing off the red stain from the strawberry soda. He thought of Peggy's unique oral specialty. He thought of how Susan and Margie had double-teamed him on the boat. He thought about being with Sofia and how he had not seen her. He thought about seeing Older Peggy again.

Susan could not respond to Margie's stories of outrageous sex and dreams induced by the magic music box. Margie's tales were scary, but they were also exciting and filled with fantasies. Margie smiled at Susan's inability to speak. She walked to her closet and took out the carousel that was still wrapped in a blanket. Margie put the bundle on her bed and took off the blanket, exposing the beautiful antique music box. Susan's eyes lit up. She found some words.

"You really do have it. Margie, you're the wildest."

Theda Moore and Rebecca Coolie stood together in the kitchen preparing the evening meal. Theda was happy she had been right about Rebecca. She had to express herself. "I knew you didn't run away. I told him you would be back."

Rebecca smiled. "I'll be here until y'all tell me to leave. I'll do my part and help in any way I'm needed. When y'all are tired of me

I'll leave. Thank you for trusting me." Fabian walked into the kitchen.

"Somethin' smells good."

Rebecca wanted to respond. "It's chicken and rice. Theda showed me how to cook it. She's a good cook. She said you like it with green peas."

Fabian looked at Theda. "You remembered. When do we eat?"

Rebecca responded again. "Soon as I heat up the peas."

Mr. King turned his Chevy off Mayport Road and onto the shell road that led to the Coolie junkyard. He stopped the car when he saw two police cars parked on the narrow road ahead of them. A young officer, they did not know, walked to the car and stood next to the car. Mr. King rolled down the driver's side window.

"Sorry folks, road's closed. You'll have to back up."

"What's goin' on, officer?"

"Can't share that information with you, sir. You'll have to back up, sir."

Another police car drove up coming from the other direction. The car stopped and Officer Short stepped out of the car. He recognized Mr. King's new Chevy. He walked to the car. The young officer moved over to the side when Officer Short approached them.

"Great car, Mr. King."

"Thank you."

He looked past Mr. King at Mary C. "What y'all doin' out here?"

Mr. King answered. "Just took a ride in my new car. Turned down the wrong road. We didn't know there was a problem. What's goin' on?"

"Well, we've got us another crime scene. Looks like we' found one of the Coolies in the woods. Don't know which one, yet. Somebody left him for buzzard food." He looked at Mary C. again. "Y'all wouldn't happen to know anything about that, would ya?"

Mary C. could not resist. "We didn't kill him, but we did send the buzzards over here to eat him. It keeps 'em away from the house." Officer Short stepped away from the car. Mr. King backed the Chevy up all the way to Mayport Road.

The dinner of chicken and rice with green peas was ending. Theda started clearing the dishes from the table. Rebecca stood up to help. Fabian was pleased with the dinner. "That was great, ladies. You two make a good team." Theda looked at Rebecca and smiled at her brother's compliment.

"When I finish the dishes, I've got to go get Sam from Aunt Wilda's. She's had him all day and I know she's probably pretty tired by now. Takin' care of a little baby ain't the easiest thing to do. Aunt Wilda ain't no young woman. It was really nice of her to give me a day without him. I got a lot of shoppin' done." Theda smiled at Rebecca, who was washing the dishes.

Rebecca had an idea. "Y'all go on and get him. I can finish cleanin' up here."

Fabian had another idea. "Just take the car. I ain't movin' off this couch. It ain't but right around the corner. Just take the car."

Theda looked at Rebecca. "I do like to drive. You sure you don't mind?"

"Of course not. Don't be silly. Go get Sam."

Theda picked up the keys to her father's car and hurried out the door. As soon as Rebecca heard the noise of the car engine she walked to the living room where Fabian was sitting down on the couch.

"So you're not movin' from that couch, huh?" She knelt down in front of him and lifted her tight pullover shirt, exposing her huge and perfect breasts to him. Fabian felt his manhood push against the front of his pants. She pulled the shirt up over her head and dropped it on the floor.

"I've been thinking about you all day. I didn't know if we'd have time together tonight. I know she'll be right back, but I can make you feel good while she's gone."

Fabian sat back and let Rebecca "Milkduds" Coolie work her sexual magic on him. She was there for his pleasure and Fabian would take advantage of her whenever she made the offer. She opened his pants. Her bare breasts covered his thighs as she moved her face down to his lap. The wet heat of her mouth on his skin took Fabian's breath away for a moment. Rebecca Coolie was a true pleaser and Fabian could easily become addicted to her body, style and free spirit.

Sofia was in her bed. She was thinking about Joe Croom. She was with him one time and hoping for more. Jason did not come into her mind. She thought about killing Clayton Steen and she even considered telling her mother. She wanted to fall asleep so perhaps all her thoughts would leave her head. But, she was afraid she would dream worse things. It was still early, but darkness was not far away from Mayport.

Margie told Susan about the wild dream she had with Sofia when they used the carousel. It had been a secret for almost a year. Margie's new alliance and secrets with Susan overshadowed her obligation to Sofia. She also told her about the time she and Mary C. used the music box at Mary C.'s house and how Margie ended up naked in one of the beds. Margie was hoping Susan would join her in another adventure with the carousel. She was afraid to use the carousel alone. The double sister attack on Jason had excited Susan to the extent she was willing to try any thing new with her older sister.

"I'm not sure if I'm brave enough to use the carousel. When do you think we can see Jason again?"

Margie smiled. "You know how hard it is to get time with him. The carousel is here when ever we want it. Just flip it on and let it spin."

"Is it really magic, Margie?"

"I don't know what it is. I just know I like it. Miss Mary C. likes it, too. They used it to bring the ghosts out at Mr. King's house."

Susan's face lit up. "To what?"

"They opened the door to the other side and the ghosts came through it."

Susan stood up. "I've got to think about this." She left Margie smiling in the bedroom.

Duck Coolie's deteriorated body was pulled out of the woods and placed in a canvas body bag. His naked and exposed flesh was easy pickings for the sharp, curved beaks of the large turkey buzzards. Officer Boos shook his head.

"I'll bet my next pay check it's one of the Coolies. Boy, those damn birds really do a job, don't they? They seem to pick 'em cleaner each time." One of the orderlies in the ambulance picked up the body bag and put it in the back of the vehicle.

"They might not be able to ever identify this one. It could be any body."

Officer Boos looked at Officer Short. "Well, it's one of 'em. I'll bet Fabian Moore knows which one it is. Why don't we go ask him?"

CHAPTER TWELVE

Fabian Moore stood behind Rebecca Coolie. She was bent over at her waist holding on to the backrest of the couch. He was deep inside her and she pushed her buttocks back toward him each time he pushed forward. Rebecca moaned to the rhythm of his fast piston-like strokes. Her huge breasts hung down and bounded against the backrest with each forward thrust. The sound of a car engine ended the addictive sexual encounter. Theda had returned with little Sam.

Mary C. and Mr. King sat at a table at the Red Barn. Mary C. had not eaten there since before Hawk died. It was right at the end of Mayport Road, so they decided to stop in for some barbeque. They both knew the conversation would be about finding Miss Stark's stolen necklace. Mary C. did not know Rebecca Coolie had returned to the Moore house. "We need to start looking for that Coolie girl before she gets too far away."

Mr. King had his concerns. "Where do we start? It's obvious she's not out at the junkyard. She probably won't go back there with the police all over the place. She most likely got the necklace when she went back there. She's got the necklace, a car and a big head start on anybody who's tryin' to find her."

Mary C. was not as concerned as Mr. King. "She's alone and she's scared. You and me know the Coolies are dead. She probably knows it, too. We need to talk to Theda and see if the girl might have said something to her that will help us know where to start."

Mr. King nodded his head as the waitress brought the dinners to the table. Mary C. and Mr. King drove back to the Moore house after they enjoyed their Red Barn barbeque. The sun was going down on the west side of the St. Johns River. Darkness would cover the small fishing village of Mayport within the hour.

The police coroner could not identify the body as belonging to one of the Coolies. Officer Boos and Short were on their way to Fabian Moore's house to talk to Fabian and Rebecca. They were hoping the two hostile suspects would shed some light on the situation at hand. The two law officers were also considering an undercover visit to Black Hammock Island.

Mary C. and Mr. King were also headed in the direction of the Moore house. They were hoping to talk to Theda about the possible whereabouts of Rebecca "Milkduds" Coolie. Mary C. liked being on the hunt, especially when there was a possibility of a priceless necklace at the end of the search.

Jason had just laid his sleeping son on one of the beds in the haunted house. He touched Billy's little shoulders and kissed the baby on his cheek. Jason was proud to be a father. The sound of someone knocking on the front door of the house took Jason's attention from his son. He walked down stairs to see who was visiting as night fell over Mayport.

Jason could see the silhouette of someone through the curtain on the small window of the door. Jason was never afraid. He opened the door without looking through the window or asking who was there. He came face to face with Margie. He was surprised to see her. The aggressive Margie talked first.

"I'm so glad you're here. May I come in?"

Jason stepped to the side and she walked past him into the house. Jason was interested in her reason for being there. "Margie, what's wrong?"

"I just needed to see you. With all these crazy things going on, I just wanted to be with you."

Susan stood in Margie's room looking at the magic carousel. She wanted to use it, but she knew she should wait for Margie. Susan had decided to go with Margie into the sexual dream world of the music box. She was excited. She did not know Margie had left the house.

Margie was kissing Jason as they sat on the couch in Mr. King's living room. When the kiss ended she had a question. "How do you feel about living in this house? Are you scared?" The passionate kiss ignited Jason's hot blood. He reached out his hand and squeezed one of her breasts. She pushed against his hand. "I'd be scared here. You think it's okay for Billy to sleep here?" Jason continued to squeeze her hard breast, but he did respond to her silly questions.

"I guess if Mr. King's lived here all these years, there ain't really nothin' to be scared of. I don't think I believe in ghosts."

The sexually aggressive Margie unbuttoned her own blouse exposing her braless, bare breasts to her admirer. "You only believe in the oak tree, huh?"

Jason did not answer her oak tree question. He grabbed both her bare breasts with both his hands causing Margie body to shiver from his animalistic and uneasy touch. Jason pinched both her nipples with his thumbs and index fingers. Margie had no more questions, as she knew she was getting ready to have sexual relations with Jason in John King's haunted house. It would be a first for them both.

Susan's index finger pushed up the "on" switch of the magic carousel. She was too excited to wait for Margie. The lights from the spinning carousel began to bounce off the walls and ceiling of the bedroom. The hundred lights entered Susan's wide-open eyes. She was getting ready to be introduced to the colorful and sexual world of the magic carousel.

Margie was leaning over the couch in living room of the haunted house. She was giving her usual demands as Jason stood behind her. "Harder! Do it harder! When you pull out I want to hold it."

Jason knew how to please Margie. His hard, pumping action caused a slapping sound when his pelvic area slammed against her hard butt. Margie knew he was pumping as hard as he could. She loved that skin-on-skin slapping sound. Margie looked around the room, just in case some of the resident ghosts would appear to her. She liked to be watched. It did not matter if the spectator was dead or alive. Jason did not have Margie's full attention. She was not prepared when Jason followed her instructions and pulled away from her. He tried to delay his climatic explosion so Margie could take hold of him and complete her usual ritual.

Margie looked back and made a new request. "Don't let it go yet, please. Relax a second." Jason tried to control his urges. Margie turned her back to him again. "Put it in my butt. I know you did that to me when we were in the carousel room. It hurts a little, but I liked it. Do it easy at first and then I'll see if I can do it hard."

Margie was wrong about who had given her the anal pleasure she was now requesting. She had no idea it would be Jason's first anal entry and penetration. If that's what she wanted, that's what he would do. He slowly pushed into her. Margie's hard butt muscles flinched as he slid deeper. One last push covered all of him. He was as deep as he could be and the incredible Margie relaxed her butt muscles. Jason could not see her face as Margie gritted her teeth from the combination of pain and pleasure

"Oh God! Easy! Oh God! Oh God! A little harder!" Jason had never felt such heat on his skin before. He felt Margie push her butt cheeks back toward him. "Keep going, please! Don't stop! Pump me! Oh God! Pump me, hard! Don't pull out. I want to feel it."

Jason started his in and out pistol-like thrusts. The heat and tightness was more than Jason could handle. As he exploded the sliding motion became easier and more pleasant. It was as if a vice-grip of flesh held him and was sucking him dry. Margie actually screamed, "Stop!" when she felt the heat of Jason's body fluids filling her, but Jason paid not attention to her request. She placed her own hand over her mouth in case she had to scream again. Jason tried not to make any noises but they were both pushing and moaning. Margie could not control her outburst when she gave out a blood-curdling scream that would have made the ghosts run for cover. Jason stopped. He was afraid Margie's final scream was heard by the neighboring Mayport citizens.

The wild sexual encounter in the haunted house was over, but they remained connected. Neither one knew what to do. Margie looked back over her shoulder. "We need a towel or something don't we?" She looked at the floor. "Can you reach my shirt?"

Jason looked down and saw her shirt to his right on the floor. He stepped out with his leg and tried to touch the shirt with his foot. He could not reach it. Margie realized the shirt was too far away. She reached out to the table next to the couch and took a white crocheted doily off the table and moved it around to her backside, cleaning Jason as he made his exit and holding it against her after he had moved. Margie grabbed her clothes and hurried to the bathroom, holding the white doily against her butt as she moved. Jason went to the kitchen and cleaned himself in the sink.

Susan was deep into a colorful, carousel, sexual dream. She did not recognize any of the faces in the dream. At first she looked for Jason, but he was not there. She was afraid and wanted Margie to be with her, but her experienced sister was not there either. She looked for the oak tree, because Margie told her the carousel would take her there, but that did not happen. Susan was afraid as more strangers walked past her. Susan turned when she heard a woman moan.

The noise was coming from a low white mist behind her. She had no idea why, but Susan walked into the mist to see who was moaning. Susan's eyes popped wide open when she saw all three of her sisters having sex with three different men. Margie was leaning over the couch at Mr. King's haunted house with Jason behind her. He was pumping Margie as hard as he could. Peggy had her face buried in a man's lap with her head going up and down. Susan did not recognize the man, but he smiled at her and stuck his tongue out and wiggled it from side to side. Susan turned away from his nasty gesture and saw Sofia. She was sitting across someone with her back to Susan. Sofia was completely naked with her long blonde hair covering her back. Susan could not see the face of Sofia's sexual partner. Her curiosity made her move closer.

Sofia was moaning as she moved her hips in a circular motion. Susan looked at Sofia's perfect body. She was jealous of her little sister's good fortune. Susan had to see who was sitting under Sofia. When Susan stepped up next her sister, Sofia turned her head and smiled at Susan, revealing her sexual partner. Susan's eyes lit up when she saw Joe Croom with blood on his shoulders and face. She turned her head away quickly and scanned the misty dream world the carousel had created for her. Her three sisters continued to have their sexual relations. Susan would only be a spectator during her first magic carousel dream.

Mr. King's Chevy rolled up to the front of Fabian Moore's house. When the car stopped Mary C. stepped out onto the ground before Mr. King could open his door. She was anxious to talk to Theda Moore and try to get information about Rebecca Coolie. Mary C. was at the front porch steps when a set of moving car lights flashed behind her. She turned to see a police patrol car driving up next to Mr. King's Chevy. Officers Boos and Short were looking for information, too. Fabian Moore stepped out of his house and joined Mary C. as the two policemen got out of the car and walked toward the porch. Fabian looked at Mary C. and Mr. King.

"What brings all this company to my door?"

Mary C. shook her head. "I'll talk to you after they leave."

Fabian nodded his head as the officers joined the three near the porch. Officer Short spoke first. "Evenin', Mr. Moore, Miss Mary C., Mr. King." Mr. King nodded, but the other two did not respond. Officer Short continued. "We'd like to talk to you privately Mr. Moore, if you don't mind."

Fabian did not want to talk to the officers. "I've got company and I've already told y'all I don't know nothin' and that ain't changed."

"Well, a few things have changed for us and we thought you or Miss Coolie might be able to help us."

The front screen door opened and Rebecca Coolie stepped out onto the porch with her milkdud breasts leading the way for the rest of her unbelievable body. It was impossible for man or woman not to look at her. Mary C.'s heart raced in her chest when she saw that Rebecca was still there and not on the run with Miss Stark's necklace. Mr. King looked at Mary C. She knew he was surprised, too and he was thinking the same thing. The priceless necklace was within their reach.

Rebecca stepped up behind Fabian. He turned to her. "These officers want to talk to you. You got anything to say?"

She stepped around Fabian, giving both officers a better look. "I don't mind talkin' to 'em. What do you want to know? I ain't got nothin' to hide."

Mary C. had to smile at Rebecca's remark. She definitely was not hiding anything. Mary C. liked the way Rebecca used her body.

Officer Boos took over. "First of all, we found a body on the road near your house. It might be one of your brothers or even your father. We can't identify it." Rebecca's facial expression did not change as Officer Boos gave them more information. "We're pretty sure it's one of them." He looked up at Fabian. "The body we found had been eaten by the buzzards, but it was obvious the person was naked before the birds got to him."

The sight of her naked brother, Duck, hanging onto the outside of the truck flashed in Rebecca's head. Theda Moore stepped out onto the porch and joined the others. Officer Short looked up at Theda.

"Miss Moore, can you tell us what happened out at the Coolie place before you made your escape? Maybe there's something you can add, now that you've had time to process it all."

Theda Moore was cool, calm and collected for a fifteen-year-old young woman. She had already given birth to a child and her maturity level was far beyond her true years.

"Nothin' much more to tell. Rebecca saved me and the baby. We took off in that old truck and just kept drivin' 'til we got here."

Officer Boos was next. "They didn't try to follow y'all? They had another car."

Rebecca Coolie chimed in. "Pa was hurt from that dog bitin' him. Remember, we told you that before? They had to stay with Pa."

Mary C. stared at Rebecca with Miss Stark's necklace on her mind. Rebecca noticed that Mary C. was looking directly at her. She smiled, but it did make her nervous. She had no idea Mary C. was only interested in what Rebecca might know about the priceless antique. All the other conversations meant nothing to Mary C. Rebecca "Milkduds" Coolie would not leave Mary C.'s sight until they had a long talk.

Fabian Moore had to join the question and answer game. "Are you arresting any of us?" He looked at Officer Boos and then at Officer Short.

Officer Short took a deep breath. "We were hoping y'all would cooperate and just tell us what you know, but it's pretty obvious all of you know much more than you're willing to tell. But, no we're not here to arrest anyone. Not yet."

Fabian was calm, cool and collected, just like his little sister. "Then, we'll be sayin' goodnight, gentlemen." He turned away from the officers. "Miss Mary C., you and Mr. King come on in the house. Theda, Rebecca, how 'bout fixin' us some coffee." He walked back into the house, leaving both police officers at the foot of the porch steps.

Mary C. looked at Officer Boos. "Guess y'all ain't invited for coffee." She was a rare breed. Theda walked into the house. Rebecca stood with Mary C., allowing the officers to get another look at her. Mary C. had to speak up again.

"What exactly do you boys think happened out there?"

Officer Short was mad, ready, willing and able to answer her question. "We think Mr. Moore went out there after the girls got here and killed at least one of the Coolies. Maybe the others got away and are on the run, but the body we found belongs to one of 'em. We think Jason was with him."

Rebecca did not react to the officer's comment. Mary C. did. "Let me tell ya what I think."

Officer Short looked at Officer Boos and then back at Mary C. "We would both like to know what you think."

Mary C. was ready, too. "Now, I'm pretty good at seein' things sometimes. I ain't no Zulmary or nothin', but it works out every now and then for me. I don't dream very much, but when I do they usually come true, or I'll think of somethin' sometimes that happens later. You know, that kinda stuff. Well, I had a vision. Call it what ya want, but I call it a vision." Mary C. looked at Rebecca. "You might not want to hear this."

Rebecca Coolie was more than interested. "I'm fine, go ahead."

Mary C. smiled. She liked the buxom beauty. She looked back at Officer Short. "I think all three of the Coolies are dead. I think the body you found belongs to one of 'em. I think you can look for the other two 'til "Doom's Day", but you'll never find 'em. I think they needed killin'. I think if that pretty young girl in there was your sister and that baby was your nephew, you would have been the first one to kill a Coolie, badge or not." Everyone was silent for a few seconds. Mary C. had a little more to share. She still directed her words to the two officers. "You two should be glad somebody did y'all a big favor and got rid of that criminal element. Why do you care who it was? And by the way, that's the only thing the vision didn't show me, who killed 'em." Mary C. looked at Rebecca. "Will you join me for some coffee?" Mary C. walked into the house and Rebecca Coolie followed her. Mr. King was left with the two officers. Officer Boos broke the brief silence.

"Mr. King, we got so many dead people around here they might be starting to out number the living." Officer Boos smiled when he realized whom he was talking to. "I can't believe I said that to you."

Mr. King had to smile, too. "I've been dealin' with the dead for a long time and you're right, the count is way out of hand. But, you know Mary C.'s right about bein' rid of those three evil men. As the law, I do know the creed you are sworn to uphold, but there are exceptions to every rule. That's a fact. This situation could qualify as one of those exceptions. I for one, hope y'all stop lookin' for the other two Coolies. Trust me. If Mary C. says they're dead, they're dead."

Mr. King was the last of the group to leave the two officers outside. He went into the house to join the others. Officer Boos and Short had no choice. They left the Moore house and had to decide what their next step would be in the case of the missing Coolies.

Mary C. sat across from Rebecca Coolie in Fabian Moore's living room. Mr. King sat in one of the soft chairs and Fabian sat next to Mary C. on the couch. Theda was serving the coffee. Fabian was concerned about the investigators.

"I'm getting' real tired to those two questionin' us."

Mary C. had no concerns about the two lawmen. "They can't do nothin', as long as y'all don't say nothin'. It's when folk talk too much that brings ya down." She looked at Rebecca. Mary C. had no bedside manner whatsoever. "This whole thing with you livin' here is really strange. If Theda trusts you and Fabian lets you stay, that's their business." She looked at Fabian. "You're a better man than most. I guess her savin' Theda and the baby makes up for her daddy killin' your daddy. She was caught up in her family's meanness, but maybe she had no way out. I hope for all y'all she's bein' truthful."

Fabian respected Mary C., but he did interrupt her. "Miss Mary C., you know how I feel about you and Jason. I know you have me and Theda's best interest in mind and I do appreciate your feelin's. I'm gonna ask you to let me and Theda handle this on our own. I'm not a little boy and I've never been stupid. Please trust my judgment and don't worry about us. I can handle what ever comes."

Mary C. smiled a little smile and nodded her head. "You're right. I won't ever mention it again." Fabian smiled at Mary C. as she turned back to Rebecca. "Now, that you seem to be a member of the family, tell us where Miss Stark's necklace is."

Mr. King could not believe what his ears had just heard. His head was on a swivel first looking at Mary C., then Rebecca Coolie, then Fabian and then back at Mary C. Fabian had no idea what Mary C. was referring to. She did not take her eyes off of Rebecca Coolie. Mary C. was impressed with the young beauty when she never changed her facial expression. Mary C. liked Rebecca Coolie; she was a rare breed, too. The room was silent as Mary C. waited for a response. Rebecca did not answer quickly enough to suit Mary C.

"Your first thought is to lie. I know that. And actually I understand that first thought. What you need to understand is that we know that you have the necklace."

Rebecca's expression remained the same. "I'm sorry ma'am, but I don't know what you're talkin' about."

Mary C. turned to Fabian. "You know Hank Haygood, don't ya?"

"Yes, ma'am."

"You heard about Miss Stark's necklace before, ain't ya?"

"Yes, ma'am."

"Well, Hank found the necklace. He was hidin' it until he met her. He thought if he showed her the necklace she would show him her big tits. I think Hank got a good look at 'em." Everyone in the room looked directly at Rebecca's breasts. Mary C. continued. "After they had their little peep show and Hank told her, what ever he told her, she went home to tell her daddy. Her two brothers went to Hank's, beat him half to death and took the necklace. Now, with her daddy and brothers dead, she's got the necklace."

Mary C. had shocked everyone in the room with her outrageous story and commentary. Mr. King had no words. He just waited to see what was going to happen next. Mary C. looked deep into Rebecca's eyes. She was looking for a quivering lip or eyelid. Rebecca Coolie did not crack at all under Mary C.'s pressure.

"I'm trying to be respectful, ma'am, but I don't know anything about your friend or a necklace." She looked at Fabian. "Fabian, I don't know what she's talkin' about."

Mr. King tried to take some of the tension filled atmosphere away. "Miss Coolie, the historical value of this necklace is priceless. Money-wise, it's probably worth millions. It has more diamonds and rubies on it then any of us have ever seen. It belongs in a museum for the world to see."

Mary C. was not as noble as Mr. John King. "John, you are a hoot when it comes to these kind'a things." She looked at Rebecca. "I know you have it somewhere. Like I said, I just know things sometimes. I also know you ain't gonna give it to no museum. This necklace can make everybody in this room rich." Mary C. turned to Mr. King. "We'll have to include Bill, he is the one who told us about it." Mr. King was once again speechless as Mary C. looked back at Rebecca and continued. "If you're sincere about become part of this family, just think what they could do with all that money."

Rebecca Coolie looked into Mary C.'s brown eyes. "If I had this necklace you're talkin' about I would give it to Fabian and Theda right now and then they could decide what to do with it. But, I don't have it. I don't know where it is. I've never seen it or heard of it. I didn't show my tits to your friend. I'm sorry you think I'm lyin', but I can see you're gonna think what ever you want. Miss Mary C., did you ever think you could be wrong?"

Mary C. smiled. "Not a chance."

The funeral for Abaddon's first human victim, Eli Sallas, was the first of three funerals to be held in Mayport during that week. It was a simple service at the Oak Harbor Baptist Church with relatives and friends who were still in shock over the loss of such a young man. Jason and Fabian were two of the pallbearers. Eli's family did not show any feelings of animosity outwardly toward Mary C. Jason attended the wake, but Mary C. did not. Hank Haywood's body was transported to his hometown of Brunswick, Georgia where he was buried in a family plot.

Joe Croom's funeral was for immediate family members only. It was very unusual for a well-known Mayport family to have such a private service. Stella Croom did not want the citizens of Mayport to feel free to attend and pay their respects. She thought there were too many people who were connected to Mary C. and their presence at the funeral would only remind her of the evil woman. It was not fair to Joe's friends, but Stella Croom did not care about what others thought. Joe Croom Sr. wanted everyone to come, but he would not go against Stella's wishes. He knew his wife was going to be a different person after Joe was in the ground. He had already seen the changes taking place. He feared the way she was challenging him to do something about Mary C.

Stoddard Moore's funeral was the following day. The Mayport Presbyterian Church was packed with relatives and friends. Mary C. and Jason sat in one of the back pews and Mr. King sat at the front of the church as one of the pallbearers. Mary C. sat on the end of the pew next to the aisle. She looked back at the main entrance as Fabian and Theda Moore walked into the church. Mary C. stepped out into the aisle and hugged Fabian before he passed her. She hugged Theda next and whispered in her ear.

"Where's the Coolie girl?"

It was a strange question, but Theda answered it. "She thought it would be better if she didn't come. Fabian thought so, too." Mary C. sat down next to Jason as Theda moved to the front of the church to sit with Fabian.

Rebecca "Milkduds" Coolie walked out of Fabian Moore's house. She carried her large duffle bag and one small bag. She got into her father's old truck. She sat behind the steering wheel, placed the two bags on the seat next to her and started the engine. The duffle bag contained her new clothes and some of her old garments. Rebecca picked up the small bag, reached in and took out a fist full of money. She arranged some of the loose money so she could fold it and put it into her top shirt pocket. She placed the rest of the money back into the small bag and then stuffed the moneybag into the glove compartment. Milkduds took a deep breath and reached under the front seat at her feet and pulled out a small black leather bag. Rebecca smiled as she pulled the leather cords, opening the top of the bag. She turned it over and emptied the contents into her hand. Miss Stark's multi-million dollar, diamond and ruby filled necklace tumbled into her steady hand. After she heard Mary C.'s commentary on the necklace, Rebecca knew she held something special. She also knew if she stayed there with Fabian and Theda, Mary C. would get a share of the antique. Rebecca Coolie drove the car out of the yard. She was a new woman and she was leaving Mayport.

Mary C. knew things. She could not sit in the church pew and think about Rebecca Coolie being alone. Jason was surprised when his mother stood up and walked to the front of the church. She walked to the front pew with all eyes watching her and asked Mr. King for the keys to his 1957 Chevy. He handed her the keys. Mary C. left the church and drove the Chevy toward Fabian's house.

Rebecca Coolie was passing the Little Jetties on her way out of Mayport as Mary C. was driving into Fabian Moore's front yard. Mary C. was right. She knew things. At that moment she knew Rebecca "Milkduds" Coolie was gone and so was Miss Stark's necklace.